The Knight's Wife

By

Nick Shamhart

Dedication

This one is for the ladies, girls, and women everywhere. But, it is especially for those who have been in a long-term relationship with their significant other, and tend to take the backseat in regards to their day to day lives as far as the rest of the world notices. In essence, for all of you who can identify with this sentiment.

…You handle all the arrangements for the picnic: food, invitations, decorations, and more; but he gets the credit. You take the kids to soccer practice every day for a decade and when they win the state championship, who gets the credit … you, or him? You do the laundry, make sure the homework is done, go to parent-teacher conferences, make sure you pick up the groceries too, and also swing by the pharmacy because little Timmy has that rash on his butt that just won't clear up, again, and you need to refill his prescription, also run to…

You get the point…….. Not to worry, your actions don't go completely unnoticed. Some guys are watching….and we appreciate it.

Acknowledgements

……..For the usual suspects…..

WARNING LABEL

This is a romance, but, not like other romance novels you may have read. I feel the need to warn you, the reader, to leave all expectations at the door when you read *The Knight's Wife*. I believe there is a strong power to the concept of love. I wanted to write you a love story, but I didn't want to go the route of the swinging single city gal who is just looking for love in all the wrong places with her wacky best friend. I don't think I have anything new to add to that storyline. I also didn't want to write the rekindled love story of the, *yes, he's a grumpy old fart, but he's my grumpy old fart* type of love story (I'm kind of living that one as it is). No, this story is about a woman placed in a precarious and exhausting situation of her own devising, where she is forced to ask herself, "What the fuck? Is this love, really? Am I putting up with all this shit for love?"

Love. I'm one of those zany heterosexual men that can type and even say the word love and not feel the need to hit or hump the object I have just said the word to. It's only four letters and one small syllable that can do so many things. Love can be the truth, or a lie. It can be a salve, a compress, a guide, a reason, a desire, a motive, a manipulation, a balm, a knife, a weapon, a decision, a goal, a dream, a nightmare…the list is endless, for just that word – love.

The Knight's Wife

Love always plays a large part in my stories. The *Balance* books are full of the various forms of love. But, please, do not expect *The Knight's Wife* to be a *Balance* book. It is something else entirely. It is a romance; it is even a romantic comedy at times, but it is about romance, of which one of the many definitions is: *Ardent emotional attachment or involvement between people*. Romance comes in odd places, shapes, sizes, and not always as we expect it. Now that you have been warned, please join me in my telling of a romance. A love story of a woman who may or may not know what that word means any longer....

One

Always a second-class citizen - second place - my place is in the home, in the kitchen doing the cooking and the cleaning; a woman's place. Well, I suppose as a knight's wife, for me, it's more appropriate to say a lady's place. A lady to her lord, the Great Sir William! Please join me in a moment's applause as we bask in the many titles of the Great Sir William: Sir William the Handsome, Sir William the Brave, Sir William the Dashing, Sir William the Lionhearted, blah blah blah, yadda yadda yadda, and so on. Do you think the swooning young maidens would still heave their perky bosoms and bat their big blue eyes at the Great Sir William every time he rode by if they knew he was also Sir William the *eats too much cabbage soup and farts like a bloated steer in bed?* I know that doesn't have that valiant knightly ring to it, but I stand by my point. So much of what makes up every hero depends on his reputation and how the crowds of peasants embrace said hero. No matter what lands that hero walks and protects. And the crowds of these lands just love the Great Sir William.

I don't want to give you the wrong impression. I'm not some bitter old crone, cackling and making fun of a hero just to get my kicks. I truly do love my Will, deeply and without regret, but after twenty years of marriage you see past all the things you fell in love with and just start loving the person behind the image. Or, I suppose you start hating them. It can go either way. But with Will I saw past the perfectly coifed black hair, the strong cleft chin and hint of dimples when he smiles that has those young maidens' breasts heaving. I saw the handsome man, sure. You couldn't and still can't miss that, but I also saw the weaknesses that he hides from the land of Thistledown, our home and the home of my ancestors beyond counting. The Great Sir William hides that fact that he is nearly blind as a bat and clumsier than a one-legged dog from his king, his country, and all the others who cheer his name and laud his accomplishments. Did you hear the one about how the Great Sir William defeated the Cyclops of Dead Horse Swamps with just his torch and a toothpick? Well the songs the tavern bards sing don't tell you that while Will was squinting to see in the dark night-shrouded swamp, he lifted his torch and the Cyclops was only inches from Will's face. Will screamed, the toothpick flew from his mouth and poked the Cyclops in the eye. Then, still screaming, Will dropped his torch on the Cyclops' foot which caused the Cyclops to simultaneously try covering his eye and put the fire on his toes out. The monster bumped his head on a low branch hanging precariously from a large oak tree, and then fell unconscious into the swamp and drowned. Try singing that to a room full of drunken peasants and see how many half-drained tankards come flying your way. The bards, even if they knew the truth, would still sing it their way. They have to sing to the masses the songs they want to hear after all. Well, if they want a tip and a free beer they do anyhow.

But I love my clumsy fool of a husband, false tavern tales and all, and I want him to return home safe. That's why I follow him on every quest, journey, or pilgrimage he is sent on for king and country. I make sure the Great Sir William does not become the Barbecued Sir William when a dragon roasts him for his temerity. He actually told a dragon once, "Be gone vile wyvern! Thy breath is offensive and thy scales are moldy!" He actually said, "Thy." He talks like that to all the monsters he fights; most of the time it just annoys them further. And, of course, when he returned home to regale me with the tale of how he warned the wretched creature but it did not heed his threats, I had to play along and say, "Oh my," and "Oh yes, dear," with the proper gasps and female fluttering at all the right places, so he would never suspect I had watched the entire thing, just out of his poor eyesight. I still haven't had the heart to tell him that wyverns cannot speak and it had no idea what he was yelling at it anyway. He does become so earnest and excited over his stories that it's like listening to a child. I couldn't risk hurting his feelings by telling him otherwise. We have never been able to have children - though not for lack of trying - so Will in his exuberant child-like state is the closest I'll ever get to mothering.

Will truly is a good, kind, and caring man. But, like all men who have retained that child-like innocence, he has certain flaws. It's not really his fault. He's attempting to live up to all the tales he heard as a small boy about chivalrous knights in shining armor and how they acted. He tries too hard to emulate those knights of yore on his quests. He isn't one though. He doesn't have the skills to be one, but that doesn't stop that little boy still inside him from wanting to be like them. Not that any of them ever were what the stories say, but that never stops a young boy from believing, does it? You can't convince that child, inner or outer, that their favorite jouster or archer is a fraud or that when gold is involved those heroes will do whatever they have to in order to win. If that means they secretly go to some hag for a potion to make them stronger or faster, you better believe that just to keep on winning their game, whatever it may be, and to retain the adoration of their fans that they'll down that witch's brew every time. Then juiced up on eye of newt or wing of bat they'll win the tournament. The boys inside the men don't want to hear that. They'll never believe their heroes aren't real until they see it with their own eyes. So, Will holds himself up to the standards of charlatans and frauds like all men do, but the problem in Will's case is he *is* one of those charlatans and the small wide-eyed boy inside refuses to believe it. No matter how hard he may try to be kind and shine in his tarnished armor, Will can never measure up to his childhood heroes. No one ever can, because they aren't real…but I suppose if you have a good heart like my Will, then it doesn't hurt to try.

We girls aren't much better with our *Prince Charmings* and how we think out of an entire kingdom, the gorgeous prince will pick us. Right, sure honey, you're average, but the stud will want you, sure, sure, it could happen. Let's not address that even then our studly prince will have all those insecurities and flaws I just mentioned above in the heroes. He'll probably be more concerned with his hair than you are with yours. We don't like the truth any more than the little boys do. It's all about growing up, I guess. I still have my big-little boy, the Great Sir William, whom you may think is a stud but is just another chivalrous dud, to take care of though.

My six and a half foot tall, broad-shouldered little boy has been called before our good king and queen to find out his next mission of daring do. I say good king and queen and actually mean it. I know that is seldom the case when you hear it from the peasants, common folk, and ladies like myself that make up the clusters of grapes in the gossip vines of most kingdoms, but here it is true. King Theodore and Queen Marissa have ruled justly and fairly over the lands of Thistledown for as long as I can remember. The worst that can be said for them is that King Theodore has *Down/Up Eyes*. Queen Marissa is as beautiful as an autumn colored forest and as sweet as bee pollen, but she is as flat-chested as any stable boy. They love each other. It shows in the way they hold hands when they walk about among the commoners or how he smiles at her while she isn't looking. He is still a man though. Since he does not receive much of an eyeful in the boudoir, whenever a lady-in-waiting or otherwise speaks with him and she has more than a handful tucked away in her bodice, his eyes are constantly dipping down to her décolleté and back up again. For a monarch, that being the worst of his vices, I don't see how anyone in their right minds could call them less than the good king and queen.

Thistledown is not a large, grand sweeping empire by any stretch of the imagination. Theodore and Marissa have a modest castle nestled in the heart of their kingdom, surrounded by a small town full of tradesmen and craftspeople. The town is then in turn surrounded by farmland of rolling hills for grains and grazing land for livestock. There are huge, craggy mountains to the north and long crystal clear lakes to the south. Will and I live on the outskirts of King Theodore's domain. It is where I grew up with my father, where Papa's body is buried under a red-leafed maple tree behind our cottage, next to the old oak where he laid my mother to rest, and where I intend to stay until my death. This land is a part of me, a part of my family's heritage going back for generations. So, since fate has decided that I will be the last of my line. That line will end in Thistledown.

We even live in the same cottage my father raised me in. It's the same cottage I was born in and the same one my great-great-grandfather built of stone and wood with his bare hands, as the family story goes, and each subsequent inhabitant has had to patch and thatch with their bare hands since. The cottage is small but quaint; solid, cluttered but clean, well, clean-ish anyway. We have a stable for our horse that doubles as a barn for the few livestock we keep on hand. There is an assortment of coops and hutches for the smaller food animals: chickens, rabbits, turkeys, and such. It's all nestled in this quiet forest glen where the northern mountains frame the tree line. I love it there and wouldn't think of ever leaving it. That was a concession Will made for me, to be away from his king – another point in Theodore's good king favor, most monarchs would not allow their greatest knight to live so far away. Of course, Theodore has no idea that I do most of the slaying of monsters and other knightly duties because my sweet bumbling husband can barely wield his sword without falling over. So intentionally or not, Thistledown's greatest knight lives barely within its borders…whether that knight is known as the Great Sir William or little old me, the Lady Gale.

Two

Will returned home this afternoon, boisterous, excited, and full of tales and ideas for his newest quest. I have to wonder sometimes how he justifies it to himself. You know he has to realize that he isn't really doing all those things the stories about him say he is doing. He isn't stupid – just clumsy. But even given that, he can't have his last conscious thought be of an ogre swinging a tree trunk at his head and then he miraculously wakes up to find the ogre dead, and then he thinks what? *I must have shown that disgusting brute what for…in my sleep?* Does he just think he is very lucky? Or, does his un-conscious mind fill in the blanks while he dreams, so that when he wakes up he is no longer sure what was a dream and what really happened?

However he rationalizes it when he wakes up, he still holds to the mysterious result. He doesn't really have much of a choice. It's not like he can ride back to Thistledown and report to King Theodore that the ogre is dead, but he has no idea how. He tells King Theodore some yarn I imagine, probably the same version he tells me, except who hears the more em-bellished story I'm not so sure of – who would you rather greatly impress, your king or the woman you're sleeping with? Either way, King Theodore goes on to tell the story to his royal bard. The bard adds his little spins and twists for the sake of rhyme and by the time the peasants have had their chance to tweak the story this way or that, it has changed so many times reality has very little to do with it. Will just smiles, shrugs, and waves to his adoring masses. And a few weeks or months later, when there is need, the Great Sir William will ride to save the day again! Just like his most recent charge.

Apparently the cattle ranchers to the north have been complaining about a troll coming down out of the mountains at night to steal livestock and even a few children have gone missing. "I'll teach that monster not to harm children in King Theodore's land!" Will shouted as he paced back and forth in our tiny kitchen. The top of his head just a hair's breadth from scraping on the low ceiling. Pounding his fist into his open palm as if imagining what he would do to the troll if it were present, and, well, small enough to fit in his hand, of course. Venting his agitation and girding up his courage, Will continued, "Theodore was very upset, as I'm sure you can imagine. Poor Queen Marissa was just beside herself, too. Two little boys and four young girls are all missing from the northern ranches and in only a fortnight! Theodore offered to send the castle guard out with me, but I told his majesty if I can't stand up on my own to some bully of a troll, then I do not deserve to serve my liege. I can only- ouch!" He walked face first into one of my frying pans that hangs from a rafter, slightly over our table. It has hung there since before my father died. "When did you move that?" Will shouted, rubbing the rising red welt forming between his eyes.

"It's always been there, dear," I said, walking over and guiding him down to sit in the over-sized chair my father built for him years ago. I couldn't just tell him to sit down - stars above no. I had a fire going in the stove behind him and couldn't risk Will mistaking the stove for a stool. So, after I helped ease him into his chair I brought him a cup of tea and asked, "When are you planning to leave, my dear?"

Taking a small sip and still rubbing absently at the frying pan indentation on his forehead, he said, "Tomorrow afternoon, after the parade." He mumbled that last part and quickly added, "Is there any honey?"

"Yes…what parade?" I asked reaching for the honeypot, refusing to ignore my *oh so smooth talking* husband's attempt at redirection. Though I knew before I asked what the parade would be, but I had to hope otherwise.

"The Sir William Day parade," Will answered around his mug, not looking up to make eye contact with me. To his credit he tried to sound as if it was no big deal and almost a touch embarrassing, really. But how many of us ever have a parade thrown in our honor? Humility is a fine quality, but when the king declares a day in your honor, to celebrate *you*, it isn't so easy to say, "Aww shucks, it's nothing."

"Sir William Day?" I asked, placing the honey as close to Will as possible so he wouldn't knock it over. And then on second thought I just started adding it myself, better safe than sorry.

"Thank you, Gale," Will said and grinning slightly he continued. "Yes, Sir William Day. I did tell Theodore not to, that I only do my duty, and wish for no such praise. My only reward is a safe kingdom for my people." He patted the top of our worn, waxed, and food-stained oak dining table as he spoke. Whether to impart a confidence he probably didn't feel or just making sure he didn't knock his tea over, I couldn't tell. But he was trying to be humble about the situation and I think he deserves some credit for that, I do.

Please don't think ill of me, but, though I want you to give him credit for trying to be humble I'm the one who has to smell those cabbage soup farts, so I had to needle him a bit. I mean, I don't want to sound petty – I didn't want it to be Lady Gale Day. But by the same token, I had done all the work that he was getting the credit for, and besides I'm the one who has to clean the Great Sir William's dirty breeches after the cabbage soup, which isn't pretty believe me. The heaving maidens may have second thoughts if they saw those stained linens. So I'm entitled. Sitting down across from him, staring with over-exaggerated wide-eyed innocence, cupping my chin in my hands, I asked, "What will they have at the Sir William Day parade? Maybe wooden Sir

William swords, signed by you for the boys? Stuffed Sir William dolls for the girls…and for some of the lonely women, too, I suppose."

"Please, Gale, stop," Will said, leaning on the table - causing it to creak as it struggled to support his weight - and covering his face with his hands. But I couldn't, ignoring his embarrassment I added, "Oh I know they'll have *Bobbing for Sir Will's Apples!* All the maidens can get down on their knees with their hands tied behind their backs and their young full lips wide open-"

"Stop!" Will said blushing, still hiding his face.

I guess I'm a softy because I did. Between you and me though, I still had a ton more, but Will was already so embarrassed it wouldn't have been any fun. I do have them mentally logged away for next year, so don't worry. I could see in the dim afternoon light pushing through the shutters that something more was bothering him. It wasn't just embarrassment over the way the young girls vied for his attentions. We'd joked and kidded about that many times over the years. It was just part of being married to a living legend. Pushing past the sarcasm and stabbing at the heart of the issue, I asked, "You're worried about the troll, aren't you?"

He nodded his head and still refused to look at me. I fished a little more, "You've never fought a troll before, have you?"

He shook his head.

"Well," I offered, absently playing with the honey stirring rod, "Papa used to run into trolls all the time when he herded bighorn sheep along the northern border." I knew that would grab his attention but I wanted to play coy, so not looking up I just stirred and stirred.

It was only seconds before Will finally looked over at me. I still stirred that weird looking fairy wand honey rod thing. I never have figured out why people didn't just use a spoon instead. I let Will sweat for a bit. He stared at me as I stirred, waiting, because when it came to forest lore and mythology Will would always listen to what my father had to say - even if it was posthumously through me. Actually that was how Will and I met. Papa saved Will once, and in a quirky twist of fate I seem to have continued the pastime. So, when I tell Will my father would say this, do this or do that, Will would listen. Perking up at the possibility of advice and no longer willing to wait for me to stop stirring, Will asked, "Hawk dealt with trolls?"

No, Hawk wasn't my father's birth name…it was Gilbert, but nobody wants to talk about the ranger and all-around sage of the woods Gilbert. So, before I was born my father started going by the name Hawk. They say it was because he could see as well as one, but knowing Papa he probably just thought it sounded rugged and tough.

The Knight's Wife

"All the time," I assured Will, staring at my stirring arm as if Papa's advice was common knowledge. Lifting the rod up and letting the honey slowly drip back into the pot, I elaborated, "Papa always said the trick to fighting a troll is to remember that they are nearly deaf, but they do have an excellent sense of smell. Just stay downwind of a troll and he'll never hear you sneaking up on him."

"That's it?" Will asked, an edge of reluctant confidence struggling in his voice.

"Absolutely," I said, reaching over and taking his hand in mine. "You'll be fine. The Great Sir William will save the northern ranchers from the troll, don't worry. Now come on to bed."

"But it's not yet supper time?" Will said, looking around in confusion.

Sighing, I leaned forward and rested my forehead against his. He winced at the pressure on his fading frying pan induced lump. I whispered, "No, but I have another game for Sir William Day, that I think you'll enjoy..." To push past Will's thickheadedness, I dribbled a tiny bit of honey from the rod onto my index finger and licked it off seductively. Then pressing my lips to his ear, I whispered, "...one that the young maidens only get to dream about."

"Oh!" he said, realization dawning on his handsome features. Subtlety is not his strong suit, but it rarely is for a knight, I guess. We went to bed and did all the things we have done over the years and a few more I've added to help him relax. He may not really be the Great Sir William everyone believes him to be, but that does not stop the pressure of living up to his own legend from pressing on him. Sometimes I think it is a harder job to be in the limelight than it is to be out among the throng. That is if the limelight is centered on your actions and deeds, not like some popinjay artist or street performer. The people who are legends for saving others are the real heroes to idolize and that stress can cut a noble life short if you don't watch out.

Sadly, though it will be his day, I'll have twice as much work tomorrow than he will. When the parade begins to see him off, I'll have to be there waving my kerchief, dressed in perfect lady-like attire, and listening to the well wishes of the crowds. "He'll be fine ma'lady. He's the Great Sir William!" or "He's the bravest knight to ever live!" and on and on, and I'll have to listen to it all. I'll have to be polite, play the part of fawning, adoring lady all day long. But, when I finally have the chance to slip away from their reassurances, I'll have to circle back around, change into more trail-fitting garb, and overtake the several hours head start William will have. Fun, fun, fun.

Oh and I'll have to leave a stew going so we have something for dinner when we return, and will you just look at those cobwebs in the ceiling corner.

The Knight's Wife

I really need to remember to clean those out before I lay down, but every day I forget until I look up ready for bed. Also, I need to… It's a wonder I ever sleep with all this nonsense running around in my head.

Three

Happy Sir William Day! Happy? Maybe merry or joyous? Oh wait, I know, a *Glorious* Sir William Day to you! The banners were flying high this morning. Flags, standards, pennants, and streamers of every shape and size, fluttered in the cool gentle breeze, from poles to awnings, open windowsills to clotheslines. The decorations were everywhere. White and blue are the king's colors and they mirrored the bright sky and fluffy clouds perfectly. King Theodore had dozens of seamstresses working night and day over the last fortnight for this morning's celebration and none of them seemed to mind. I didn't hear a single groused or grumbled word about the work from anyone with sore and calloused, some even bleeding, fingers. They all loved Will and were more than proud to have helped add to the festivities. The fruits of their hard labors made sure that Will's chiseled features looked down on the peasants from every banner. Some just depicted his face or profile. Others were of him astride a horse, or battling a monster of some sort, but wherever a person turned on this fine Sir William Day they saw Will's face.

I was actually right about the wooden swords and the dolls, too. The creepy, scary little things, with oddly disproportionate bodies made me shudder a bit every time I saw one. So far no bobbing for apples but the day is young; wait until Will leaves and the kegs of beer and the casks of mead really start flowing. I'm sure there will be all manner of lewd, inebriated Sir William themed events. But this morning and early afternoon the festivities have been wholesome and family orientated. I think King Theodore made sure of that. Knowing how easily embarrassed Will can be, the king wanted the day to truly be Will's – until he leaves on his quest, of course. Then who knows how inappropriate things may become?

Young boys, pages, and squires have been running around all morning, in small groups and clusters, fencing with their Sir William Day wooden swords. The clack, crash, smack, and occasional cry over too rough a strike echoed among the closed shops and empty homes, as everyone was out at the celebration and festivities. A more creative gang of hooligans had tied a pair of brown burlap wings onto a stray dog and were chasing it up and down a shadowed alley in imitation of the time when the Great Sir William banished a giant bat from Echo Caverns. The maidens were giggling and swooning whenever Will strode by. They'd also wave their hands franticly in an imitation of fanning themselves if they were talking heatedly about a particular story like *The Great Sir William saving the errant milkmaid from the pack of ravening Wargs.* All of them mentally taking the place of the milkmaid and becoming the object of Sir William's post-battle lust. That story is completely a work of fiction, mind you. It never happened, but that did not keep them from sounding like a bunch of hyperventilating geese when they talked about it. And yes, I was right; some of them were holding Sir William dolls. I shudder to think of what those dolls will see, tucked away on a shelf as a keepsake, on some lonely, sleepless, fantasy induced night.

When I left the hero of the day he was perched up on a dais with the king and queen, watching as a band of traveling entertainers tumbled about for their slapstick viewing pleasure. I should have been up there with him, most other women would, but I'd rather not have the crowds' attention directed my way, thank you very much - the Aloof Lady Gale, that's me. I'm fine with that. I'm polite and friendly when the commoners talk to me, but I do not want to make a spectacle of myself either, like those oxygen deprived gigglers. Oh for the love of the sun! I wish they'd stop making those noises! They sound ridiculous. Girls please, take the advice of an old hand, well not that old, but old enough to know the score anyhow, the hero won't look over at you no matter how loud you laugh. In Will's case he's so damn blind he's just as likely to grin roguishly at an old crone or witch as the young maidens. But if the hero you're giggling at is really the stud you think he is, you'd be better off just flashing him your boobs. He still may not notice you, but at least you'd have put some effort behind it. Giggling does not catch a guy's attention. It never has and never will…but oddly enough a well-placed giggle in the bedroom can get him off quickly so you can finally just go to sleep. Go figure.

Advice to the young and swooning aside, I stashed my trail clothes and sword in an old, abandoned orchard north of Thistledown. I can change on the road and follow Will from there. He is, stars above be my witness, very likely to get lost at least twice before I can sneak away from the well-wishers in town. I just hope he finds the trail north again, at some point, so I don't have to go back and look for him.

As all my problems and plans ran through my head a shadow fell over my shoulder and a soft feminine voice asked, "How are you holding up?" Damn it. I jerked my head up. How did Queen Marissa manage to sneak away from the festivities, and without me noticing? Papa would be disappointed in my lack of observational skills. He used to press on me to always be aware of my surroundings because I'd get lost in my thoughts like now. He'd say, "The distraction from the most harmless daydream can cause the largest amount of damage. Be on your guard little Nightingale. I won't always be there to watch out for you."

"Fine, your highness, thank you for asking," I said, covering my surprise and tucking Papa's voice away. I knew I'd hear it often enough while I trailed Will later. I can't be in the woods and not think of my father; the two are inseparable for me.

25

Queen Marissa smiled and nodded, paying my distraction little notice. Her dark hair, with only a touch of gray, was gathered up in tight ringlets and bounced with every motion. She took my wrist in both of her delicate hands and leaned in, conspiratorially whispering, "I can't imagine how hard it must be for you. Will always running off to all that danger my Theodore asks him to face. And you're left home alone, all the way out in those woods, without a soul to keep you company while you fret. It must be horrible."

Oh your majesty, if only it were that easy. Instead I smiled demurely and said, "Oh, it can be hard sometimes, I guess. Late at night it gets a little lonely when he's gone."

"I thought so," Queen Marissa added resolutely. She nodded her head very lady-like and proper. Then placing her hands on my shoulders, she continued, "That settles it. When Will journeys off to fight for my husband you are going to come stay with us here at the castle until he returns. I should have done this years ago, but I'm sorry to say I never thought of it. I guess getting older makes you see the bigger picture, so you will stay with us and I can keep you company, be a shoulder for you to lean on while you wait for Will's safe return."

Oh crap. I should have seen that coming.

"That's very kind your highness," I said, trying to look demure, attempting to convey a causal reluc-

tance; an unwillingness to put her out or be a burden.
I looked at my feet hoping to buy some time. Staring
at my dress boots I remembered how much the damn
things pinched my feet (and pained toes aside) I decided that instead of inventing some half-assed excuse she was likely to downright refuse, I would go
with the less popular, but more effective, vague ac-
ceptance and hope that she would get drunk tonight
and forget the whole thing. I said, "It would be nice
not to have to worry alone." See, nice and vague.
No, I'll be by later this evening after I run home and
pack a few things. Nothing definitive she could hold
me to, or that might stick out in her mind as *made
plans*. Papa's voice climbed back out of my memory
and uttered one of his favorite sayings, "If you don't
make a promise, you don't have to keep a promise,
little Nightingale."

"Good, I'm glad that's settled," Queen Marissa
said, steering me back toward the tumbling act and
the cheering crowd gathered around the stage. "You
simply must see this gypsy juggler. He isn't all that
good, but he certainly is gorgeous."

"Oh, really?" I added, see vague again. It's kind
of awkward when your queen talks to you like that. I
know she is just a person like everybody else, but as
a ruler they sort of get placed higher on our mental
shelves, don't they? Not that they are better than us,
but it is a kind of leftover childhood ideal that our
leaders are above such vain concepts as finding an
entertainer cute. They should be worried about laws,

taxes, or feeding starving orphans, and not the flippant daily minutia of sexual attraction.

"I tell you, Gale, once you see the way he grips his *balls* it will take your breath away," she said with an added giggle sounding entirely too much like the maidens attempting to gain my Will's attention via their coquettish nonsense. Besides, Queen Marissa has more than twenty years on me. Sex is sex, but you don't really want to hear your aging monarch – woman or man, I don't care which – say *balls* in that insinuating double entendre tone of voice. Would you? I mean think about it…Oh, oh my…so I take it back. If the young man with the long black hair was the gypsy juggler Marissa was referring to, then my queen can ogle his balls all she wants. She is human after all.

I could still breathe, but if those young maidens were looking between the Great Sir William and the pretty gypsy juggler, then I could see why they may be a tad lightheaded. Not giggle worthy, but looking between the two of them was like looking back in time. The juggler looked like Will at twenty, bouncing about playfully, every step full of assurance and energy. Then sitting beside King Theodore was Will at forty, strong and weathered, less vigor and zip, but more tempered and calm, confident with the weight of years.

"See what I mean?" Queen Marissa asked in a whisper, exceedingly close to my ear. I could smell by the mead accompanying her voice that the queen had already been celebrating. She added, "You know I would never say anything inappropriate about another woman's husband, Gale, but you'd have to be blind not to see how handsome William is. Then with the two of them in such close proximity, Will and the gypsy, well it's enough to give any honest woman very dishonest thoughts."

Alright, that was a little gross, but she did have a point. With the exception of the fact that the juggler must have better eyesight than my Will, he could have passed for the younger version that my father saved and brought to our home so many years ago.

"Gentlemen and ladies," the juggler announced to the crowd as he caught all five balls he had been tossing behind his back, "Your highnesses and today's hero Sir William, I, James Vayruin, thank you from the bottom of my heart for your rapt attentions to my humble act of dexterity."

The crowd erupted into cheers and James smiled roguishly, patting his hands out in front of him to quiet the audience down. "Please, I'm but a simple entertainer," he added bowing from the stage toward the higher placed dais. Pointing up to the king and Will, he added, "The man who deserves your applause is the knight who keeps the beautiful kingdom of Thistledown free from monsters, creatures, and villains. Save the cheers you give to me and give them to the Great Sir William!"

The crowd's efforts doubled and James added his own applause as well, somehow around his heaping handfuls of…well, his balls. King Theodore even clapped and turned on his throne to face Will at his right hand. I could see Will's blush all the way down at stage side where Marissa and I were standing. James the juggler could work a crowd that was for sure. I suppose that was his job, but still I had yet to see them this excited before, and Theodore had thrown many celebrations in Will's honor. Not an entire day, but still a party is a party. As the ovation died to murmurs, James bowed once more and left the stage. He jumped down, nimbly with feline grace and strode toward Queen Marissa and me. He gripped Marissa's hand in passing and kissing the top of her knuckles, he said, "Your Majesty."

Turning to grin and tossing a wink my way, he added, "My Lady."

Four

Banishing thoughts of the handsome - and hopefully only passing through Thistledown - gypsy juggler James, I fled north from the late evening Sir William Day festivities. It seemed every Thistledown resident wanted to wish me well and give me some measure of reassurance before I could leave, "It'll be fine my lady. He's the Great Sir William!" Gee, thank you Mr. Baker, I never would have known that without your help. I've only been doing this for nearly twenty years, but your beer-soaked reassurances calm me so.

The sun had set and the moon had yet to rise over the orchard I used as a shortcut and place to stash my gear anytime Will was sent north. It was overgrown and neglected after its owner passed away without an heir to see that the homestead continued to produce. There were plenty of early season apples swelling to the proper picking size. Between the bugs and birds poking and prodding at them many had prematurely fallen. The misshapen lumps, hidden in the grass, made the quickly darkening glen difficult to navigate through. The cloying smell of decaying fruit lingered into the night from the hot afternoon when the sun warmed the rotten apples. I had almost reached the spot where I had stashed my trail garb – a deep knot in an old oak that stood sentinel over the smaller apple trees in the middle of the orchard – when I heard a twig snap. The broken twig was quickly accompanied by a quietly muttered, "Damn apples."

I circled back around, not knowing who my fumbling stalker was. As I said the orchard was abandoned and well off the common path of travel, so anyone out there late at night must have been there for a reason. I hurried down a side row, well what used to be a row, with the orchard gone to seed the original grid work design had pretty much been wiped out. Branches twisted in and around, grasping and grabbing, without pruning and proper mainte-nance the trees looked like they were trying to hug each other. Papa had taught me that if you ever want to move silently in the forest it isn't about tracking and trailing prey through woods and over streams. It's about blending with the forest, becoming a part of it, sort of an extension of it – until it is hard to tell where you end and it begins. I linked with the grasp-ing, grabbing trees. I became one myself. Thirty years with Papa and quite a few more on my own had given me plenty of time to perfect my skills at becoming part of the woods. I love the deep forests and the trees, and I'm at home there – day or night. It was quite obvious that my follower was not.

Within minutes our positions were reversed and I was the one trailing *him*. I could tell it was a man by the way he moved. He had grace, but in the dusky half-light of the stars I could see he was a bit stilted and jerky about how he navigated. To my eyes he wasn't much more than another shadow in the gloom, even from a few paces behind, but the outline was definitely male, or a really tall broad-shouldered woman, I guess.

I keep a six inch stiletto tucked into a sheath on my thigh at all times and also one under a wrist bracer when I'm in full armor. It may or may not be very ladylike but I figure better safe than sorry. Plus, I apologize if you hadn't figured this out by now, but I'm not much of a lady. No I don't go for the accessorizing mentality of *Oh gosh, does that razor-sharp half a foot of metal really go with that dress or not?* It's not the way I think. I can't be worried about such trivialities as fashion while I'm busy. Most of these quests end up with me having to kill something, and to kill another being – monsters though they may be – you have to be a bit cold inside. I don't think they make too many fashionable accessories to go with death, practical ones sure, but not fashionable. So unladylike or not I drew my stiletto; those of us who are cold enough to strike for the kill like to keep our *fangs*, forged or naturally grown, always at the ready. Blade in hand the key became picking my moment before I struck. Your perceptions are thrown off in the forest at night. We are visual creatures and when our strongest sense is taken from us we weaken and make mistakes. Do not attack by night. In the dark it is best to stalk your prey and wait for it to make a mistake instead. It's all about patience.

A single misstep or another tumble on a rotting apple was all I needed. From the way his leg buckled and his half-uttered, "Damn it!" I suppose it was the latter. He tripped, stumbled a bit wildly, arms flailing about a bit comically, and fell to a knee. His right hand was planted precariously out in front of him as he tried to regain his balance. His head was drooped forward while he attempted to collect his composure. See, the perfect moment always presents itself; you just have to be patient. I slipped in behind him and quickly laced my free hand through his hair. Pulling forcefully on my fistful I straightened his neck back and placed the blade's sharpest edge to his throat. A tricky move in the dark, I could as easily have nicked an artery as not. Without the telltale warm gush or trickle of blood running down my hand I must have done it right. So, jabbing my knee into his lower back for leverage, I leaned down and harshly whispered by his ear, "You need to give me a very good reason why I shouldn't slit your throat."

I know, very melodramatic. It kind of sounds like something out of a bad stage play, but a woman alone at night needs to exude confidence and establish authority from the outset of any confrontation. And threats of death, ham-handed theatrical dialogue included, do that very nicely. In fact, shy of grabbing hold of his balls and pulling you don't get more dominant than a blade resting against the Adam's apple. He stammered a bit before saying, "The queen paid me to follow you."

The Knight's Wife

"What?" I asked, pushing the knife a bit closer for effect. "Why?"

"My lady," he said, breathing quickly, certain death will do that to you every time. Fear: the world's greatest cardiovascular motivator. Trying to catch his breath, he stammered, "The queen wanted to make sure you returned home safe. Then I was to escort you back to the castle tomorrow morning, once you'd packed your things. She said you knew all about this."

Damn it Marissa. Well so much for vague. Now on top of saving Will's ass from the troll I needed to figure out how to get away from my escort and invent a buyable excuse to give Queen Marissa next time I saw her. Wonderful, when it rains it pours, and when it pours it floods, and I have to remember to empty the rain barrels because it looked as if it would storm tonight and we need fresh water for the garden and…damn it! One thing at a time; focus on the guy with the knife to his throat first.

"Up," I said and stepped back, letting go of his hair - his dark, black, glistening in the starlight, shoulder length hair. Damn it again, Marissa! I knew who it was before he had completely turned around. Once James the gypsy juggler had regained his feet, he stammered, "My lady, I apologize for startling you. I meant to call out to you once you were in sight, but you obviously know these woods better than I do and heard me following. I am sorry."

"You're the juggler, aren't you?" I asked as if I only had the faintest of recollections of him from the day's festivities. Fat chance of that, I'm a married woman, but I'm not blind. Not like my poor Will. Will! Crap I had to stop being distracted and ditch this juggling gigolo so I could help Will. I could only hope he had detoured half a day's ride in the wrong direction…which given past experience he probably had, if not more, so that I could easily catch up to him.

James smoothed out his shirt and ran a hand through his hair, visibly calming after the little jolt of fear I had sent his way. He smirked in the early rising moonlight as if my recognition of him somehow validated his cocksure identity and said, "Yes, my lady. My name is James Vayruin." He dipped into a sweeping grandiose bow, of the kind reserved for the stage and ballrooms - *May I have this dance?* or *Thank you all, you've been a wonderful audience* type stuff. I know I should have been flattered, but he just looked like a moron doing it in the middle of an abandoned orchard at night. So I laughed instead and patting him on a stooped shoulder in passing, I said, "Sure, Jimmy, come on. This isn't the throne room, nobody to impress out here and we have miles yet to put behind us."

I don't know if he was still out of sorts from being caught unaware at knifepoint, or if he just wasn't accustomed to having a woman not swoon and giggle at his charms – sorry kid, but I've had plenty of experience with pretty packaging. Whatever the case was, he lagged behind, and I had to clap my hands like I was encouraging a small puppy dog, "Come on, Jimmy, this way! Chop-chop, quick like a bunny!"

When he finally started to follow me I had trouble not saying, "Good boy, who's a good boy?" and rubbing his belly. He struggled to find his footing behind me, but managed to grumble, "It's James, my lady, not Jimmy. Jimmy makes me sound like a little boy."

Not bothering to turnaround I called over my shoulder, "That's nice, Jimmy." I smiled into the dark night ahead of me when he didn't respond. Oh crap! Had I actually started to flirt with the kid? Crap again, yes, yes I had.

Remonstrating myself I realized I had no intention of either returning home to gather my things and then go back to the castle while Will was away, or allowing Skippy the pretty boy to follow me around all night like a good puppy dog - especially if I was going to flirt with him. I have nothing against a bit of harmless flirting, but you may have noticed that I also have a tendency to get distracted. I did not need the distraction of pretty blue eyes, flowing black hair, and a mischievous grin that made you wonder what he was thinking about - damn! See what I mean?

There is a beauty to the woods by night, so I focused on that instead. Different shades of black and shadow on shadows as the moon's light filtered through the thick canopy of leaves. But no matter how bright the moon, that beauty can be deceptive. Low hanging branches that you would typical duck under by reflex are obscured or hidden. It may seem to your night-tricked eyes that a branch is farther away than you think. Trip hazards like exposed roots and twigs that you would be looking for in the daylight are dangerous – even deadly if you fall incorrectly – in the dark. Deadly beauty, isn't that life.

Gathering inspiration from the night I realized I needed to circle around, again, to get back to my trail gear and weapons, but first I needed to lose Jimmy. Preferably by means not as lethal as him falling and impaling himself on an exposed root, but after a half an hour's wandering I started to become a tad flexible on the mortal wound issue.

"My lady?" Jimmy asked tentatively, "haven't we passed this clearing before?" as we did just that.

Crap, so he was pretty and competent, wonderful that's all I needed.

"No, Jimmy, we haven't," I snipped, holding my head high and tipping my nose toward the sky in my *What is that smell?* Ladylike manner. "The forest by night all looks the same. You're just unfamiliar with the area."

The Knight's Wife

"If you say so, *my lady*," he added with sarcasm dripping from his words. Okay, fine, I kind of, sort of, hoped he did fall on a stick after that, Mr. Smart Mouth. When I decided I had wasted enough time on him. I started running. Not, light-footed *oh tee hee* I'm a fleeing deer type of running. I mean sprinting like a dragon is chasing you to blow a cloud of fire up your ass type running. Jimmy didn't have a chance. After seconds my heart was beating rapidly in my chest and I could hear Jimmy trying to keep up over the rush of blood in my ears. The jolt of danger, spiced with the physical exertion added a level of joy and spring to my step. I flew through the night, over rocks and roots, becoming another shadow among many. A loud thump followed by a yelp of pain broke through my enjoyment and echoed over my pounding heart. There, that should have done it. It was time to get back to the old oak. I looked up at the stars to gather my bearings. I needed to head off - "My lady please! I'm hurt."

Crap. If I just ignored him he'd quiet down.

"My lady, please," his voice quavered on the night breeze in fear and pain. "I told the queen I'd make sure no harm came to you, but I seem to have harmed myself."

Nope, I didn't hear that. It must have been an owl.

"I think…I think my leg may be broken, my lady."

Sigh, fine.

I headed back toward where Jimmy was calling from. When he came into view I could see a good sized lump forming on his forehead where he must have struck it on a low hanging branch. Blood, black in the moonlight, was trickling down the side of his face where a gash had opened on his scalp, and he was crouched over his shin, rubbing at his lower leg, rocking back and forth childlike. When he saw me, he breathed out a sigh of relief and said, "Oh thank goodness, my lady. I don't think it is really broken, but I wrenched it quite painfully. I don't believe I can follow you home. Perhaps we can build a fire and make camp here." And pausing in his speech to think he added, "Why did you run from me?"

Not broken? Alright chatterbox that was enough. I kicked him hard. I mean *hard*, right on the temple and he dropped unconscious instantly. It's a risky strike. Any blow to the head can be even if the combatant is properly trained. It could have killed him if I'd struck too hard, but I had other things to do. The clock was ticking. It was worth the risk. I know what you're thinking, but, remember, *Hello, nice to meet you, cold killer here.*

I checked for a pulse. He was fine and out like a light, so I ran back toward the old orchard. I was further behind schedule than I was comfortable with – Will had probably course-corrected after my sidetrack and was most likely well on his way north. It would be a long tiring night, but I would have to press on at a run and hope that I was not only not too late to save the bumbling Great Sir William, but that I also still had enough energy and my wits about me to slay the troll. They say a woman's work is never done. I wonder if the people who came up with that one took into account saving your husband from slack-jawed, foul-breathed trolls and still having to come up with something for dinner. Crap! I forgot to put a stew on before I left.

Five

 I ran, oh stars above how I ran. I dressed on the run, cinching down my leather armor and strapping on weapons as I ran, which is not an easy task let me tell you. All I could think of was my foolish, yet honorable, Will standing in front of the troll and yelling something idiotic like, "Get thee gone, vile troll! Or I will smite thee down!" as the troll swatted him around like a fly. Those thoughts quickened my pace further and when I reached the northern road I sprinted. The lightly colored road grit reflected the moonlight enough that it made searching the hard pack for signs of Will's horse easier. After a few minutes I found what I was looking for – a small *W* engraved in the horseshoe print. I pay the blacksmith an extra silver piece to add the *W*. He thinks it's a vanity issue for Will, and that's fine by me, but the purpose is for times like this when Will goes far enough out of my sight that it is easier for me to track him. I spent hours off and on running or sprinting until I could barely breathe then I'd stop and check the roadway for another *W*. I followed that pattern of run, breathe, look, and repeat until dawn broke over the trees. Mostly it was that light gray you early birds know well, but the oranges, reds, and true light of day were close behind. That's when I found Will curled up against his horse in a small clearing beside the trail. Both of them cozily snuggled up next to the remnants of his campfire.

I had run and exhausted myself for hours while he slept under a nice warm blanket – one that I knitted too, mind you. While I ran so hard that the leather from my chest piece had chafed my nipples raw and the sweat running down my breasts was stinging the wounds, Will had slept. I should have been happy to find him safe, and I was, but have you ever done that? Exhausted yourself over worry, only to find out that the thing that had you so worked up was just fine without you? It stings your pride more than a little, and in my case it stung my nipples, too.

It was still early enough that Will would probably sleep for another few hours. He's a heavy sleeper. That's not a fact you hear much about in the tavern songs is it? How the Great Sir William sleeps like the dead. I once found a pair of faeries arguing over whether one of them had placed a glamour on him as he snoozed away the morning, because they could not believe that a human could sleep so deep naturally without fae aid. For once one of his weaknesses worked in my favor. I had a chance to rest, maybe catch a quick nap, before I had to wind my way through the underbrush on either side of the trail to get ahead of Will when he did start to travel again. I climbed the nearest maple tree that had a large amount of foliage to cover me from sight, found a secure enough perch, tucked my arms around my sore throbbing nipples, and let my chin fall to my chest. I was asleep almost instantly.

It seemed like I was just as instantly woken up by Will's horse whinnying when its nearly blind rider kept jabbing it with gear as he tried to load it up. Once a frying pan caught the poor thing just above the eye – thank goodness it was a pan and not his sword. That's happened before.

I was exhausted, just weary to the bone. You know that feeling where you realize you're supposed to get out of bed, you have things you need to do, but even lifting your eyelids seems like too much work? The thought of doing anything but sitting still for a very long time seemed impossible. I really could have used another few hours' sleep, but instead I waited until Will had moved along out of the clearing and back to the northern road. While I could still hear the clinks and clacks of his barely secured load, I slipped down from my perch. My feet landed lightly, never making a sound. I lined the bottom of my boots with an extra piece of suede before every mission. Will may be blind, but he isn't deaf. I have had to use every scrap of forest lore my father taught me to stay silent on these mutual quests of ours.

Papa taught me everything about the woods. I know the lands of Thistledown better than any trapper or ranger. I know the plants, the trees, and the wildlife too. There is a small overgrown deer run that edges the left side of the northern road. Not many people know about it. It's barely more than a path with fewer weeds, stuffed and choked with brambles and thorns. But it works well enough to keep me out of sight, so long as the leaves are in. If its winter I'm basically screwed. I have to stay so far out of earshot and eyesight it's ridiculous. I dread winter missions. I figure if the day comes that I'm ever too late to save my husband it will be a winter morning. You could call that poetic for the soul, but I call it just bad luck.

My mother died on a winter day giving birth to me…maybe its destiny for me to lose Will in the winter, too. Papa died on a winter morning. I guess if you believed in curses the cold months would be cursed to me for sure. It was a good thing it was a late summer day that had me edging my way up and around the deer run past Will and his current horse – Duke XII. Please, don't ask me about the previous eleven. I already told you about Will's improper stowing of large pointy objects like swords, so just go ahead and use your imagination for the rest. We had the first three Dukes back when Papa was still alive. So, I guess the average of about one Duke a year isn't so bad. Well, maybe the Dukes would beg to differ, especially number VIII, who was sat on by a giant. But still, not bad given Will's track record as a whole.

Duke XII could smell me. I could tell by the way he started bucking and chomping on his bit when the side trail circled too close to the north road. That was

45

always a hassle, because I stable our horses as well –
like I don't have enough to do already, right? But
they know me, better than they know Will, so when
a horse thinks its real owner is nearby it would rather
go be with them. I could hear Will try to soothe
Duke, saying, "Easy girl, we're not in troll country
yet. Don't worry."

See what I mean about the blind thing? If you've
ever had a male horse or happen to have seen one get
a bit randy, it's kind of hard to miss…unless you're
the Great Sir William, of course.

I pushed myself a bit harder to travel further up
the trail. Hoping that if I could get upwind of Duke
he'd calm down and if I made any noise as I tore
through the brambles, Will would just assume it was
a deer bolting and that had been what Duke had
smelled.

Once I was far enough ahead of them I left the
side trail and started using the north road instead.
The travel was easier on the wide maintained path.
None of the underbrush of the deer trail could have
torn any of my armor, but I checked for damage anyway. It's good sturdy, quality leather, my armor. I
work, reinforce, and tailor it myself, too. I let the
blacksmith handle Will's, but I craft my own, thank
you very much. That way I know any of the flaws
and don't find out too late in the field, well, kind of
like my now raw nipples. I'd have to remember to
install some kind of nipple-guard or padding when I

returned home. Then again I'd rather have sore nipples from armor that I crafted than a dagger in my side from a chink in poorer quality goods that somebody else tailored.

The temptation to push myself a bit harder to place more distance between Will and me, so I could find a spot to hold up in and catch a nap, was hard to resist. If I went too far, he may run into trouble he couldn't handle, or he could get lost, even on such a well maintained path as the north road. He could wander into the brush for a pee and lose his sense of direction. No, it was best to stay just out of sight and keep my pace slow. Even if I went too slowly and Will caught a glimpse of me, he would just assume I was another traveler on the road. When I follow Will I keep my hair bound up tightly and my face hidden under a mask that only leaves my eyes exposed. I've kept myself prepared for such an encounter. It is inevitable that one day he will spot me, that's why I have the mask, and I heavily darken my eyes with coal. It may give me some exotic southern pleasure slave type look when I see my reflection in a stream or glass, but, then again it might also just make me look foolish. I don't care either way. It works to obscure my identity and that's all that matters.

With sore aching feet and other sore sensitive places I started to pass the first northern cattle ranches an hour or two before nightfall. There was a small copse of alders slightly past the second ranch. I settled in, obscured from the view of anyone passing along the road, yet still able to see traffic from either direction. I had kept a slow enough pace, whether through exhaustion or skill I'm not sure, but I only waited minutes before Will rode into view on Duke. The sky was quickly darkening and I had a moment's hesitation when I thought Will might stop for the night in the very same copse I had chosen to camp in, but at the last second a loud booming voice echoed from the hillside, quickly accompanied by its owner, the nearest rancher. "The Great Sir William will not have to sleep outdoors on my watch!"

The heavyset rancher rode into view on a horse that was fresher and younger than poor Duke XII. Neither Will nor the rancher dismounted as they stopped alongside each other. The rancher stuck out his hand for Will to shake, saying, "Gar Jinkins, at your service sir."

Stars above! I hadn't seen Gar Jinkins in years! Those years must have been good, because the old rancher was twice as fat as he used to be, and he was never what anybody would call slim to begin with.

Will shook Gar's pudgy hand and said, "A pleasure to meet you, Gar. King Theodore tells me you are having some trouble with a troll up here?"

Gar nodded his head and looking down, he sadly muttered, "It took one of my grandbabies, sir. I…" He trailed off as emotions threatened to overcome him. Will is a good honest man. He may not be what the legends say he is, but he still cares about people, how they feel, how they hurt, he is more than willing to empathize with their troubles, and that is more than can be said for most heroes who have actually done some of the deeds they are given credit for. Will reached over and patted Gar on the shoulder saying, "I will take care of it, my friend. I promise. I only apologize that I did not hear of it sooner. Please, if your offer of hospitality stands, let us head to your homestead and talk of these matters by a fire, over a drink to ease the pain and warm the body, yes?"

Gar nodded and wiped at his eyes with the back of his calloused workman's hand. They were gone in moments, up the side trail Gar had so recently ridden down, back toward the Jinkins' homestead. I could see the lights from Gar's ranch flickering to life at the crest of a hill as the two figures rode in that direction. The Great Sir William makes a promise, a noble one, but still I'm the one who has to keep it. Not to mention, he gets a warm bed, a hot meal, and goodness knows what else while I sleep out in the cold on the hard ground with an alder root getting frisky with me no matter how many times I changed positions. I'd do it anyway though, Papa traded with Gar a lot when I was younger, and he'd have wanted me to help the Jinkins clan out. Nice warm bed or not, sleep was sleep, and I needed some badly. I was out like a light with the sun, but just as darkness fell I couldn't help but feel like something was watching me. The woods at night can do that to even the most seasoned traveler, but it is still disconcerting. The best way I've found to sleep with that possibility of unease, is to place my back to a tree and keep my knife in hand. Lord help the foolish woodsman to ever come across me taking a nap and mistake me for *Sleeping Beauty*. He'd be the first *Prince Charming* to sing soprano that's for sure.

Six

I woke up early the next morning and ate a meager trail savvy breakfast of hardtack. A few strips of venison jerky and some biscuits, washed down with stream water, mmm mmm I've never been so stuffed. Thistledown is a small kingdom. I don't know what terms of measurement you use in your lands: leagues, miles, feet, or something else, but you could hike from one end of Thistledown to the other in about a week at the longest. So I usually don't have to pack too heavy on the provisions for these excursions. Plus, Papa taught me how to gather the foodstuffs the forest provides if I really need them. I know what berries and fruits are in season when and which greens are edible and which ones will have you running for the privy if you eat too many. I even use most of that outdoor cooking lore in my day to day recipes – it saves on growing crops.

Of course a couple of stale biscuits and a few strips of dried out dead deer were no comparison for what Will was surely served up on the ranch: hot tea, slabs of bacon and sausage, with countless eggs, plus sweet breads. I could smell them all wafting down the hillside on the early morning breeze. Then again, I didn't have to spend all night and probably some of the morning listening to the entire Jinkins clan talk and cry about how one of the littlest Jinkinses would never see another holiday, or never grow up and have more little Jinkinses of her own. On second thought the idea of having to eat that huge steaming hot repast while looking into Gar Jinkins' red-rimmed eyes made my cold trail breakfast seem like the better deal.

As I ate I tried to stretch some of my sore muscles and aching joints. The previous night and day of hard running and hiking had taken their toll on my aging body. The days when I could push myself to exhaustion, then sleep on the cold hard ground, and not pay for it the next morning were long behind me. So some stretching and massaging were definitely in order. Looking around my campsite as I stretched I even found a bit of chamomile and ground it into a paste to soothe my raw nipples. It helped with the inflammation and made my breasts smell like tea. What more could a woman want? The entire time I went about easing my body back into some semblance of function I could not shake the feeling of being watched. At night that unease can be shrugged off as the human dependence on sight as their primary sense, but in the daylight it was a feeling to be suspect and wary of for sure. I scanned the horizon past the copse of alders with their scalloped leaves rustling, expecting to maybe see the troll that had been the cause of this trip to begin with, but I saw nothing. Only the rolling hills bathed in the light from the early sunrise and the herds of cattle that must have been some of Jinkins' and some that must have been from the other ranchers, marching out to do their daily grazing - but no troll. That is another

of the drawbacks to the whole cold killer thing I was
telling you about. The cold killers, we always expect
the worst out of others, so it makes us more than a
bit paranoid. The feeling I had of being watched was
probably just a byproduct of that cold killer paranoia
… probably … maybe, but you never know.

I lost my chance to dwell on that feeling overmuch when I heard Will's voice shout, "Fear not my
friends! I will avenge little Daisy and I shall return
with the barbarous creature's head for you, Gar. I
promise." I really wish he wouldn't talk like that
sometimes. It drives me crazy. He doesn't speak the
same way at home as he does to the masses. I don't
hear, "Fair maiden would thee mind passing the
salt?" I guess in any relationship you have those tiny
inconsequential things that the other person does that
make you want to strangle them, until every last
Thee, Thou, and *Wouldst* can't make it past their
stupid, pompous…um, okay, so I get a little cranky
when I'm tired. It happens.

Anyway, Will rode astride a much refreshed
looking Duke as they sauntered down the same path
they had ridden up toward the homestead last evening. Will had turned in his saddle to wave heroically
at the Jinkins clan that had assembled on the hillside
to see him off. I gathered my gear, what little of it I
had, and crouched behind a large alder to wait until
Will had passed. I did not want to get ahead of him
this time. The chances were best that he would encounter the troll sometime today or tomorrow and I

always give him the opportunity to slay the beast on his own. It has never happened yet, but hey I'm an optimist, there's always a first time. There's also the possibility that I could be wrong and the monster could kill him with the first strike, don't think that hasn't crossed my mind either. It's a gamble, but if I go running ahead and slay the troll before him – which admittedly would just be easier – then Will could become lost, searching endlessly for a villain that is already dead. He may also find the corpse and start to wonder more about all those times he's been knocked on his ass. Always a risk, always a hassle. So I watch and wait like any good hunter.

We traveled further north along the road into the mountains as morning turned into afternoon. The dew and damp of dawn had long since been burned away by the sun, and the mountains were looming larger and higher before us. The road disappears altogether at the base of Mount Crenshaw, deep, deep in the Northern Mountain Range. I hoped we would not have to travel that far. It's a long road, and more dangerous things lurk in the heart of the mountains than trolls. Things that would keep you awake at night if I told you they existed and things that are so ferocious, yet rarely seen that they don't even have a name, at least that's what Papa told me.

I had barely started to think of the nastier things that call Mount Crenshaw and its surrounding peaks home, when Duke started to buck and thrash about. We were miles from the nearest ranch and the road was deteriorating quickly in evidence to how little it was used up here. I had stayed very close, just down wind and out of eyesight – Will's eyesight that is, you or I probably would have seen me ten times over. Will leaned down in his saddle to calm Duke, gently stroking the steed along his neck and mane. That miniscule movement, a hairsbreadth bent in the saddle, actually saved his life. The troll tore out of the underbrush to Will's right, ferocious and slobbering. Matted black hair cascaded in tangled ringlets down its back where the skin mottled between a grotesque shade of dark green and a rotting corpse gray. It was eight feet tall, lanky but strong. The troll leapt with the force of a panther, plowing into Will and Duke, sending all three of them tumbling from the trail into the thick brambles along the other side of the road.

Smaller trees snapped with the force of their struggle. A wild turkey screamed and shot out of the brambles, disturbed from its hiding place by the grappling threesome. That must have been one hell of a rise and shine for that bird. I could hear Duke shrieking that high-pitched whinny horses only use when the threat is mortal in nature. If you're familiar with horses you don't hear it often, but when you do it means the poor thing is in real danger. Will grunted and groaned. The troll snarled and bellowed. I had to sprint to catch up to them; at least they were making enough noise they were easy to follow. When the miniature cyclone of destruction that was my husband, his horse, and the monster came to a stop I could see I was faced with a decision that I'd had to make only a few times before. The troll had its long fingers wrapped around Will's neck and it had used its size to pin my large, but not larger than a troll, husband to the forest floor and was quickly choking the life from him. The decision was how long should I wait before I stepped in? How long could Will fight before he blacked out, and even more important, was his neck strong enough to stand up to the crushing force the troll was placing on it? Did I risk Will seeing me by stepping in early? You would think I had been faced with these choices a lot before then, but I hadn't. Thankfully most of the monsters around Thistledown had the attitude of superiority that makes things like ambushing the hero seem beneath them. This troll did not have that superiority complex. No, he was a cold killer, too. Crap.

I drew my short sword with my right hand and held my stiletto firmly in my left - the smaller blade defensively riding along my bracer in a reverse grip. I don't like shields, it's too hard to maneuver and counterstrike when you use a shield, so I use my stiletto defensively when infighting. A word of advice, if you ever find yourself going up against a cold killer; don't pussyfoot around. If you have your shot or strike and you know your opponent would take it in your position, then you better make your move and honor be damned. That is if you want to walk away, of course. I could no longer hear my Will struggling for breath. I snuck up behind them and with one thrust, placed between the troll's shoulder blades, broke his hold on Will's throat. The creature roared and spun around so fast my sword was yanked from my grasp. It turned to face me with the point of my own sword still sticking out from its chest, dripping black blood in the bright noon sun. The troll looked down at the metal protruding from its chest, then looked up dumbfounded at me, then back down at the sword point, and roared again. I had missed the heart strike. Stupid trolls and their stupid weird ass centrally located organs. I eased back into a fighter's stance, with my stiletto being my only weapon I switched it to my dominant hand and led with my left bracer instead. It was not an enviable position – going up against a much larger opponent with very little in the way of weaponry. I was in trouble.

The troll stopped roaring and picked up a stone. At first I thought he was going to throw the rock at me, but then, grunting with the effort he pushed on the protruding tip of my blade. It stuck at one point during his crude operation and the troll started to hammer on the sword tip hard and repeatedly until sparks flew from his chest. It slid out of his back and landed with a thud on the recently torn-up forest floor. Then the troll glared at me. His eyes were deep, dark, hate-filled pits from which I swore I saw more sparks fly. Crap. Not just a fellow cold killer, but a badass too. That's all I needed. Yeah, I was in really big trouble.

The troll roared a battle cry and sprinted at me like he had through the brush when he surprised

57

Will. Size can be a huge advantage in a melee fight. It gives the larger opponent reach and strength, but it also has its drawbacks, too. If the larger fighter throws a punch full-force or runs all out to tackle the smaller combatant they are committed to the move. All that mass has trouble redirecting itself if the fleeter fighter can, as the saying goes, stick and jab. I'm neither short nor tall for a woman. But, average height for a woman still puts me at almost half the size of a troll. I crouched even further down as the troll barreled past me, ducking between the charging brute's legs as he stormed past. Oh, and I stuck and jabbed at the nearest weak point. No, get your mind out of the gutter. I didn't stab *that*. I sliced the artery that runs along the inside of all bipeds' thighs wide-open. I mean *wide-open*. I could feel the hot gush of blood as it soaked into the elbow joint on my right arm's bracer. I spun around quickly to face the troll as it stumbled past. It was a mortal strike, but sometimes big badass cold killers just don't know when they're done.

The troll crashed with its missed tackle. I don't think it even realized it had been cut. That's the beauty of a clean strike – over and done. It was able to regain its feet once, but it staggered and fell before it could reach me again, groaning. Then it shuddered once and became still and silent. Please, don't judge me. Most of you probably don't have the stomach for what I do, but maybe you could if you were doing it for the same reasons I was, I don't know. But mortal wound or not, in my line of work you don't leave anything to chance. I ran over to the downed troll and placing all my weight behind the strike, I drove my stiletto deep into the base of its skull – better safe than sorry.

I was hunched over, heart pounding in my chest, and in the quiet of the deep woods as the battle-rush flooded my body with energy – that hyper-alert feeling after you realize you're going to live another day – I heard a voice. In fact, I heard the words I have been dreading for almost twenty years. "Who are you?"

Crap. So, the troll hadn't choked the life out of Will, thankfully. But it also had not been able to choke him into unconsciousness. Thanks a lot pal - you just can't find decent monsters, willing to work at their jobs anymore can you?

Not looking up or acknowledging that he had spoken, I wiped my blade off on the troll's filthy loincloth. Keeping my back to Will I lifted my stiletto to use as a mirror to see where Will was. The reflection told me he had managed to struggle up to his elbows, but he was still mostly lying down where he had been. Good.

I spun around and as fast, if not faster than the troll, I covered the few yards separating us and kicked Will in the head, just like I had done two nights previous with Jimmy the gypsy juggler. Will flinched with the blow, surprise giving his features a comical expression before he fell back to the ground, out for the count.

Hey, I did what I had to.

Seven

Alright, so I kicked my husband of almost twenty years in the head to knock him unconscious. It was for his own good, really, you have to trust me on that. How many times have you heard a lady say that, huh? Well the *for his own good* part at least, probably not the kick to the head part. On second thought maybe you're into that kind of thing. You never know some people are, so I don't judge. Then again, if you've been together a long time, maybe it's at least something you've fantasied about a time or two. Trust me; kicking somebody you love extremely hard in the head, well, it just isn't as satisfying as it may sound. Feel free to try it yourself sometime, but remember I told you it wouldn't be as good as the fantasy.

I didn't have much choice though really. I mean sure I could have just run away. If I fled into the woods Will never would have caught up to me. He can't track for squat and he'd probably have tripped over a log and knocked himself out again anyhow. That makes more sense in retrospect, it would have had the same result and been less domestically violent, but in the heat of the moment my brain yelled, "Kick him! Kick him in the head!" What that says about both me and my brain I don't want to think too long on. How about we say I'm impulsive. At least that sounds better than psychotic.

Give me some credit though, I checked to make sure Will was still breathing before I retrieved Duke so he would be there by Will when he woke up. The horse had a few bumps and scrapes, but it looked like we didn't need a Duke XIII just yet. Once everything appeared to be in order I fled to a nearby maple tree. It was large enough for me to scamper up and hide out of sight, behind the thick foliage and branches, until Will awoke. I loved climbing trees as a little girl, which turned out to be an occupational bonus, because it seems I spend more time up in them now than I did as a child. Crouched behind a large branch, I examined the end of my sword that the troll had pummeled out of its chest with a rock. It was dented and burred, great, one more thing for the *To Do* list when we returned home. Obviously I didn't have what I needed to reshape the blade with me up in the tree, so I watched Will sleep. He slept - yeah I'm going to call it sleep and not unconsciousness even though I knocked him out - for about an hour. Just when I started to get antsy from a twig jabbing me in the ass and constantly having to switch positions, Will groaned and sat up, holding his head in his hands.

Duke trotted over and nuzzled the back of Will's neck as he rocked, trying to clear his head I imagine. He mumbled, "Atta girl, thanks. What happened, huh?"

His voice was uncertain; kind of woozy and garbled like the village drunk that always seems to sound intoxicated, no matter how long it has been since he had a drink. You know that kind of tone, maybe you have an uncle that visits on holidays that sounds like that – lots of slurs and impediments. Slowly, using Duke's reins to pull himself up, Will stumbled and tripped several times before he finally had his feet steadily under him. That stability only lasted long enough for him to turn around and trip, falling headlong over the troll's corpse. I had a spilt second when I thought, *Stars above, how does he function at all without me?* But before I could follow that thought too far I felt that damn sensation of being watched again. Cold killer paranoia aside, I knew somebody was watching me that time.

I didn't make any sudden movements. I didn't want to give away that I was onto my stalker. Figuring that when I had looked before, earlier that morning, my motions had alerted my watcher that I was aware of them, giving whoever or whatever it was a chance to hold back and hide. I scanned the underbrush as nonchalantly as I could. Keeping my eyes mainly focused on Will, I only watched the shadows with my peripheral vision in hopes of catching a glimpse of my pursuer. Nothing. Nada. Zip. Zero. Zilch. Crap.

Will's voice intruded on my remonstrations. "A promise is a promise, right girl?" I looked down directly at my husband as he pulled his sword from its scabbard along Duke's saddle. It's a beautiful weapon, elegant, well-balanced, but huge, I could never wield something so large – effectively at any rate. With a sound of disgust, and a panicked whinny from Duke as the sword barely missed us needing that number XIII after all, Will lifted his broadsword over his head and brought it down in a two-handed blow at the troll's neck.

It took him three chops, four if you count the time it got lodged in a tree trunk a yard away. I'm still not sure how he managed that, but he did eventually remove the troll's head from its body to take back to Gar Jinkins. Weird and creepy, I know I'm not in his place, but men and that whole vengeance thing of "I want his head" or its head or whatever, just seems kind of twisted to me. Once revenge has been served, it will not bring your loved one back to lop somebody/thing's head off as a trophy. Maybe he wanted to see it as proof and he'll just burn it. I can see how that could be somewhat cathartic. But for me, personally, if it had been somebody I loved that the troll had taken I'd have been out here killing the damn thing myself…but, that's that whole cold killer thing cropping up again, I guess.

Holding the nasty trophy by its greasy lank hair, Will hauled himself up into Duke's saddle, and let the horse find its own way back to the trail. Not having the forethought to pack Will a canvas sack for decapitated head transportation, he had to hold the gross ball as it dripped greenish-black blood the entire trip back to the Jinkins' ranch. I knew the way, of course, but if I hadn't I could have followed the trail of troll blood, ew.

Once again Will rode onto Gar's lands as the sun was setting. It had been a long day for him this time as well as for me. He was a bruised and battered hero, returning from a quest instead of setting out upon one. His promises fulfilled and only carrying the grim satisfaction of justice, well and a troll's severed head, to a family that would still be grateful to house him once more. A family that would clean and care for him. A family that would help spread the word of the wondrous deeds of the Great Sir William! Troll slayer and child avenger…but even after the stories were told and retold that family would still be broken. I doubt that no matter what he does to that head, Gar Jinkins will never have that same sparkle in his eye or ruddy colored smile I used to see on him when I was a child. It might surface from time to time, but the shadow of that loss will always come back. He'll see a flower that was his granddaughter's favorite, or a swing he had set up for her in the backyard, maybe a stuffed animal she left on her bed, and he'll spiral back down. Loss never leaves you, funny huh? The one thing you can't lose is loss.

I guess maybe that's why I do this. Not only to protect my Will, but because somebody has to. Somebody has to stand up against the monsters in the world and if Will can't actually do it, then I better. It's hard not to berate yourself for not being there sooner, to save whoever it is that needs saving, but you can only be so many places at once, meaning one. I thought about that while I snuggled down into the same copse of alders, hearing the cries of relief and renewed sorrow drifting down on the evening breeze - interspersed with the occasional cheer for Will. As I drifted off to sleep, tired and worn, but still ready to fight, I realized how sad it is that there can't be somebody always there to watch over us, especially the children, to keep them and us safe…but again, the world has too many heartaches and too few heroes.

Eight

I woke up just before dawn. The sky was still black and blanketed with stars, all but for a slim gray section lightening the eastern horizon. It took me a second to gather my wits as to what had pulled me from my deep post physical exertion sleep. You know that small jolt of fear that your unconscious mind sends your way when it notices something that you, snoring away soundly, ignore. It's a survival mechanism but it still can scare the shit out of you. Then another twig snapped providing my conscious mind with the reason I was awake before I wanted to be. I'd had it with whatever was following me. I sprang to my feet and into the still dark trees, I yelled, "Who's there? I know you've been following me, just show yourself."

The nearby bushes rattled some more - twigs snapping, branches breaking, leaves crunching - as my pursuer gave up all pretexts of stealth and tromped toward me. I readied myself for another troll, drawing my dented short sword to accompany my already drawn stiletto. Maybe it was the jilted, yet slightly smarter mate or brother that had been trailing me while its partner pounced on Will. Or it could have been that I had misjudged Gar and the old rancher had wanted a piece of the troll after all. Maybe he had snuck down from the ranch the previous night because he had seen me concealed in the alder copse and wanted to confront me, thinking I was a poacher or cattle rustler. Who knows? I would have believed and fully expected any of those. What I did not expect was Jimmy the pretty boy juggler to brush past a wild rosebush and smirk as he strode fully into view as the gray dawn brightened.

Crap.

"What are you doing here?" I growled, holding my stiletto out and bringing him up short when the point did not drop or waver at his approach. Knife aimed at his abdomen or not he still smirked, saying, "It is you, my lady. I wasn't sure. I thought I had followed the right trail, but from a distance I could have been wrong - especially when I saw the mask and coal-darkened eyes. I still wasn't completely sure until I heard your voice."

Crap. Crap. Crap.

Losing his smirk completely and looking much of his maybe twenty years, he sat down suddenly. Rubbing at his temple with a genuine frown of concern, he accused, "You kicked me in the head."

Sighing deeply I turned away and sheathed my blades – the spurred short sword stuck slightly in its scabbard so I had to forcefully jam it in. My back turned to him I grunted with the effort of wrestling with my sword, and said, "Yes, Jimmy, I did. Now answer me, what are you doing here?"

The Knight's Wife

Whether he was willfully ignoring me or if he was really that innocent, or maybe stupid, my jury was still out on that case, he added, "You kicked Sir William in the head too. I saw the whole thing. You killed the troll not Sir William. He was about to be turned into a pulpy mess, but you stepped in and killed-"

"Jimmy!" I interrupted him. "Do you want me to kick you again?"

Miracle of all miracles he shook his head. "Then answer my question," I added grinding my teeth as the sword finally slid into place.

He cleared his throat and started right back up. Stars above that boy loved to talk. He said, "Well my lady, I promised the queen I'd look after you. I wasn't sure why you ran off like you did and I was worried something would happen to you. Then the queen would blame me. I was kind of hoping to stay in Thistledown. I like it there and my troop has already moved on. I figured if I could get in good with the queen I was sure to be welcomed. So when I overheard her talking late the night of the festival how she needed someone to go after you to make sure you were safe, I volunteered. It seems kind of pointless after watching you slay that troll though. You can really fight! I mean I've never seen a woman kick as-"

"Shut up, Jimmy," I snapped. And apparently I was blessed with a second miracle in as many minutes because he did. What was I supposed to do? My secret was out. Will's secret was out. All because some dumb chatterbox of a pretty boy wanted to impress Queen Marissa. Crap…but then again, maybe the cat wasn't out of the bag just yet. I mean only Jimmy here knew. I could real easily slit that young muscular throat, right? It wouldn't be too hard. I was tired but I was pretty positive I was faster and better with a blade than he was. He was almost as thick as Will, but strength is meaningless in a knife or sword fight. It only takes the littlest of pressure, a pound at most, to break human skin. I could dump the body…

Oh fine! I wasn't going to. You don't have to look at me like that. I was just thinking that I did have options. Jimmy must have read some of what was going on in my mind in my eyes because he jumped to his feet and started yammering on again, but this time with the stammer of someone nervous and not his typical Mister Confident *look at me ladies aren't I stunningly handsome* voice. No, he sounded more like a pre-ball-dropped squire when he said, "I'm not going to tell anybody, my lady. I mean it's none of my business how well you fight or if this was a one-time thing. Yes, I'm sure that's what all this was, right? Just a one-time thing, where you happened to be in the right place at the right time to save Sir William who normally does this sort of thing all the time by himself. And you just happened to wield those blades with some innate skill that you didn't know you had or…or…or something.

Right?" He looked hopefully at me. When the only response I gave him was a glare he blurted out, "Please don't kill me."

Crap.

The sky had lightened to full dawn. Ranchers and farmers rise early, it's part of the lifestyle. I could hear Will and the Jinkins clan coming down the path again. This time the clan was cheering my bumbling husband the hero's name and not wishing him well on his quest, but profusely thanking him for making their lands safe again. They would be within eyesight of the copse where I was hidden with Jimmy the stammering juggler in moments. I had to decide what I was going to do and fast, before Will was within earshot. The chances of him seeing us would be slim no matter how close we were, but Jimmy apparently was lacking the capacity to shut up. He was still yammering on as I paced a bit, keeping my back to him. I had stopped listening to what he was saying and I just nodded appropriately to let him believe I was actually paying attention to his blathering.

Okay, so maybe I might, just might, mind you, it's nothing confirmed or definite, only a might, have some emotional problems when it comes to patience with other people. I know, I know, admitting it is the first step and all that, but when I need to make a quick decision it usually ends up with me stabbing, cutting, or kicking something. So, given those options I think the roundhouse kick I landed to the side of Jimmy's head was really the best choice, don't you? I mean he fell to the ground, mercifully silent, but not gushing blood from a stab wound which was his other option, as Will rode Duke onto the road, heading south toward Thistledown. I checked his pulse again, just to be safe. He was fine. Young people in their twenties are made of rubber, you know that. Look, I know I kick things a lot. Sorry, but nobody's perfect.

Nine

After leaving Jimmy safe and sound - unconscious but not gushing blood - in the quiet alder copse, I ran. Again. Gee, Lady Gale how do you stay so thin? I run my damn ass off girls, literally. You want to stay thin? Chase your nearly blind wannabe hero husband all over your kingdom, trust me, that'll work better than any healthy diet. Of course if he isn't a nearly blind wannabe hero you'll probably creep him out stalker-like, but it will still work to keep those hips and thighs trim anyway. I didn't necessarily have to haul ass quite so much this time because I knew Will would report in to King Theodore before going home. He didn't have to, his majesty had told Will on more than one occasion that it would be alright if he went home to see me first, or just to have a good night's rest, before reporting in. But Will is a stickler for detail. He isn't obsessive about it or anything. He just likes to complete a task start to finish before he rests. It's kind of funny when you think that he never really does complete the task either. But he sure wants to see it done right.

The reason I galloped over the countryside, taking shortcuts through fields and over pastures I knew well was the fact that I forgot to leave something out for supper. I know that's ridiculous after all I had done over the last three days, but if Will comes home and there isn't a meal ready he's bound to ask why. More than likely he'd say something stupid like, "But why isn't dinner ready? It's not like you have anything else to do." And if history is any kind of teacher I'd probably end up getting pissed off over such a remark and kick him in the head. So, as you can see, racing to make sure I was home with enough time to spare wasn't really the overkill it may seem, but more of a way to keep my marriage working smoothly…with less head trauma.

I had other concerns on my mind as well. What was I going to do when Jimmy the juggler eventually regained consciousness enough to go tattle on me to Queen Marissa? Not only had I violated the kid's trust, I had abused him, condescended to him, and the pretty boy had also figured out my biggest secret. I could always kill him. I probably should have. I know, you're thinking even Gale isn't that cold…well, okay, you're right I'm not, but still, let's not shoot down any options at this point, alright? There is always the chance that he would be too embarrassed with his failure to bring one little old housewife back to the castle, and he may just up and leave Thistledown to rejoin his gypsy clan. Not likely, but possible. He did get his butt kicked by a girl, twice. So, maybe he'll hightail it to the next kingdom. Or, maybe Queen Marissa won't believe his story. I mean sure I'm sassy, some might even say spunky, but I've never given anyone in Thistledown the impression that I was more than a good wife and woods woman. They know Papa was a ranger - Hawk the badass fount of forest knowledge - but I doubt they believe or suspect that he taught me how to fight, and that when I was twenty he told me I was a better swordsman than he ever was. So, disbelief is an option, too. Nice to think people's lack of confidence in me could actually be a good thing.

I hate it when people tell you to take your problems as they come, don't bite off more than you can chew, don't make mountains out of molehills, don't count your chickens before they've hatched, blah blah blah. The way I see it if you don't worry about all the possibilities headed your way and all the crap that could go wrong, then you are simply setting yourself up to be blindsided when things actually do go screwy. And they will. They always do. That's life, always looking to screw you over.

Even utilizing every shortcut I knew of, including one that had me swinging ape-like from a rope over a chasm full of sharp rocks – aptly named *Sharp Rock Pass*, Thistledown is not exactly blessed with creatively named places, or creative people for that matter. I know a farm family that has named every one of their sons Phil, all eight of them – crap, sorry, sidetrack, but even using all my knowledge of shortcuts it still took me late into the afternoon before I set foot back inside our cottage.

I stopped by the red maple tree where Papa rests, touched the rough bark, leaned my forehead against it for a minute or two, and placed a leaf at the base. I do that every time I return safe from a mission. I pluck a leaf before I go to let him know that I'm leaving, and as a way of hoping that he'll watch over me and help keep me safe. The leaf connects me to him and the tree, no matter how far away I travel. It stays tucked in under the stiletto sheath all during the journey. When I do return home, more or less intact, I place the wrinkled and sometimes dried leaf back at the base of the tree to let Papa know I'm home safe again. Silly, I know, but it helps me and it doesn't hurt anything. It's only a young girl's superstition, but those tend to stay with us don't they? Papa used to do the same with leaves from the nearby oak tree he buried my mother under. So I figured he'd like that I do the same for him. I don't take one from my mother's tree. That isn't callousness or anything. I didn't know her. I love her. Papa told me endless stories about her, but the leaf is for the person the bearer knew, not someone they wished they had.

Leaf in place, and yes, eyes wiped on a handkerchief thank you very much, I went inside and stoked the fire in the stove back to life. It had gone completely out, not even the smallest of sparks were left in the ash. Three days to cool will do that. After coaxing the fire to roaring again and placing a pot of saltwater on a burner, I went out back to clean my troll blood-stained armor in the washbasin. It was black, crusty, and smelled like a dead cow left in a field to bloat in the summer sun. Hell, one sniff of myself and I realized I smelled like a dead cow left in a field to bloat in the summer sun. Once the nasti-

er stains were removed, I stashed my breastplate –
making a mental note to add nipple padding – and
the rest in a cobweb choked alcove in the stable. I
left my already stained and bloated bovine smelling
blouse on when I slaughtered a rabbit from our
hutch. Why dirty another shirt? I hate killing any of
the animals I raise, even for food. Funny how I have
a hard time skinning a sweet bunny rabbit to eat, but
bathing in a troll's lifeblood is all in a day's work.

Rabbit skinned, chopped, diced, and added to the
pot with some potatoes and carrots, I had a coney
stew cooking. I stripped out of my torn and rather
ripe smelling trail clothes, setting them aside to soak
and launder overnight - that aroma wasn't coming
out without some kind of pre-treating, believe me -
and finally attended to my scrapes and bruises. The
sun had dropped low in the sky and the trees were
darkening the corners of our cottage when I finally
had the chance to sit down, put my feet up and rest
after *now* four hard days of labor and running – lots
and lots of running. No sooner had my feet touched
down on the ottoman than I heard Will coming up
the trail on Duke. Figures, doesn't it?

Ten

See, a woman's work is never done, never. Clean something and it gets dirty again. Fix something and it's just going to break. Cook a meal and it gets eaten, gone, poof! Now I know this may sound overly dramatic, but there are times when I actually look forward to dying. Seriously. Not the whole makeup running, snot dripping, *my life is so horrible and hard I want to die* type dying. I mean take today as an example; I had maybe sat down to rest my feet for five minutes before I had to hop back up into action? Really? So, to me, death sounds like a nice long nap. Sure, I'd miss sunsets, cookies, sex (when I'm in the mood sex, not that damn thing poking me in the small of the back until I just give in, when all I want to do is go to sleep sex), and a lot of the other day to day pleasures. Sure, I'd miss those things, but simply the idea of resting without limits sounds awfully good most of the time. With my luck there'd be an afterlife and whatever ruler or god that runs the joint would come racing up the second I place my head on a fluffy white cloud for a nap and say, "Thank me! Gale's here everybody! It's about time; the laundry hampers are overflowing with dirty robes! Oh and when you have a moment the eternal privy is clogged, too."

I could hear Will brushing Duke down and stabling him while I drug my aching, tired body out of my chair, and scraped together dumplings for the stew. He was taking longer than he normally did; maybe the bruises and gashes he sustained from the troll were slowing him down. More likely he was still mulling over the incident and how I, the masked woman, had actually done the slaying. Whatever the reason, either or both, the sun had fully set by the time Will squeezed his large frame through our backdoor. Doing my best to smile and hide that I was fully aware of what had happened, I asked, "How'd it go, dear?"

He grunted noncommittally and flopped into his overlarge chair at the place that I had set for him at our worn kitchen table. Rubbing at his temples with a large dirty hand, he leaned heavily on the tabletop and it groaned under his weight. He refused to meet my gaze. Yep, mulling or sulking, either one, same result. Adding more perk to my voice than I felt, I said, "I'm making rabbit stew with dumplings! One of your favorites for the conquering hero."

He grunted again, but at least he slid his hand from obscuring his eyes and smiled weakly at me. Easing back in his chair – it creaked under his weight, louder than the table had, like the two were competing as to who was suffering more under my husband's bulk – Will broke his silence and simply said, "Sounds good."

I knew what was wrong. How could I not? I was what was wrong. Not me *me* as far as he was concerned, but me the masked woman me. I still had to ask even though I knew. Will is honest, forthright, and all those fine qualities, which means he can't play games that involve bluffing and he can't lie without becoming grossly uncomfortable. Dumping the dumplings into the stew, I walked around the table, grabbing a bowl of warm water and a washcloth as I went and I knelt down next to Will. I started to clean some of the blood from his armor and asked, "What is it? What's wrong?"

Will grunted again, but closed his hand around mine to stop my progress. He looked down at me and said, "I stayed with the Jinkins clan. Your father was a friend of theirs right?"

"Yes," I answered.

Nodding his head Will said, "I thought so. They're good people. It was sad. They had lost one of their children to the troll, Gar's granddaughter Daisy. Her mother showed me some pictures Daisy had drawn. Cute little stick figures, everyone smiling...The smiles were hard to come by when she was gone. It's over. The troll is no more. But it's had me thinking the whole journey home, how we never had children and how sad that is, but it's even sadder to have had one and lost it."

Holy crap!

Twenty years of marriage. Day after day, week after week, month after month, year after year after year and you think you know someone. You think you know how they are: noble, unable to tell a lie, true and honest to a fault…and then he lies right to your face! Wait, Gale calm down. He didn't actually lie. He could and probably does feel that way, but he chose to tell you about that in hopes that it will convince you that is why he is sulking and not the fact that he finally had to come face to face with his own charade. Maybe…or maybe he's a filthy liar! Again, either way.

He leaned forward and took the washcloth from my trembling (hopefully he assumed with sadness, not pissed off wanting to punch him in the head anger) hand and said, "I'll finishing washing up out back, thank you, Gale. Dinner smells great." And he stood up, taking the washbasin with him. Before he went back outside into the dark, he turned and said over his shoulder, "Oh, Queen Marissa said that she wanted you to go see her tomorrow."

Crap.

Acting as if I knew nothing of what that could possibly be about I asked, "Does she? Did she say why?"

"No," Will said, shaking his head, "just that she wanted me to let you know she wanted to speak with you. I figured it was only woman stuff. I'm sorry, should I have found out more?" He said the last with concern and interest breaking through his original dismissive explanation.

"No, no, it's perfectly fine," I said waving him out the door. "I'm sure you're right, that it's just woman stuff, gossip probably, you know she loves to chit-chat. Go on, get cleaned up, I think dinner is all but ready."

He smiled in the candlelight, content with the explanation that has contented men for eons, *woman stuff*, and leaned in to kiss me on the cheek before he went out.

Crap. Apparently Jimmy the juggler is also quite the fast hiker, too. Unless he did take off and Marissa is just curious as to why I didn't come to the castle like she requested. Or, if he did flee, then Jimmy's disappearance has her concerned. Maybe, either way…crap.

Eleven

I left early the next morning to go to Thistle-down Castle and see Queen Marissa. Will could mope around and pretend that it was poor little lost Daisy Jinkins that had him depressed, but I knew better. He had risen and gotten out of bed before me, something that he was never very good at doing. I caught sight of him out in the backyard by the vege-table patch - it needs weeding…crap, of course it does - swinging his sword. Not with the practiced strokes of a master going through a routine, mind you. There was none of the flow and comfortable ease those skilled with a blade can achieve when the weapon almost becomes a metallic extension of their own body. No, these were the wild swipes and chops of an amateur…or more like a blindfolded kid bat-ting at a candy stuffed party favor. I could see that he was trying to reassure himself that he was the Great Sir William which meant I was in deep shit. Confidence is all any public figure has, without it they are nothing. Yes indeed, I was going to have a rough few weeks ahead of me. I could feel it in my bones.

But Will's confidence issues could keep for an-other time. I had to figure out what I was going to say to Queen Marissa. That, of course, all depended on what, if anything, Jimmy the juggler had told her. It isn't a very far walk to Thistledown Castle from our cottage, half a day at most, small kingdom remember? But, since Will was so absorbed in his "training" that he didn't need Duke and since I was about dead on my feet from the past four day's activities, I rode the journey instead of hiking it.

Having left home so early that morning, I strode under the castle's portcullis before the servants had started to prepare the noon meal. The town itself is very quaint and charming. The buildings are made mostly of native granite or oak and shingled with cedar shakes. There are lots of brightly painted shutters and doorframes and a fountain shaped like a blooming thistle in the town square, with water spraying out from the center of the blossom. The streets are cobbled in some kind of stone. I don't know what type. Maybe they're just called cobblestones, I don't know. They're brown and tannish, that much I can say. I know flint when I see it or other rocks that have a use in the woods, like a whetstone, but as far as road stones go? They are better than mud, and that's good enough for me. There have been days like this one where the blue sky, peppered with fluffy white clouds set against the castle as a backdrop, that give me second thoughts about living out in the woods and not in town. Then a small boy ran by screaming at the top of his lungs, "Johnny is a Poopy Head! Johnny is a Poopy Head! His breath smells like moldy bread!" and I realized I liked my quiet homestead just fine. Nice and far away from Johnny and his loud-mouthed slanderer.

The Knight's Wife

Queen Marissa met me at the stables before I had finished passing Duke off to the stable hand – who beamed at the idea of rubbing down the Great Sir William's noble steed. Marissa was out of breath. She must have seen me coming from a window in the castle and run all the way down. Panting, she pulled me into an open stall and smoothed her rumpled, aerobic jostled dress back into place. Composed and queenly once more, she looked all around to make sure we would not be overheard before she snapped, "I cannot believe you!" And she flicked my earlobe, hard, like an upset schoolmarm.

Ouch and crap. I flinched, wincing at the tone of her voice as much as the flick. Rubbing my ear, I said, "Sorry, I just lost track of time, your highness."

"Lost track of time?" Marissa asked shock evident on her elegant features. Then she repeated herself, flicking my earlobe with each word, "Lost track of time!"

Ouch, ouch, ouch, and ouch.

I stepped back and rubbed at my ear. Queen Marissa threw her hands up in exasperation and started pacing the confined space. The scent of hot hay and horse manure baked up from the stable floor as the sun beat down from its zenith. Smoothing her dress again, taking a deep breath, and looking calmer, at least no longer in danger of ear flicking, Queen Marissa said, "I should say so. Lost track of time my royal ass! I always thought you and Will were happy. I never figured you for the affair type, Gale!"

Hold on, what?

I stared blankly at my queen, past the dust motes and mites that danced in the sun rays separating us. If I didn't let her know I had no clue what she was talking about, she might break first and give me a bit more to work with. It was not a moment to be hasty.

She relented, throwing her hands up again in exasperation and then, as if changing her mind, held her palms out in placation as she said, "I'm not judging you, Gale. I'm on your side. Goodness knows I could see how pretty he was, who could blame you? Certainly not me, I love my Theodore, but if I were ten years younger I may have jumped him myself. I just didn't really expect you to...well, you know?" She said the last, bobbing her eyebrows up and down suggestively.

Oh crap! Oh crap! Oh crap! She thought I'd had an affair with Jimmy the juggler and boinked the whole four days away while Will was out slaying the troll. *I just lost track of time*, Gale you moron! Wait...I could use this. If she didn't plan on telling anyone, she had said she was on my side, then I could cover up my lie with another lie. This lie could help solve the problems with my old lie, maybe. If I confirmed it and stuck to the story then she wouldn't want me to come to the castle to stay whenever Will was sent off on a mission because she'd figure I was doing some bedroom gymnastics with the gypsy. I could still save Will's ass – assuming I could get him his confidence back, of course – and not have to make up an excuse for why I didn't come to Thistledown Castle. Oh yeah, this was perfect, this would solve everything, this…this was definitely going to bite me in the ass. I could just feel it when, eyes beseeching, imploring for compassion, I said, "Please your highness, don't tell anyone. It…it wasn't something I planned. It…kind of sort of just happened by accident."

Sure, Gale, that's how all affairs happen – by accident. The guy falls over on top of the woman, who just happens to be lying down naked and spread-eagled somewhere, flat preferably, and trips up and down for a few minutes to an hour if he's really clumsy. But she bought it. Marissa was more than willing to play the confidant - the big sister who gets a chance to live vicariously through her younger sibling's escapades. She looked around again to make sure we were unobserved, before sitting down on a hay bale. Patting the space next to her she motioned me to do the same and said, "Of course your secret is safe with me. But, I want details, that's my payment and price. James refused, he said he was a gentleman, and a gentleman never kisses and tells. So cough up, my dear, I want to hear the naughty stuff."

He what? Oh crap, crap, crap! Next time, if there was a next time, I'm not sure that I wouldn't kill him. See, I knew I should have just slit his throat in Jinkins' alder copse. Stupid pretty boy with his stupid, perfect, gorgeous, long, black hair…crap. Gentleman my ass. Crap.

Twelve

So, I was now an adulteress without having any of the fun that would typically go along with having an affair. Great, yeah that's fair! Not only that, but I had to make up as many sexual depravities as I could to satisfy my queen's curiosity and to ensure her continued silence and help. Maybe you have more experience in that sort of thing than I do, but when push came to shove I was drawing a blank. Honestly how creative are you? What would you say if a friend asked you, "Quick, tell me something dirty you just did over the weekend with some twenty-something stud?" Even if you had actually done something, would you be able to rattle it off lickety-split?

I ended up pulling out all kinds of pieces parts from local tavern tales I'd heard over the years. He's dead now, but for a while there was this wandering bard aptly called Lewd Larry. All of Larry's songs pretty much involved the exploits of various nymphomaniacs and well…nymphs, that he had supposedly known - all of them conveniently hailing from distant lands that rhymed with different sexual acts or female body parts. I'll let you use your imaginations on what the maid from *Hortatio* liked to do and the gymnastic scullery wench from *Send Grover* whose house was *Near the Pass*. Needless to say, as far as Queen Marissa was concerned, Jimmy and I were well accomplished in all those places. I was sure that though I'd lied to protect mine and Will's secret, it was still going to bite me *Near the Pass*!

Once the stories were told to Marissa's satisfaction I sent the stable boy to fetch Duke. The poor kid nearly had a heart attack when I popped up from what he thought was an empty stall. He ran off and fetched my horse and Queen Marissa gave me a kiss on the cheek, saying, "It's alright, your secret is safe with me. I'll send James out to your cabin the next time Will leaves." Oh great, my queen the pimp. Wonderful.

I was still so confused and flustered...and well, pissed off that Jimmy had told Queen Marissa that he and I had had an affair that I barely noticed most of the ride home. I let Duke take his time, moving at a nice gentle trot through woods and meadows, while I was lost in thought. So distracted was I that I almost ran over said liar when he jumped out from behind an old oak tree on the trail home. I was at least another hour's ride from the cottage and the afternoon was quickly headed toward evening. To be honest that little voice that controls my cold killer tendencies almost blurted out, "Oh just run the little prick over. That would solve most of your problems right there. Oops, sorry constable sir, he ran out in front of my horse and I didn't see him."

But I didn't. Both me and the little voice chickened out at the last second. Stupid little voice.

The Knight's Wife

Jimmy was frantically waving his hands, attempting to get me to stop. I ignored him, swerving Duke *around* him (stupid voice), and kept on trotting toward home. Jimmy stopped waving and ran alongside instead, panting and out of breath he said, "My lady, please, wait. Allow me to explain. I tried to catch you before you made it into town, to warn you, but you had left so early this morning that I missed you."

I pulled back hard on Duke's reins and the stallion bucked, raising his front legs up and stomping them back down aggressively. Turning to look down at Jimmy, I snapped, "Explain what? How you told Queen Marissa we had a wild four day affair?"

He had flinched back and was holding his arms up in a warding gesture. With his arms blocking his face I couldn't make out what he was mumbling, so I snapped again, "What?"

He peeked out tentatively from behind his crossed arms, black hair falling curtain-like over his pale blue eyes, and said, "Please don't kick me in the head ... again."

Well if a woman can't get the satisfaction out of an affair, at least a consolation prize of fear and respect is something. A paltry second place award compared to the orgasmic things I'd told Marissa we had done, but still I'd take it. Sighing I said, "I won't kick you, Jimmy. Now explain."

"Really?" he asked, looking more like an innocent schoolboy than he had any right to. Especially after some of the things we had supposedly done together. He took a bashful step backward and dropped his warding hands to his sides, saying, "You promise?"

Oh for the love of... "Fine, sure, whatever, I promise not to kick you in the head, cross my heart and hope to die, stick a needle in my eye and all that crap, Jimmy. Now explain or I'm going home."

He fidgeted a bit with his fingers before he spoke, picking at a hangnail. Then looking down at his feet he scuffed and kicked the dirt around his boots a bit before finally nodding his head as if he were agreeing with someone I couldn't hear and said, "I didn't really plan for that to happen, my lady. Please believe me, I'm sorry. I went back to the castle...after I woke up when a pair of tree sprites started poking me with sharp sticks for snoring too loudly in their quiet copse." He glared a bit accusingly at me as he explained his unconscious predicament as if I was supposed to care.

When he realized there would be no sympathy directed at him from me, he looked down at his feet again when he continued. "Well, once I was back at the castle. I realized I had beat Sir William there. He must have gotten lost along the way or something. The queen was very upset and wanted to know where I had bcen and where you were. I honestly didn't intend to tell her we had an affair…and come to think of it I never really did say that. When she asked me what had happened I blanked. I couldn't think of what to say. If I said you kicked me and beat the crap out of me, she might or might not believe it. Then I realized who was I to accuse the Great Sir William of being a fraud? I'd have been laughed out of Thistledown, if not stoned in the streets for my temerity."

So pretty boy Jimmy wasn't just a nice package to look at, he was also clever enough to examine the situation rationally. I could use that. Stupid may be fun in the bedroom, but since that wasn't happening, rational would help me cover my tracks, or at least collaborate my lies. He finished (still fidgeting in the dirt with the toes of his boots) by saying, "The queen took my silence and inability to choose what to tell her as an admission of an affair. By the time I'd figured out what she was implying, it was too late. So I simply told her a gentleman never kisses and tells."

He looked up at me with those soft blue eyes pleading for understanding, for some measure of compassion. Crap. He was very nice to look at and it seemed he was not without a conscience. I could easily believe Marissa had crafted and construed the story as Jimmy had relayed it to satisfy her bored royal fantasies. It may very well not have been his fault…but then again, he could have come up with something. He could have explained that the bruises on his forehead were the result of being accosted by

93

highwaymen and that he had been lying in a ditch somewhere for the past few days. That he had only now been able to scrape himself into some shape that would allow him to travel to her with his news. Crap. See I could think on my feet, why couldn't he? Calm down, Gale, not everybody is as practiced and as good of a liar as you are. I don't know what Jimmy had hoped for me to say – that I forgave him, that it wasn't his fault, or that these things happen. Who knows?

Whatever it was he had been hoping I would say I could tell by the surprised look on his face that he did not expect me to lean over and punch him, closed fist, right on the nose. He fell to the trail, leaking blood from around his fingers, and whining over and over, "You promised."

I nudged Duke back into a trot and called over my shoulder, "I promised I wouldn't kick you, Jimmy. I never said I wouldn't punch you. Now if you please, I still have to make dinner. Do not follow me again, Jimmy."

I was beyond earshot and down the trail, so I don't know if he even responded. Hey don't look at me like that. I didn't kick him, did I? I didn't even think about stabbing him with my knife, not once! I think that's called progress, don't you?

Thirteen

By the time I returned home, Will had switched from wildly swinging his sword to vigorously punching a sand-stuffed burlap sack he had set up over a thick oak branch out back. He may have been a joke of a swordsman and a clumsy martial artist, but in close, where only fists matter, he actually was quite the brawler. It was the one aspect of the Great Sir William sham that he almost resembled. He had broken up many bar-room brawls in his youth when he was a lowly palace guard. Perhaps that was where some of the legend grew from originally; taking on multiple drunks, even overly-inebriated ones, and winning is still an accomplishment. Too bad he couldn't convince a dragon to settle their dispute with a boxing match…never mind, he'd still get his ass kicked there, so bad example, but you see what I mean.

I unsaddled Duke and brushed his mane gently. Then, when I was through grooming him, I set him to graze in the small pasture we have set up for him alongside the cottage. Will, bare to the chest and dripping sweat, was still grunting and pounding away when I went inside to fry up some pheasant for dinner. An hour later when the food had been set on the table and Will had yet to come in, I went out to fetch him. I knew before I saw the blood-stained rags he had wrapped around his fists that my problems had finally shifted from fake affairs and cover-ups to how I was going to help Will regain his confidence. Lucky me.

"Will dear, dinner's ready," I called, back far enough to be out of fist range. Will has never struck me in all the years I've known him - sad I can't say the same - but Papa always taught me never to sneak up on a person, talented or not, while they were practicing their craft. That goes for artists, potters, painters, seamstresses, blacksmiths, and any other learned trade you can think of. But, that rule was held to be especially true if that craft involved very pointy objects or closed fists. Bathed in the dusk's shadows, the huge, hulking, and sweat soaked form of my husband jumped at the sound of my voice. See.

Will grunted once, nodded his head, sending drops of sweat cascading from his brow, and refusing to turn around, said, "I'll be in in a moment dear. I need to finish up here first."

"No, Will," I said firmly. "You're finished now."

I didn't use my super bitchy tone of voice that I reserve for small children that talk too loudly indoors or for the local clerics when they come calling about saving my immortal soul and as an added bonus asking for donations. No, I used my caring, stern wife knows best voice – which when you think about it sounds a lot like my day to day voice. But that only stands to reason I suppose.

The Knight's Wife

Will didn't argue. He nodded his head and turned away from the misshapen, blood-stained, now leaking in two small places, burlap punching bag. Exhausted on his feet I guided him into the kitchen and had him sit, as always, at his over-sized chair while I unwrapped his hands. Will is strong…but weak, too. It's sad when somebody realizes that they are not what they thought they were. Self-image is still an image, and all images can be obscured or ruined. It doesn't matter if it's a blurred reflection in a mirror, a tarnished painting, or a mental image that crumbles over time with the aid of doubt and burns up quickly when reality is forced upon that false perception, self-image.

I was hoping that in this case Will's image was only slightly out of focus and I could help him see that, doubts or not, he was still the Great Sir William, even if he didn't feel like it anymore. The tricky part for any fighter isn't greatness, wins over losses, or even triumphing over unlikely odds. Nope, every fighter gets to deal with those, or at least any good fighter does. No, it's getting back up after life kicks you in the gut - that's the tricky part. Will had been kicked. And, yeah, I know, I'm the one who literally kicked him, but that's not what I meant. He had two choices: he could mope around the farm, working himself to death in hopes of proving to himself that he was still the warrior the kingdom thought he was – which looking at his pressure split knuckles as they oozed a mixture of blood, sweat, and grime onto my kitchen table, seemed to be his intention – or he could shake the whole episode off as a hallucination. That when the troll had ambushed him he had hit his head and imagined the whole thing. Head trauma can do that to a person. It can make the trauma victim feel sleepy or give them the obvious headache. It can cause hallucinations, strange dreams, plus many other symptoms.

Delusion is such an easy out. Look, I'm not lazy, but would you want to spend day after day coaching your husband back into thinking he was still the world's greatest warrior when in reality he was any-thing but? That's a shit-load of work ladies. So, un-less you're rich enough to have servants at your beck and call to do all your chores and then some, you'll understand why I considered nudging Will down the easier path to delusion.

"Will, what's wrong?" I asked tossing the blood soaked rags into the cast-iron stove. I was not going to try and scrub the stains out of those filthy things. He ignored my question and still refused to meet my eyes. Screw it; fine be that way, it was time to go with delusion. Reaching out and cupping his cleft chin in my hand I made him look at me. When I had pulled his eyes up to lock on mine, I said, "Will, you can tell me. This cannot be over the Jinkins girl. That is a tragedy, but that is life. You and I both know that, so what is bothering you?"

"It's nothing," Will mumbled, pulling his eyes away from mine once more. But he kept speaking, quietly and haltingly, he continued, "Do you ever wonder… how, how I slay all those monsters when I cannot…cannot…well, you've seen it. You know, how I cannot keep from walking face-first into frying pans that have been in the same place for decades?" He pointed up as he finished. If you're interested, he had pointed nowhere near where I keep the frying pans, but that only proved the point twice over.

Oh yeah, I was definitely going with delusion.

I smiled and spoke softly, sitting down on his lap and throwing my arms around his bare neck and shoulders as I did so, "Will, darling, so you're a little clumsy. So what? You complete the mission, the monsters all rue the day the Great Sir William is sent after them. Does it matter if you have a bit of eyesight trouble, or that you cannot aim without peeing all over the privy seat? At the end of the day the monsters are vanquished, right? So who cares?" He grunted a not very enthusiastic affirmative. To seal the deal and move onto the closing of this topic for as long as I could, I reached up and casually started to stroke the back of Will's head. Letting my fingers run smoothly through his sweat slicked locks. It was a subtle gesture. Hey, I can do subtle!

When I felt enough time had passed and Will seemed to be getting drowsy, I rubbed at a random spot on the back of his head and asked, "Will, were you injured when you fought the troll? Did the murderous brute land a blow?" Okay, so not so subtle with the whole "murderous brute" line, but still it worked.

Looking confused and trying to find the spot I was indicating with his swollen and damaged fingers, Will winced and said, "Actually, Gale, you're right I was. Duke was spooked at bit, too. The troll ambushed us and knocked us into the underbrush where we tussled. Then, I..." He trailed off as I'm sure memories of a masked woman dispatching the troll flooded over him.

I smacked him, playfully, on the shoulder to scold him and bring him back to me instead of his memories. "Will, why didn't you tell me this before?"

"I don't know. I didn't think it was all that important," Will said absently, still trying to rub a sore spot that didn't exist.

"Not important?" I scolded again. "Will, head wounds are very complicated things." I wandered over to my pantry where I kept different salves and balms. Grabbing the one I actually liked the smell of instead of the one that was for contusions, I pulled a chair around behind Will as a perch and started to comb his hair, looking for the imaginary wound.

"There!" I exclaimed with what I hoped was the proper amount of wifely concern. Applying a bit of the lavender and lemon balm, I added, "Papa, always said that head wounds were the worst. A man that was struck too hard on the head could vomit uncontrollably for days, or go to sleep and never wake up, even see things that weren't really there."

"Really?" Will asked, perking up. "Hawk used to say that? Ouch!" He had said the last because I'd poked the imaginary spot with a toothpick. Hey, if it didn't sting, he wouldn't believe there was a wound. I had to seal the deal. But to his excited question I said, "Sure thing." Okay, so sometimes I am just the tiniest bit ashamed at how easy it is to manipulate him. It's wrong, but it's for his own good...and I'm pretty damn good at it too, not to mention it's kind of fun...I know, I know, it's wrong. But...

"Sure," I said again, still combing and balming. "Papa even said one time he fell about six feet out of a tree when he was trying to get a better view. He struck his head against a branch on his way down. He could have sworn he woke right up and danced with a group of fauns and satyrs. He told me that one of them even gave him a pipe flute to play as they danced the afternoon away. He then walked all the way home got into bed after kissing my mother on the cheek, but he woke up in the middle of the night still under the same tree he had fallen out of. The whole thing had been a wild dream, but he could have sworn it was real. Head wounds are not something to be messed with, even if you're the Great Sir William!" I said the last as I patted him on the shoulder and started cleaning up my medical supplies.

When I turned around after putting my unnecessary ointments away, Will was smiling and tearing into a pheasant leg with more enthusiasm than I had seen from him since before Sir William Day. He smiled at me, covered his mouth with his napkin, and said, "This is delicious, honey, thank you."

Fourteen

Weeks went by and though I know he still had his doubts, for the most part, Will seemed to have his confidence back. He had a boyish spring to his step as he went about all those public relations things. You know, all those *hero on his day off* storybook fodder you always hear about and kind of groan over inwardly like: taking "gently used" toys to the orphanages for the poor to play with, kissing or tickling the occasional baby in passing, reading to the elderly (which is really funny because their eyesight is probably better than Will's), feeding and clothing the various vagrants and vagabonds, and a bunch of other make the hero relatable type stuff.

When he wasn't smiling and giving a positive thumbs-up for the portrait artists and town-criers, we did all the things people do when no matters of state, family, or friends are pressing; which is, of course, pretty much just sat on our butts and did nothing. I mean we did eat, we relaxed, we had sex, we puttered around the cottage fixing things that needed mending (you know those things, you probably have them too, stuff we had kept putting off until a slow time such as then), but more often than not we sat around and did nothing. I finally swept away that stupid cobweb in the corner of the bedroom ceiling that I kept forgetting to until I laid down to sleep. It was nice. Quiet, peaceful, and nice.

I know you're expecting the great hero, even one who is only a hero vicariously through the deeds of his wife like my hero, to constantly be racing off battling injustice. That's what the stories always tell you, right? Please, they don't sing about the everyday in the tavern tales. It would be too mundane to hear the tale of the Great Sir William's battle with hemorrhoids or the Great Sir William versus the squeaky chicken coop door. But, heroes have their downtime, too. If the king truly cried out for his champion everyday nobody would do the job. In fact, if the king needed help that badly, all the time, I think most people would be fleeing that kingdom faster than you can say, "Political ineptitude." For us, and for all heroes, living is pretty much just like your life, only every now and then we wait for the king to send word of peril and off we charge. But if all goes well, it's right back to the doing nothing part after the action.

It must have been a month, maybe a little more, before Will was called away again. I woke up to find him sitting at the table, squinting at a piece of parchment that had King Theodore's sigil embossed on the front. After pouring myself a cup of tea, I pulled out the chair closest to Will, and sat down asking, "What is it?"

Looking up from his literacy struggles, Will gazed at me through spectacles as thick as bottle glass. Not an image you're likely to see sewn into any pennant or standard – the four-eyed knight valiant. Heck, I was just happy he wore the damn things at all. When I had a chemist build them for me, Will's first response was to call them *alchemy* and then the even more creative *devil goggles*. Like most men, heroic or otherwise, he didn't want to admit to a weakness or flaw. But, like so many things in life necessity tends to shove that pride right down your throat after a few years and given time, Will was willing to at least wear his glasses at home. He looked at me over the parchment, his brows creasing, and said, "Oh, there's apparently a group of dwarves causing some mischief down to the south, near Lake Weldon."

"King Theodore wants you to go send them on their way?" I asked around a sip of tea. Then reached for the honeypot, and a cold biscuit I had baked the night before. I left them out to make my morning a bit slower-paced. I don't wake up all chipper and bird-song. I like to take my time and be lazy when I can.

"Mmm hmm," Will answered absently, going back to his eternal struggle with his eyes, and glancing at the letter once more.

"When do you plan on leaving?" I asked.

"Oh there doesn't seem to be too much of a rush on this," Will said dismissively and laid the letter down. Reaching for a biscuit as well, he continued, "I think I will go call on King Theodore this afternoon and see if he wants me to run the troublemakers off this instant or wait a bit. Maybe it is more desperate than he has made it sound in this letter, but if all the dwarves are doing is stealing a few pies off of windowsills and poaching the village fishing nets. I don't see why I should rush off to break a few smallish fingers just for that."

That in and of itself should have been troubling – Will typically takes any opportunity he can to add to his growing legend and show (even petty thieves) the bad guys what for. He hadn't shown any signs of his post-troll malaise since the night I'd all but told him it must have been a hallucination caused by head trauma. So was this *I'll wait and see* idea just Will using a bit of caution. Hey miracles do happen, ladies, or had he been putting on a brave face for my benefit this past month? Wonderful, the lolls between stretches of stress and worry never last long enough, do they?

The real question was did I need to follow Will to see King Theodore, or was he safe enough to do that much without me holding his hand? He would always go and receive his orders and then return home to tell me the what, why, and where he was going before he did so, and typically I had no need to follow him, so I'd stay home. All these doubts, all these questions, things were never simple before, but one stupid troll sets one stupid ambush, and all of a sudden a twenty year system of success gets tossed into the crapper.

The Knight's Wife

After a few nervous hours of mentally hemming and hawing over it, I figured I was being paranoid, so I waved to Will's retreating back as he rode off that afternoon to go see the king. I'd take my chances and hope that I might have a quiet afternoon all to myself, with nothing to do but perhaps putter around in the garden, or read a good book under the willow tree out back, or simply lie down and watch the clouds roll by. It sounded nice in theory at least, but as the top of Will's head vanished over the horizon I had that sensation of being watched again. I hadn't seen Jimmy the juggler since I had punched him in the face a month ago, but to be on the safe side I yelled into the early autumn tinted woods, "I told you not to follow me, Jimmy! If that's you I will kick you!"

Nothing. Please, be my cynical creepy paranoia for once, please.

I went back inside and poured myself another cup of tea. In the peaceful void of perhaps ten, fifteen minutes at most, I relaxed and started contemplating how to add some extra padding to my breastplate to minimize nipple rubbing when a shadow followed by a young handsome face filled the open upper-half of my kitchen doorway. Jimmy grinned and said, "I figured you'd have a harder time kicking me if there was a wall between us."

He said all that with a shrug of his broad shoulders and a grin that dared butter to try and melt in his mouth. He even tossed a wink my way. Oh wonderful, so it only took a month for the cocky stage performer to bounce back from being beaten up by a girl, good to know. Jimmy, dressed in a simple black leather vest the same color as his hair (no cumbersome shirt underneath of course), reached up and placed his hands on the top of the doorframe so he could lean in, all charm and flexing biceps. Should I have told him that there was a hornets' nest right above his head that I hadn't gotten around to removing yet? Eh, maybe, but he was so cool and confident, surely he was prepared for such an eventuality. So, I sat sipping my tea instead and asked, "What do you want, Jimmy?"

He smiled again, and though he was cute, more than cute really, that was the difference between him and my Will. Not twenty years, no the weathering of time had nothing to do with this. Will was very handsome, he knew it, but he didn't use it. He never tried to be charming. He'd probably hurt himself if he did anyway, but Jimmy? Oh he knew how handsome he was and he was more than willing to use it at any opportunity. Around his sweet, butter wouldn't dare melt smile he said, "I was in the neighborhood and thought I'd stop by to see how the *real* Sir William was doing. The Great Knight-in-Gale!"

Ignoring his sarcastic flattery and word play, I asked, "In the neighborhood?"

The Knight's Wife

"Well, I was the one the king chose to deliver his message to Sir William." He winked solicitous at me and added, "At the suggestion of the lovely Queen Marissa, of course."

Breaking his calm, juggler gigolo routine, for a second to wave away a hornet buzzing around his ear, he added distractedly, "I figured I'd wait around until after Sir William left. You didn't follow him, so that leads me to believe that he has only gone calling on the king and not run off to show those naughty dwarves the error of their wicked ways. Either way, if I went back to the castle the queen would suspect that something was amiss with our little tryst. Out of respect for your secret and out of a selfish desire to be thought of as the Thistledown roguish heartthrob, I stayed behind. After you obviously noticed me – you are very good at that, let me say – I figured why sit out all day in the woods with no one to talk to but the trees. Why not visit and have a chat with my make-believe mistress?"

Two hornets were now buzzing around Jimmy's perfectly coifed hair. He swiped at them, but missed. One lodged in his long flowing locks and he didn't know it. He was right though, arrogant, but right. If he was willing to take that much consideration for me I suppose I should let him know about the hornets' nest. "Thank you, that's very thoughtful, Jimmy. You should-"

Too late. The calm heartthrob rouge of Thistle-down wailed and shrieked like a little girl as the hornets attacked in force. Hands flapping and brushing around his face and hair, he ran off into the woods screaming.

Fifteen

I spent the next hour coaxing a very frazzled and very un-rouge-like Jimmy out of a nearby river. Taking my tea with me, I had followed in the wake of his screams and shrieks figuring he might need some level of medical aid if he ran headlong into a tree or off a cliff side in his flight *from* the bumblebees. He had jumped into the nearest and deepest section of river he had stumbled upon, staying under as long as he could hold his breath. When he resurfaced it was only the top of his head, eyes, and nose that emerged from the water. He glared at me where I stood on the riverbank, one hand on hip, the other clinging on to my favorite mug, saying, "They're gone now, Jimmy. You can come out of the water. I even burned their nest." I had. It was quick and easy work with all of the hornets away from the hive chasing Jimmy.

"You did that on purpose," Jimmy accused, sending another hate-filled glare my way and surfacing just enough for his lips to crest the river. "You knew they were there. I don't think there has been a time I've been around you that I did not get physically injured in some way. You need help, *my lady*, you have problems!" He said the last petulantly and sunk back down to nose level.

111

"Gee Jimmy, you think?" I yelled across the river at him. "I'm a woman, we're all like this. I thought you were better with the ladies than that."

His glare deepened a few notches as he stared at me without responding. The current continued to splash around the side of his face. It was a bit comical and endearing to watch him try and ignore the river slapping him on the cheek while he glared at me. I sighed, "Look, I promise not to hurt you if you come out of the river. I'll even help you put some ointment on the welts that are forming from the hornet stings, you big baby!"

"I don't trust you!" He surfaced enough to shout, then bobbed back down as if those extra few inches of water would help insulate him from the hornets…oh alright, fine, or insulate him from me.

"Good, you aren't as dumb as you look," I chided. "You should never trust someone who has kicked your butt as many times as I've kicked yours. But your choices are simple, either stand there in the river all day, fighting off the snakes, or…"

I didn't need to finish with Jimmy's alternatives, he was out of the river before I'd said *or*. I didn't actually know if there were or were not any snakes in that river, but I figured I was on such a roll with the whole lying to the men around me to convince them to do what I wanted and make them think it was their idea thing, why stop now?

The Knight's Wife

We hiked back to the cottage together, Jimmy a squelching, sodden, and dripping mess behind me. When we reached the backdoor I turned around and said, "Strip."

"Excuse me?" Jimmy asked, eyebrows raised, no longer cocky and self-assured. He was back to the rambling, babbling insecure kid I'd knocked unconscious a couple of times.

"I'm not having you drip river water and mud all over my clean kitchen," I scolded, hands on hips. "I need to clean up and tend to all those stings anyway. I'm sure they didn't conveniently stick to exposed skin, so strip. You can hang your clothes out to dry while we get you fixed up. Here!" I said, reaching around the open upper door and tossing a towel at Jimmy. "Wrap this around your waist before you come in."

I went inside to gather up my supplies: tweezers, in case there were stingers still embedded in his skin, plus a few homemade lotions and balms for the swelling…Did I take a peek out the kitchen window at pretty boy Jimmy in the buff? You're damn right I did. I'm human, but it was more for the eventual stories I would have to tell Marissa, you see. Details, it was about details, lots and lots of, um well, details, larger details than I'd expected to tell the truth.

I had assembled my insect first aid supplies on the table, when Jimmy wandered in, clutching onto the knot in the towel for dear life. I suppose I shouldn't blame him. We are at our most vulnerable in the nude, and I had given him more than enough reason to be afraid of me. Couple that with me ordering him to disrobe and I think anybody would hold onto their last scrap of dignity with rigormortis-like strength. I pulled out a chair and said, "Sit."

He did without question. I lit an oil lamp and hung it up on the rack with my pots and pans to provide more light to work by. I gently touched the side of his head and he stiffened. Okay, I probably deserved that reaction. But, he eased a bit as I started to wash, tend, and mend his wounds. No matter how afraid we are of something, when that something starts to ease our pain we gradually become less and less leery. I've even heard of some people who fall in love with their tormentors. They end up craving the abuse or something. That's a little too freaky for my tastes, but I guess it could happen. Working out lodged stingers and applying soothing ointments to welts, I noticed many other scars, mostly along his back and shoulders, areas where his vest covered just right, some scars were fresher than others. A few were still the pink of only a year or two old and the others held that dull almost chalk-white pallor of decades.

"Who are you, Jimmy?" I asked, tracing a finger along a very old scar. It wound down from a shoulder blade all the way to where the towel obscured further inspection. He flinched again, maybe it was at my touch, or maybe it was at the reminder of the scar. The ghosts of pains past came hurtling back to knock him off his ease. He stiffened a bit more, but didn't shrug me off or away as he said, "My name is James Vayruin. You know that and you still insist on calling me, Jimmy."

Okay, fair enough, he didn't need to give me his backstory. I had my secrets, of which he knew plenty, that was no reason that I should pry into his. Reaching around Jimmy, across the table for the cap to my ointment jar, I said, "Sorry, Jimmy. It's none of my business. I shouldn't have asked."

He reached over, placed his hand on my wrist and said, "No, it's alright. I just don't like thinking about it. About home..."

He leaned into the touch and so help me, I didn't stop him. He looked so vulnerable and child-like, sitting there, back covered in scars that held more pain for him now than the original wounds. He leaned his head against my chest and I held him there. Pain is an odd thing. I have no trouble dishing out physical suffering. I hurt and I kill, but present me with mental pain and anguish, and my unused maternal instinct kicks in.

We held each other for what must have been minutes but felt much, much longer. All I could think of was how many times I had hurt this boy, despite his age he was still very much a child, and here I was comforting him. Sure, way to go, that was all his confused mind needed, Gale. He so much as said he got those scars at the hand of a parent, someone who was supposed to care for him and love him, but offered him pain instead. And now there I am, a person who has done more than her fair share of harm to him, offering solace and succor. That wouldn't mess with his mind at all, no, never. I didn't care. His head was hot and warm against my breasts, from both the swollen welts and his tears. It felt good.

At least it did until I heard the jingle of reins. Crap!

I had a mostly naked man in my kitchen, whom I was hugging to my chest, mind you. A man whom the queen was under the impression I was having a sordid nasty extramarital affair with, and my husband the nearly blind greatest hero of the land was about to walk in on us. Yeah, crap!

I had to get Jimmy out the backdoor, fast. It was obvious that he had no clue Will was about to come home. He was still lost in his own painful memories and clinging to me like some kind of shelter in a storm. I pulled away as quickly and as gently as I could. Jimmy startled a bit, but I leaned down and said, "Jimmy, you need to leave. Now!"

"What?" he mumbled, looking confused, "Why?"

"Will's almost home," I said, trying to pull Jimmy to his feet.

The Knight's Wife

"But, but," Jimmy said awkwardly, "we haven't done anything wrong."

"I know that, you know that, but what do you think will happen when Will walks in on a naked man holding his wife? Do you think he'll say, 'Oh well, obviously you two have done nothing wrong'?"

"Oh," was all he muttered. He stood up and started staring around in confusion as to what to do. I pulled Jimmy's still damp clothes in through the kitchen window and tossed them at him. He caught them and the towel fell down around his feet. Crap…and wow, nice. But mostly, crap!

I could hear Will unsaddling Duke outback and I knew I had barely missed him seeing men's clothing that was not his on the wash line. I looked out the kitchen window to see him rubbing Duke's flank and slowly turning to walk toward the backdoor. Spinning around I saw Jimmy with only one pants leg up. Crap. Gathering up the clothes he had dropped, I stuffed them in his arms and whispered, "We don't have time for that. Get dressed on the road. Go now."

I shoved him toward the front door. He stumbled out, still clutching to his damp vest and pants. But that wasn't the worst part. Right before I closed the door I acted on impulse. You may have noticed how impulsive I tend to be, right? Hey, I don't point out your short comings alright, so let's not dwell overmuch on mine. But, I kind of, sort of, smacked him on the naked ass as he was headed out. You know a kind of hurry up and move gesture. He couldn't read too much into that, right? I mean women smack men on their naked butts all the time, right? It doesn't mean anything…right? Yeah … I know…crap.

Sixteen

Will opened the backdoor just as I was closing the front door. The latches clicked simultaneously in one of those weird, quirky coincidences. I jumped at the sound and turned around, saying, "Oh, I was just going out front to meet you. How was your day?"

If he noticed that anything was even remotely amiss, like me brushing my hair back nervously in a very un-Gale-like schoolgirlish manner, Will did not let on. He stumbled a few steps into the kitchen and pulled out his oversized chair, flopping down with a sigh and a groan from both him and the chair, he said, "My day was a little strange to be honest. King Theodore was fine with me waiting a few days before I head south, that wasn't the problem, but Queen Marissa kept acting weird, trying to get me to stay for supper and when I said I had to go home she kept bringing me pickle jars to open. She said it was because none of the kitchen staff was strong enough. I must have opened eighteen pickle jars this afternoon, very strange woman sometimes." He chuckled and shook his head a bit at the memory.

Nice, Marissa, real subtle.

"She is sometimes, yes," I agreed and stopped fussing with my hair. Pulling out the chair next to him, I sat down and asked, "So you're going to wait until next week to take care of the southern dwarf problem?"

"Hmm?" Will mumbled, absently playing with the ointment I had neglected to put away. Crap. "Hmm, oh, a yes," he said looking up. "Yes, next week should be fine." Holding the open jar out toward me he asked, "Did you clear out that hornets' nest? You didn't get stung, did you? I was going to take care of it, Gale, honestly. I just forgot."

Alright, that'll work. "Oh, it wasn't such a big deal, Will. It's only a sting or two. I just wanted to clean them up and make sure they didn't get infected." Most days I don't really have to lie. People come to their own conclusions, and I kind of, sort of, nudge them along in that direction by telling them what they want to hear.

He nodded and capped the bottle for me, handing it over as I placed all the rest of my tools back in their proper places. When I put the ointment jar down, I teased, "Hey, you didn't screw that on too tight did you? I don't want to be stranded when I need it if Queen Marissa calls you back to the castle because she has a pickle craving." He laughed politely while I started on supper. I was dicing up carrots for a soup, enjoying that feeling of disaster averted, stress and anxiety released, when I heard Will shout, "What was that?"

"What was what?" I asked, turning around so fast that I knocked half the pile of carrot slices onto the floor in the process. Instincts and training kicking in with my alarm, causing me to swap may grip on the paring knife around defensively, ready for a fight. I don't know what I thought I could go up against with such a tiny weapon – a rabid potato, maybe a very malicious ear of corn?

"There!" Will shouted, standing up so quickly he knocked his chair over in the process, and pointed out the kitchen window. "Right there, I could have sworn I saw a naked man running through the backyard. There right past the barn." He pointed past my evil vegetable defensive arm, toward the barn where Duke lazily munched on a cluster of alfalfa. Seeing no immediate movement other than our horse eating, Will's certainty started to falter, but I knew better.

Jimmy you moron, what now?

"Don't be silly dear," I chided in my best *there's nothing wrong* tone of voice and bent over to pick up the spilled carrots. As I scooped them up, placing them in a separate bowl to be washed again before I added them to the soup, I said in a low whisper that I knew he'd still hear, "You can barely see three feet in front of you. It was probably a deer or maybe a drunken gnome at most."

Chuckling, Will leaned out the window, the sill creaking under his massive weight. After squinting and staring for the entire time it took me to assemble the soup, Will laughed again and shaking his head ruefully, said, "I guess you're right. I could have sworn it was a naked man though. It even looked like he was struggling with a snake. The damnedest thing…I'm having the strangest day, Gale. I think I'll lie down for a bit before dinner."

He kissed me on the top of the head in passing and went into the bedroom to lie down. Over his shoulder he called, "Come get me when dinner's ready, will you?"

I said I would, but I was already trying to see where Jimmy had gone. Absently, as if talking to myself, I said, "I think what this soup needs is a little fresh parsley. Yes parsley, I'll run out to the garden and cut some…maybe a sprig or two of basil as well."

Grabbing a bowl and my garden shears for effect; improvisation is the key to a good performance, right? I went out the backdoor and marched over to the herb garden, scanning the yard with my peripheral vision the entire way. I leaned over to snip a parsley sprig, brushing away a few honey bees that were collecting some late summer pollen from a nearby chive blossom, and a small pebble landed by my feet. I hadn't been observant enough to see which direction the stone missile had come from. Standing back upright I looked around in hopes of seeing Jimmy, and caught the second pebble right on my lower left butt cheek. I hissed, "Ow, damn it!" loudly enough that Will called out from the cottage,

"You alright, dear?" at the same time I heard Jimmy whisper, "Sorry."

Shouting toward the cottage, I said, "I'm fine, Will, just a straggler from the hornets' nest. It must have come back for some retribution." I could hear him chuckle softly, but neither the drapes in our bedroom or kitchen windows stirred so he must have taken me at my word and didn't get up to check. I glared over at where Jimmy's voice had come from to see him crouched under our rabbit hutch, holding a dead snake in his hands. I could see he was about to say something so I motioned for him to be quiet. Then I pulled a few bug-ridden vegetables from the pile I keep for the rabbits and pretended to go over and feed them. Sticking a half-rotten turnip through the hutch door I harshly whispered, "What in the name of all that is holy are you doing?"

Jimmy whimpered a bit before he said, "I crossed that stupid river, and one of those stupid snakes you warned me about bit me. But, I...well I didn't want to get my clothes all wet again, so I didn't bother putting them on. Then when the snake bit me ... I dropped my clothes into the river and ran to shore with the snake still biting me. I don't know where my clothes are and I don't even know if this snake is poisonous or not?"

He pushed the limp body of the snake out from under the hutch for my inspection. It dangled there limply and he shook it a little. I don't know if it was

on accident or if he just did it for emphasis, but with
the heightened stress of the day, and him crouched
down in a pile of rabbit manure shaking a limp snake
at me, what could I do? Well I started laughing, that
dangerous kind of laughter that hurts your stomach
because you're wrenching it so hard. And, worse
still, I had to muffle it so Will didn't hear and come
check up on me. Then I thought of it from Will's
perspective, seeing Jimmy (both big and little) naked, wiggling a dead snake at his wife, and I started
laughing harder. Jimmy hissed, yep, he hissed, "It's
not funny, Gale!"

It was, and the snake wasn't poisonous; Jimmy
would be fine, naked, but fine. At least I now knew
that there were snakes in that river, you learn something new every day. And that set me to laughing
even harder. After several long minutes of thinking
non-funny thoughts: dead kittens, virgins widowed
on their wedding nights, little Daisy Jinkins' stick
figure drawings? Yeah, that did it. Sighing I said,
"You'll be fine. It's not poisonous. Wait here, I have
some old rags of Will's that should fit you and there
are a few blankets in the stable. You can bunk with
Duke for the night if you want, but tomorrow you
need to return to Thistledown, do you understand?"

A feeble, "Yes," wavered up from under the
hutch. I knew he was lying though. He would try to
hide in the woods and wait until Will left for the
south. Then he would follow me when I followed
Will. One stupid act of compassion, one stupid mo-

ment of empathy for somebody and I had earned myself a new puppy dog. A puppy dog that though pretty on the outside was weak and beaten on the inside. Just great, that's all I needed.

Seventeen

I don't know where Jimmy hid until the next week. He stayed quiet and out of sight, that was all that mattered. Will had no more visions of naked men wrestling snakes in our backyard. Even when Will went off to cut the ribbon at a tavern grand opening in town, Jimmy didn't pop in to say hi. Maybe he was scared of another hornets' nest, or kick, or punch to the head, or maybe he actually listened to me and stayed away. I don't know and the why doesn't matter in any event. I had a peaceful week until Will left on his mission to rid the south of their pesky dwarf infestation. It was a two to three day ride to Lake Weldon from our cottage, on the opposite end of King Theodore's realm, which, of course, meant a two to three day run for yours truly.

I allowed Will a few hours head start as well - whenever we leave from the cottage that has been my typical allotment. I didn't want to set off right after him, even though it would make the mission easier for me if I did. There was always the chance that he may get lost or double back because he forgot something, then, if he found his way back to the cottage that is, he would want to know where I was. So, a head start was always the way I did things. At any rate it gave me time to stretch and move about in my new – nipple padding improved – armor.

The Knight's Wife

I set off when most people would have been sitting down for their midday meal, having not bothered to leave anything out for Will's return supper. With a journey as long as Lake Weldon nothing could keep until we returned. I would just have to race ahead on the way back as I had done the previous time. Tiring after such a lengthy trip, yes, but I was well rested and this time I did not have the cumbering addition of a Sir William Day festival to break myself away from. I traveled at a light and easy jog for the bulk of the afternoon; weapons tightly strapped so they didn't bounce and a light pack with the barest necessities snugged to my back. Will had managed to stay on the road and not get lost as was evidenced by Duke's engraved horseshoes leading in a straight line due south. The markings were evenly spaced. Will was allowing Duke to trot at his pace and not pushing the stallion into a gallop to make time. With a nice easy day's travel for a change, I would be caught up to them before nightfall.

It turned out not to take even that long. I stumbled around a bend in the road and skidded to halt, jumping into the underbrush at trail-side. Duke was standing along the road's shoulder, chomping on grass and flicking his tail at the late season insects. Will was standing a few feet off the road, leaning against a tree, relieving himself. From where I was crouched, obscured by a bunch of rhododendron, and in fact, spiting flecks of leaves out from my awkward, rushed concealment, I could see that he was

127

resting his forearm against a trunk absolutely covered in poison ivy…of course. It would be fine as long as he didn't use that hand to…Oh Will…well anyone want to bet that doesn't end up in the tavern tale of this quest? The Great Sir William ran off the southern dwarf clan with a poison ivy rash all up and down his pecker. I don't think there'd be many drunken shouts of, "Sing the 'Itchy Crotch' song!" Eh, when I say it like that who knows, men are odd, maybe there would be.

Surprisingly, that didn't happen as often as you may think, not the relieving and poison ivy pecker part, he pees as much as anybody, but the me stumbling upon him unexpectedly part. I don't know if the added distractions lately had been affecting my judgment and woods-sense, but typically I try to stay far enough back to avoid the pee stops. Having too many things on your mind can be fatally dangerous in the deep woods. You could wander off a cliff, run headlong into a bear or mountain lion, stumble into a fairy ring, or all kinds of unpleasant stuff. I had to try to keep focused.

When Will had finished, he looked around, kind of like an owl fed too much tea and sugar – all jittery and wide-eyed. I had been worried about that. I don't think he had heard or noticed my close call and mad scramble into the brush. No, he was looking for the mystery woman who had saved him from the troll. Whether he had convinced himself that it was a hallucination caused by head trauma or not, he was still paranoid enough to be on the lookout. That would make my job even harder, yet again. I would need to stay further back to avoid detection. I could at least take some measure of comfort that his first mission post troll was only to banish a few kleptomaniac dwarves and not slay a dragon. Maybe after this quest went off without a hitch he could truly start to believe in himself again. I hoped that with the dwarves, Will showing up would be enough to run them off and there would be no need for a battle of any sort. A win-win situation for everybody. Hey, a girl can hope, it's not against the law or all that unlikely. It's only unlikely because the universe seems to hate for me to have it easy at anything I do, so maybe it's against some universal law of Gale's workload or something. But I can still hope.

When Will eventually stopped for the night we were still a day's ride from Lake Weldon and the small fishing village that dotted its northern shore. Blind though he may nearly be, Will always did seem to pick great campsites. I had stayed in this very glen with my father once when he took me south on a trading mission. A thick cluster of pine trees hid the small meadow from the trail like a natural fence and crumbling shale cliffs led into a river valley as a backdrop. It was beautiful. At night you could lie on your back and trace patterns in the stars. Papa used to do that with me all the time. He would always tell me the stories that went along with the patterns. They would change every time, so I'm pretty sure he was just making them up and not going by any actual legends. But no matter which story he told me, he would always find a way to add my mother into it as well. She would be watching from there, right there, see those three stars make her dress and those five her heart-shaped face. It was a comfort to a girl who never knew her mother to feel as if she could see her, and that she was in turn watching her daughter every clear night from the heavens.

While Will grunted and snuggled in close to his campfire for warmth, I pulled out the drying red maple leaf I had tucked under my bracer before I left. Turning it over in my hands, lying on my back I traced a pattern in the sky and told myself the story of the lovely maiden and the rugged ranger. How he slew monster after monster to make his lands safe for his maiden…and yet, a monster he could not defeat carried her away. Death had stolen the maiden from him and the gift of life had left him imprisoned here on the earth. He watched her from the ground as she shone among the stars. He watched over and protected the life she had given him, a life that kept him prisoner, because without it he would have thrown himself at Death and joined his maiden. He loved his little life too much to abandon it though, so he never begrudged or mistreated the little life. He cared for it, taught it everything he knew, loved it, and told it stories of the maiden, of how beautiful she was and how the little life looked more and more like her every day. Until one morning, when the little life had grown and could take care of itself, it found the rugged ranger cold and asleep on his bed. He had left the life that no longer needed him and joined his maiden, where together they watched down from the sky as the life used all they had given it to help others. They were happy. They were proud. But the life, no longer so little, still missed them and watched them every night the sky shown clear.

I fell asleep holding the leaf close to my chest. My stiletto was out, oiled and gleaming in the starlight in one hand – a drying red maple leaf in the other.

Eighteen

The next day was completely uneventful, just the way I like it. Will kept Duke at an even pace that I was easily able to follow. He was still more on edge than was his typical, still looking about owl-like, but he caught no glimpse of me...or of Jimmy, who I had no doubt was somewhere behind me, following like a stray puppy dog.

I felt him watching me that morning when I woke up, stiff and cold in the early autumn dawn. There are times when I miss the resiliency of youth. Sleeping on the cold hard ground and having to rise and shine for an early morning jog was definitely one of those times. I still hadn't seen Jimmy, but I knew he was there alright. I suppose my woods-sense was not as dulled as I was worried it had been. Don't ask me how I knew it was Jimmy and not someone or something else. After a while a hunter can tell you when he is tracking *his* buck or *his* bear. There are subtle connections that the mind does not realize it is consciously making. I'm not comparing what Jimmy and I had as a hunter/prey relationship. That would have been easier. Leave scraps of food out for any wild animal and it will gladly take them, with caution. Leave more and more, and the animal will slowly become accustomed to you. That's how our ancestors domesticated cats and dogs. The same holds true for scraps of emotion and people, but that's even harder to stop than turning your back on a hungry animal. Turning your back on an emotion starved person? Even I'm not that cold. It would have been easier if I was.

I had to play it aloof though, or at least distant. I couldn't turn my back on Jimmy completely. That would be cruel, easier, but cruel, not something the ranger and the maiden would look down proudly on. But, then again, I don't think they'd look down too proudly on me screwing Jimmy's brains out either. And, if I was honest with myself, that's where I could feel things heading. So, warm, nice, polite, maybe only one kick to the head, you know, friend stuff?

The village on the shores of Lake Weldon didn't have a name. It was part of Thistledown and protected under King Theodore's banner. But, a dozen shacks, a combination bar and boardinghouse, plus a fish processing lean-to reeking of decaying guts, heads, and seaweed down by the docks was hardly worthy of a name anyhow.

It was late dusk by the time we – Will riding Duke in the lead, me trailing right behind, and Jimmy somewhere behind me, an odd caravan if ever there was – came upon the unnamed village. There are times when I think that Will's ability to arrive at any of his destinations right as the sun was setting and all those in need of aid were done with their days' labors and were sitting around talking about the hero they needed, was just as much responsible for his legend as all the monsters I killed that he got the credit for. Nothing claims to the world *the hero has arrived* as a lone knight, riding his steed, with the setting sun in the background.

There is a quiet hillside that overlooks the lake and the village, sort of an unofficial campground, really. I planned to spend the night there so I could finally have a fire for warmth. Travelers were very common around the village; trading in surplus fish and salt were always a draw for merchants. A fire up on the hillside would go unnoticed and if noticed, it would be shrugged off as just another trader. I had settled in with the wind gently blowing across my back as I used an old fire ring of stones another traveler or trader had left behind. A spark was gently bringing my tinder to light as I heard a raucous shout bellow out from the pub down below, "Three cheers for the Great Sir William!"

And those cheers subsequently followed, thrice, and one patron perhaps a tad slower or drunker than the rest continued on for a fourth cheer, but stopped halfway when he realized no one else was cheering. I snorted a bit at that and heard a similar sound carried on the wind from the bushes behind me. Sighing I said, "You can come on out, Jimmy. I know you're there."

The bushes rattled and shook, dry leaves, yellowish and brown with the changing of the season fell to the ground as Jimmy stood up and walked toward me. He started apologizing before I had the chance to reprimand him. "I'm sorry Lady Gale, I didn't know what else to do. Queen Marissa would assume I was with you, so I followed you to be with you…but not *with you* with you." He stumbled when I glared at him. Grinning a bit mischievously he added, "Though I wouldn't be opposed to being *with* you."

Crap. See, give a mouse a cookie…or give a beaten gypsy a hug…it works out to the same thing. The damn critter always wants more.

Glaring across my growing fire I added more tinder and said, "I'm old enough to be your mother, Jimmy."

He matched my glare with a look of equal parts charm and dubiety. Sighing I conceited, "Oh okay fine, your very older sister. There how's that? Now put a lid on the charm and take a seat. We might as well share the fire instead of you building your own."

The set of his shoulders drooped a bit, but he sat down across from me instead of next to me. So that was a start, I guess.

I had found a duck along the roadside with a broken wing a few miles before we arrived at the lake. I snapped its neck and placed it in my shoulder bag to clean for dinner. Jimmy winced as I started methodically plucking the feathers from it. Shaking my head at his squeamishness, I asked, "How do you survive, Jimmy? Do you travel around with different gypsy troops, relying on your looks and charm to cook your supper, or what?"

"No," he said rather primly. "I can cook when I need to. I simply prefer that someone else does the dirty work. That's how most people are, Lady Gale. They don't take quite the joy you do in harming others."

"Ha," I laughed and shaking a handful of feathers at him, I continued, "Everybody takes joy in hurting others to some degree, Jimmy, it's about control. It may not look like it, but I don't take all that much joy in what I do. It's more that I'm cold about the things I feel are necessary. Somebody has to be…I have to be."

"Maybe," he mumbled in concession. Rubbing at the side of his head where I had kicked him on more than one occasion he grumbled, under his breath, "Bullshit."

"What was that, Jimmy?" I asked, using my stiletto to gut the duck. I may or may not have used a bit more zeal in the cutting than I needed to.

Knowing damn well that I had heard what he had mumbled, Jimmy said, "I said, looks good. I love duck, can I have some?"

The Knight's Wife

Spitting the now dressed bird, I crushed some wild berries and herbs I had gathered along the journey and rubbed them into the skin, before I placed it on the makeshift rotisserie that the last occupant of the campsite had conveniently left behind. Not looking up from my preparations, I said, "Oh I don't think so, Jimmy. You see those of us who like hurting people so much, well, we aren't too big on feeding the hungry either. It gives us joy to eat in front of them."

"Alright, alight," Jimmy said in placation. "I'm willing to believe that maybe you don't get the kick out of it that you appear to. But you have to admit the evidence from my perspective leaves you pretty incriminated. This is what, the sixth time you and I have been alone together and it is only the second time that I'm not writhing in pain or been knocked unconscious."

I couldn't help it. Honestly, I didn't mean for it to sound so flirtatious, but I looked up, grinning, and said, "The night's still young, Jimmy."

He smiled, not the smile of a man who thinks he's going to get lucky, but more the smile of a man who wants to indulge the bully that might kick his ass at any moment. I suppose I should take that as a blessing. I didn't want to lead him on anyway, but I was a bit insulted that I had lost enough of my feminine wiles, if I ever had them I guess, that he didn't take it as flirting - getting old sucks for more reasons than your back aching because you ran too hard or slept wrong.

Instead of flirting back, he shifted position on the rotting log a previous occupant had rolled over for a seat. Rubbing his hands together and warming them in the now roaring fire, he said, "You asked me who I was, Lady Gale?"

Shaking my head, I said, "Forget it, Jimmy. That's none of my business."

"No, no," he continued, looking into the flames instead of at me. "I know more of your secrets, whether by accident or fate, than anybody else on earth. So I guess if anybody is entitled to know about me…it's you. I…I would only ask that you tell me something else first?" He phrased the last in a question as he looked up from the fire. His eyes burned past me, through me, and into me. I nodded. With the way he was looking at me he could have asked me just about any question and I would have nodded.

Breaking the gaze first, he asked, "How did this happen? I mean you doing what you do for Sir William. His name is known throughout more lands than just Thistledown. How could this have been going on for so long, and no one suspects a thing?"

I shrugged my shoulders and said, "That's an easy one, Jimmy. I love him. He can't see a damn thing. His eyesight is very poor, always has been. It makes him clumsy as a one legged dog. I don't want him to get hurt, so I watch out for him. Haven't you ever loved someone enough to do that, Jimmy?"

"No, Gale," Jimmy said, his voice husky with emotion as he stared back at the dancing flames. "I don't think I've ever loved anyone."

Nodding, I said, "I had suspected as much. Jimmy, love will make people do stupid things...some really stupid things. Slaying dragons so your husband doesn't get eaten is the least of the stupid...well maybe not the least, but there are defiantly stupider things love can make you do. My papa saved Will on his very first mission for King Theodore. Papa killed the giant that Will was supposed to after the giant knocked Will unconscious. My papa was a great man, a legend in his own right when it came to these woods, but he didn't want the credit and he didn't want young Will to be a laughing stock, so I nursed a badly beaten Will back to health in our cabin. Papa had lied and told Will that he had found him next to the slain giant's body. Over the weeks of rehabilitation we started to fall in love. When Will went back to King Theodore, I followed. I've been following him ever since."

I poked at the firewood as I told my abbreviated story of stupid love. Stupid blind love in Will's case. I looked up and Jimmy nodded, saying, "I'll take that. It's not the romantic sweeping fairytale I had been hoping for, but it is the more realistic one...one that suits you, Gale." He said my name with a warmth and familiarity that implied we had known each other for years instead of weeks. It was odd, but not unpleasant.

He went on to tell me his story. When he was done, I wished that he hadn't. I needed sleep on the eve of any battle that Will may need me for, and I was not going to get much sleep after hearing of Jimmy's life. My feelings were already mixed and…and fine I'll admit it, a bit on the hormonal side. I'm attracted to the wounded, the weak that need protecting and nurturing. Things that are broken…and James Vayruin was very, very broken.

Nineteen

Dawn crested over Lake Weldon, bringing the valley said lake was nestled in to life with reddish-orange light. Looking down I saw the warm orange glow kissing Jimmy's smooth youthful forehead, where he still had it resting in my lap as I stroked his hair. I know, I know, I gave the mouse another damn cookie. I couldn't help it. You don't rip open someone's past - their wounds that are barely healed - until they are a weeping mess of emotion, looking for something solid to cling to for support, then you roll over and say *goodnight, here's a handkerchief, try not to get it too dirty*. No, I exposed his pain; it was my responsibly to help cover it back up. Even if that meant I had to rock him to sleep with his head in my lap like a scared little boy, then so be it.

When I glanced back at the fishing village I could see Will leaving the bar and boardinghouse from the rear entrance, so he could quietly saddle Duke and resolve the issue with the dwarves. Not wanting to wake Jimmy, I slipped my balled up travel bag under his head and eased out from under him. He grunted once or twice, but repositioned and fell back to sleep. Working the kinks and cramps out of stiff legs, I quietly made my way down the hillside until I was crouched with my back up against the stable as Will rode out on Duke saying, "Alright girl, we have some dwarves to take care of. Are you ready?" And when Duke obviously didn't answer him, he added worriedly, "I hope I am…"

He rode east along an old road that the fishermen used. It ran the circumference of the lake and was already busy with bustling fishermen hauling in the morning's catch. I stayed far enough behind that Will would not hear or see me. I even dodged in and out of the trees and bogs along the trailside so the fishermen wouldn't see me and suspect me for some villain set on ambushing their beloved hero. Decked out in black leather armor and coal-blackened eyes complete with tight facemask I did give off that whole *crazy assassin woman* vibe. It made for a harder day's travel than I'd like, but visions of villagers with fish-scented pitchforks (don't ask me why the pitchforks would smell like fish, it's my weird imagination, so just except it) and torches kept me edging through the woods instead of brashly following the easier route by using the road.

When the main trail split, one branch headed over toward the nearest lake to Weldon - Lake Cashsham - the other, smaller side trail wrapped around the southern tip of the lake and would take a traveler back to the village. Will chose neither path. He plunged Duke into the thick underbrush between the roads. Duke bucked and whinnied at first, not wanting to break trail in such thick swampy undergrowth. The white stallion's hooves quickly became coated in mud and muck. Squelching sounds accompanied his chuffs and nervous whines as his rider pushed him onward. Will leaned down, saying, "Easy girl, it's only a little further. The innkeeper said the dwarves had been hiding past the southern swamp because no one wants to come out this far. We'll show those thieves somebody has the courage to get a bit dirty, alright?"

His words did seem to calm Duke, somewhat, and all three of us trudged on until early afternoon. Have you ever tried to traverse a swamp quietly? Probably not, I can't imagine that it's a common problem. I've only had to do it a time or two myself, but if you have you know how difficult it can be just to wade through as is, let alone without the added need for silence. Every time you place your foot down incorrectly the ground decides the displaced air from your boot should sound like the explosive gas of a bugbear that's eaten nothing but chili for a week. Having experienced both, the swamps and the chili-fired bugbear, I can't decide which of those smells worse. So add a desire to constantly gag onto the already rough task of silence and you'll see how hard it was. To ensure the squelching noise from my boots was masked I had to time my steps with Duke's – not an easy task to match a biped's gait to a quadruped's, believe me.

It was hours later and I was covered in slimy muck and mud when we finally stumbled onto solid ground. In retrospect it should have sent up a mental red flag that Will rode directly into the dwarves' camp. No hesitation, no doubling back or searching through the underbrush for marks to track. He was not a skilled woodsman, I'm sure you've gotten that point by now. So, when he rode right in among their tents and fires, slowly roasting the day's noon meal as if he knew right where they would be I should have guessed something was up. Without dismounting he bellowed to the confused, some maybe slightly intoxicated dwarves, "Your thievery is at an end you vagabonds! Get thee gone from my king's land!"

At least one of the dwarves was not caught completely off guard. A large, heavy burlap sack struck Will in the chest, knocking him head over heels in a kind of reverse somersault off of Duke's back. By the wet thudding sounds and smell emanating from the dripping sack it seemed to contain the pilfered fish for that day's meal. Will grunted, but sprung back to his feet, dripping lake water and fish scales, and challenged, "I was going to go easy on you ruffians, but you will pay for that insult!"

He charged at the offending dwarf. A very fat and bald fellow no taller than a stable boy, but with the heavy drooping mustachios of a grandfather, only his facial hair was black instead of gray. The surly dwarf yelled, "Let's see what you got pretty boy!"

Men: short or tall, young or old, brilliant or dumber than dog shit, it doesn't matter. When faced with a fight they always need to figuratively whip out their cocks and swing them around verbally to see whose is bigger. Now women? We'd rather spread rumors about our enemies' sexual or eating habits. Psyche them out first, then slip in and stab them in the back. Less theatrical, but more effective I say.

Will charged across the camp at the droopy mustachioed dwarf, fists pumping and legs kicking, to show him exactly what he had. He didn't make it. Instead he tripped on a tent spike and tumbled past a cooking fire, rolling with the grace of a bull on ice skates. He struck his head on a rock that one dwarf was still sitting on drinking a mug of mead and knocked himself unconscious. The seated yellow bearded dwarf didn't even pause to look down where Will landed on his back, unmoving, until the drink was finished.

The entire camp stared in disbelief. All seven dwarves stared at the hero that had intruded on their camp and been knocked unconscious without any help from them. I stared from the nearby tree line, embarrassed again in a long succession of embarrassments. It even looked as if Duke was staring down at Will in disbelief, large equine eyes almost rolling in his sockets as if to say, *You have got to be kidding me.*

Droopy mustache dwarf wandered tentatively over toward Will as if he thought the hero might be faking it, ascribing a level of cunning to Will that I had always doubted my husband possessed. When

Droopy pulled out a large scaling knife and started to crouch down toward Will, I broke cover and yelled, "That's enough, Droopy!"

I had both my short sword - honed and sharp once more - and stiletto out and at the ready. Stalking toward the boss dwarf with the grace, skill, and menace Will could not, I said, "Drop the knife and back up, slowly."

Without showing any surprise at my sudden appearance, he did as ordered. Funny, both Jimmy and Will hardly ever listen to me. I have to yell or kick them in the head first. But, these guys, these dwarves were cold killers like me and they recognized malice and intent to maim when they saw it. I suppose I should be glad that the people I cared for were not cold killers, but it still would be nice if they listened to me and did what I said as easily as the dwarves did. And, yes I realize I just admitted to caring about Jimmy, but this was neither the time nor the place for that. So, as I walked past I kicked Droopy's scaling knife into the cooking fire. "Hey!" Droopy yelled, "That was me best blade, woman!"

I leapt across the few feet separating us. My knees absorbing the shock of impact, bringing me down to his height with my stiletto stopped short of breaking the stubble covered skin on his thick tree trunk-like neck. He swallowed hard as I growled, "Do you want mine?"

The Knight's Wife

Holding his hands out and up at his sides, long hanging mustachios quivering, Droopy stammered, "Look sheila, I don't know who you are and I don't rightly care. Me and me boys were paid to play this up. But, I'm not taking a knife to the throat for a few fish and a couple'o pieces of silver. Do you hear me?"

"Who are you?" Will ordered from behind me. I glanced down at the reflection on the blade I held at Droopy's throat to see a completely unharmed and fully awake Will standing behind me with his hands on his hips.

Crap. See what I mean about retrospect and giving him credit for guile?

I didn't respond. What the hell was I supposed to say? Instead I kicked Droopy back a step so I could at least turn to face Will. No, I didn't kick him in the head, which come to think of it would have been the easiest thing to do since he was so short, but I was trying to cut back on the head kicking. The dwarf stumbled backward and his six compatriots caught him, keeping him on his feet.

Eyeing both Will on my right and the seven dwarves on my left I eased into the best fighting stance I could. Given the fact that my back was to a large cooking fire with a giant cast-iron pot of boiling soup perched atop it, I think I did alright. And, yeah, I know, seven dwarves? Ever since that traveling bard and his brother, what was their last name,

147

Dour? Dismal? Gloomy? No, Grimm! Ever since the Grimms passed through Thistledown years ago, every group of dwarves has made sure their gang consisted of seven. Fads, go figure, who knew dwarves would be subject to conformity too, and people say women are bad about that kind of thing?

Will barked, "I knew you weren't some trauma induced hallucination," rubbing absently at the back of his head and continuing, "Who are you and how long have you been following me?"

I shook my head. I wasn't going to give him the opportunity to recognize my voice. "Fine," he stated resolutely, "have it your way." He turned to the dwarves and said, "Gentlemen, on the count of three, we charge."

"No way, pretty boy," Droopy said, rubbing at the spot on his chest where I had kicked him. "We did our part. This be your fight now. That sheila has teeth and claws. I lost me a good knife and I ain't losing anything else, but good luck to you." He saluted Will with his first two fingers to his forehead and wandered over to fetch the sack of fish he had thrown earlier.

The other dwarves dispersed as well. Some went over to help Droopy gather up the spilled fish for their supper, some even brought logs over to sit on and watch our standoff – dinner theater, great, just what I always wanted to be. I was still in trouble. I couldn't dodge around the camp with all its obstacles before Will caught me and unmasked me. I'm nimble and he's clumsy, but still that wasn't a viable option. He knew it. And he knew that I knew it because he was slowly edging toward me, forcing my hand.

"Stop!" I growled in my best, deepest, toughest attempt to mask my voice. It came out husky and throaty. I realized it was a good thing Will had never been into that whole dirty talk in the bed stuff or he would have recognized me, even displaced as I was from the woman he loved. Pointing my stiletto at him, I growled, "I mean it hero. Do not come any closer."

"Or what?" Will asked. He isn't stupid, remember. "You've been saving my life all these years, right? So you'll go ahead and kill me now? Just to keep your identity secret? Don't be silly."

Narrowing my eyes, I growled, "There are plenty of things I can cut or cut off that won't kill you. So don't push me!"

The audience of dwarves chuckled at my retort. One even grunted, "I like this sheila. It's a shame she ain't three feet shorter. You boys think maybe she's got a beard under that mask? She sounds dwarfish to me."

Another one chimed in with, "Who cares if she ain't got a beard and is twice yer height? ... As long as all the right parts line up when yer doing the nasty!" His squat arms and hips gyrated in mime to emphasize his point.

Ew, gross! Dwarf sex.

My eyes had shifted over toward the catcallers and when I looked back Will had edged a bit closer. Close enough that even as nearly blind as he is, he was able to read the disgust in my eyes at the thought of sleeping with one of the dirty, hairy, smelly, obese creatures, because he smiled and chuckled a bit. Crap. Not good.

If he was close enough to infer an expression in my coal-darkened eyes then he was too close. He was a step or two from recognizing a gesture or mannerism and figuring out who I was and twenty years of heroics would be over. Not to mention probably our marriage, too. I needed to get out of there and fast.

I don't know if it looked as cool as it did in my head, but I had an idea. It required a level of gymnastics, balance, and timing that I hoped, and I mean really hoped I could pull off. I edged back until I could feel the heels of my suede boots touching the large stones circling the campfire, then I took a deep breath and leapt backward, up and over the fire. As I started to come back down everything seemed to take on that dramatically slow feel harrowing situations produce for me sometimes. I could feel my body falling back toward the ground, directly over the fire. Scary, but what I wanted. I could see the

look of astonishment on Will's face and the faces of
the dwarves. When I was about to plunge feet-first
into the roaring fire I kicked out at the giant cast-iron
cauldron. It was a huge cooking pot meant to serve
the main meal for all seven dwarves. Dwarves eat a
lot. You could have bathed two children or one adult
in that cooking pot. My feet struck out, momentarily
touching the bulbous middle, and with all the force
of gravity and the remaining power in my legs, I re-
directed my momentum and sprung backward. Now,
it probably would have looked even cooler if I had
had my weapons sheathed. If I had, I could have
done a backflip. But, I'm not that *good*, so I fell
backward, past the fire, landing flat on my back with
a thump that knocked the wind from me. The cauldron tipped over, spilling tons of boiling broth all
over the raging fire. Steam and smoke shot up and
out in all directions. I heard Will grunt and swear
and the dwarves scream like scared children. Sheathing my weapons and gagging as I tried to drag air
back into my lungs, I fled into the woods and hoped
I hadn't hurt Will too badly with my escape. Burns
were a lot worse than kicks to the head…it seemed
my troubles were escalating.

Twenty

Maybe Jimmy was right. Maybe I did like hurting people. Maybe not on purpose, of course, nothing sadistic or malicious as he had been implying, but at such a level that I wasn't aware of it, because I kept finding myself in situations where I ended up hurting people, even and especially myself. I don't mean the stupid physical aches like the possible broken ribs I was cradling, but the hurt of putting myself in such a moronic, idiotic, daft situation to begin with. Those thoughts kept running through my head as I blindingly fled into the unfamiliar forest and swamp.

That is one of the worst, and I mean the worst, things you can do. You never run wildly and blindly into a forest you are unfamiliar with. You shouldn't even do it in a forest that you *are* familiar with, but at least then when you stop you should be able to gather your wits and find your bearings. If the forest is unfamiliar, as the southern reaches of the swamps and wetlands of Lake Weldon were for me, you could find yourself in a world of hurt really, really fast. And when you did stop to get your bearings, assuming you didn't plummet off of a cliff or tumble down a deadfall, it wouldn't matter because (except for the sun and stars to guide you, again, assuming your navigation skills are what they should be) you could be royally lost…the cruel bitch of it is, you could be lost, and be only a few yards from a well maintained road. You could die so close to salvation and never know it. Those are more lessons from Papa there. They're good lessons and I knew them well, but I was so flustered, so hurt, and so embarrassed that I refused to remember them. They say that's the number one killer of people who get lost in the woods and need to rely on themselves for survival – shame. Shame will kill you every time if you let it. I ran from my shame. I ran until I was good and lost…and then I ran some more.

When I finally ran out of steam, both physically and emotionally, I yanked off my facemask and in a petulant, childlike gesture I flung it to the ground and curled up into a small ball. I had no idea where I was and I didn't care. I wanted to be alone and I wanted to hide. Glancing around, I spotted a nearby rocky overhang and wriggled over to it. In the leeward side there was a bit of a natural shelter, so I wedged myself down in and covered my face. I was upset. I was stupid. I was too brash, too cocky, and overconfident. I should have known Will would have been wondering all these years how he did the things he was given credit for and when he finally realized what was going on he wasn't going to just let it drop at my suggestion of head trauma. I didn't give him enough credit. I never would have thought him capable of paying the dwarves to lay a trap. That went way beyond lying about poor Daisy Jinkins being what had him upset. Entrapment was a whole new level of subterfuge that I had assumed was beyond Will's goody two-shoes mentality. The lies we keep from each other just amaze me sometimes. I bet there was no new stupid tavern opening last week. I bet the son of a bitch went and sent word to the dwarves with the bribe. Oh, he's just a helpless baby, Gale. He'd never be able to do anything without *you*! Stupid ego, stupid Will, stupid dwarves, stupid ribs that hurt like shards of glass with every sob, and just stupid everything.

I don't know how long I sat there crying, an hour maybe less. I hate crying. I rarely do it. I'm not some *oh look at the little baby*, isn't it so sweet and here come the waterworks type girl. I never have been, but when I do cry, boy howdy is that something to see - I let it all out. It's not pretty, huge racking sobs (which really hurt with my ribs), snot rolling down my upper lip, and red puffy eyes that look like somebody poured kerosene into them. I wish I could do that delicate flower, one tear rolling down the cheek stuff that the composed royal ladies seem born and bred to do. But no, I look like a drunk walrus gagging on a fish.

Evening was approaching, even in an unfamiliar woods, I could tell night was coming by the length of the shadows. I didn't care. I wanted to stay in my secure, tight little ball of sadness, and just be left alone. I still had my weapons and so help anybody or thing that tried to take advantage of my moment of weakness. Sadness can be turned into a tool of aggression real quick.

The Knight's Wife

Then the dried leaves nearby began rustling as if fate wanted to test that very theory. I pulled myself up and sat with my back to the rock overhang, wiping a disgusting, monstrous glob of snot on the back of my bracer in the process, and glared at the moving brush. It was several yards away and even in my overly emotional state I had picked a decent hiding place. I had a clear vantage point on anything that came snooping around. I was wrapping my right hand around my stiletto and preparing to draw it when I heard a whispered shout, "My lady? Gale? Can you hear me?"

Crap. It was Jimmy. Crap.

I could. No, let me restate that. I *should* have let him go and not called out. I told myself later that it was because I was worried that he would wander around these woods, which were unfamiliar to me, and become lost and die just trying to find me. I told myself a lot of things to justify my actions over the years, but that one at least had a decent enough measure of truth to it. So, I called out, "Over here, Jimmy." Whether I should have or not I guess is a matter of opinion.

The brush and bushes rattled more heavily as he approached, following the sound of my voice. He stumbled into the small clearing that I had used as my hideaway, sweeping a few loose bits of twigs and leaves out of his hair with a cocky grin. He started to say, "That was amazing! I saw the whole

155

thing! With the jump over the…" He trailed off when he got a good look at my post-fish-gagging drunken walrus state, coal-darkened eyes probably smeared and looking like some psycho bride that's been left at the altar. Realizing how awful I must have looked, I scooped up my thrown mask and started using the fabric to wipe at my eyes and nose.

Jimmy hesitantly walked over and crouched down next to me. He didn't start babbling right away, which in and of itself was a damn miracle. We sat there quietly, tucked away in an unfamiliar woods, in an area that I wasn't even sure was still part of Thistledown, and just kept each other company. Occasionally my breath would catch or hitch like it does after you've had a really good cry, and every now and then Jimmy would shift or move to a more comfortable position, but he said nothing. We stayed silent. When it became obvious that night was falling and I had no intension of moving, Jimmy gathered some wood (what dry tinder he could find in that musty forest come swamp) and built a small fire. The ground was very damp and Jimmy knew enough to build the fire on a platform. Papa would have liked him for knowing that. It always bothered Papa how little Will knew about the woods. Jimmy even knew to build it in layers: green logs covered with a layer of stones which he inspected to make sure they weren't porous or excessively wet, so they wouldn't explode when the fire heated them. He used my flint and saw-edged blade to light our meager fire from my travel bag which he had brought with him when he followed me. The one I had left him as a pillow that morning instead of my lap. That morning? Wow, isn't it amazing how when the bottom drops out on us we lose track of time?

When there was no light left but for the fire Jimmy broke the long silence. Over the pop and hiss of the damp swamp wood, he asked, "Are you alright, my lady?"

I didn't answer him. I just stared at the fire. I know you're probably thinking, *What's her problem? It's not that big of a deal. So, she messed up a bit and her husband isn't as stupid as she thought he was. Why did she fall apart over that?* Twenty years, that's why. Twenty years of always being on the ball, wound tight and all but sprung for action, and having to do a million things at once. Twenty years of stress. Twenty years of wondering if this battle would be the one I was too late for, or would the king insist on sending other soldiers and they'd find out what a doofus Will really was? Twenty years of worry. Seven thousand three hundred days. You want me to give you the minutes? It adds up. Combine that with all the other things we keep with us, but don't really talk about. Things that still weigh us down. I missed my papa, and always would. I missed never having children. All those things can sometimes take one instance that really wasn't all that fall apart worthy and send us down a freak out spiral into a major breakdown. That's why.

Jimmy pressed a little more when I didn't answer him, "You didn't expect Sir William to set a trap, did you?" He scooted around our meager fire, pulling my travel blanket out of the bag as he did, and draped it around my shoulders, whispering, "It's alright. You don't always have to be strong. Sometimes…sometimes it's okay to be weak. I don't even see it as weak to need somebody. That's all *you* need, my lady, just someone else to be strong for you."

I made the first move. I refuse to lay that blame on Jimmy. He didn't push for it. He didn't even ask for it outside of a flippant comment made when he was pretending to be the cocky and confident young man that he really wasn't. The young man he showed the rest of the world, but not the young man that he had let me see. Draping a blanket over someone's shoulders and telling them everything is okay, is not the first move. That's showing compassion in a world that is sorely low on it. But me, leaning into his arms and kissing, softly then firmly, the hollow below his right ear, yeah that was the first move.

The second, and how he was willing to go there with me looking like the drunk gagging walrus ghost bride was another miracle, was me sliding my right hand along his strong jaw and pulling his face toward mine. Listing the moves numerically after that would become a bit tedious and methodical, and plus at a certain point it would be the same move repeated over and over again to a quickening pace, so I won't.

Have you ever made love in front of a roaring campfire? It's very romantic sure, but, and it didn't happen that night so don't worry, I want to remind you that though romantic, you have all sorts of sensitive areas out and about, exposed to the elements; like wet tinder that pops and throws sparks around indiscriminately. So, if you ever find yourself carried away out-of-doors, with a fire blazing near your nether regions, I suggest you maneuver your lover around on top and let his ass catch the sparks…unless he's really hairy, maybe then you could risk an ember or two dancing down your back or cheeks. Who knows, maybe you'll like it.

I maneuvered Jimmy around, hey he's young and sparse on the hair, I found that out when I ran my hands down his smooth chest. Not quite as thick in the muscle department as Will, but to be honest I always preferred lean and strong to bulky and massive. He slipped out of his shirt – the temperatures were too cold to sport just the black vest, no matter how good he looked in it – and reached for my face once more after he was less encumbered. Pulling my mouth to his as if he needed me to be close to him, to taste him, to feel his breath, warm and coming in quick gasps against my lips. I wound my arms around his neck, stroking his long black hair, and delicately unlaced my bracers as to not ruin the moment with tedious armor removal. Instead of the ar-

159

mor protecting me from injury it was in the way –
still protecting me, I suppose, if you want to look at
it philosophically – but I didn't want to think. I
wanted to act. Thinking had only caused me pain,
perhaps acting would ease the pain, and if I was
lucky give me a bit of pleasure, too.

We could have yanked and pulled at the different
pieces of armor, tugging like animals, grasping,
grunting, and swearing until enough was removed
that we could at least accomplish the act we were
both so very much anticipating. We didn't. Jimmy
for all his awkward and scared innocence with emotion, knew his way around physical intimacy quite
well. He used the armor as part of the whole package, instead of just the wrapping. He teased his
tongue along my neck and clavicles where the edges
of the breastplate met skin, deftly unlacing knots and
unhooking clasps as he went. I wear a lot of armor.
Most days when I'm tired and exhausted from hiking
and running in it, I consider all that weight and cov-
erage a burden, but then, with Jimmy teasing his
tongue along the seams and creases it felt like I
wanted more, like I couldn't have enough. I wanted
Jimmy to have to peel back more and more layers
just so he could tease and taste as he went. When I
was unarmored, completely, Jimmy removed the last
obstacle in our way, his pants.

We spent a very long, warm in some places and
cold in others, night together. Seeking comfort and
escape in each other's arms, in each other's bodies.

The Knight's Wife

Holding on as tightly as we could, long, long into the night, neither of us wanting the moment to end, but both knowing that it inevitably would. I held Jimmy, as he thrust into me again and again, watching the stars over his shoulder and eventually I closed my eyes, not wanting to see the judgment that I knew wasn't really there. For one night, for just one damn night, I wanted to be weak, to let someone else be my strength. I let the young, broken, beaten gypsy juggler be that strength, and I do not regret it.

Twenty-one

Morning dawned and for the first time in my life I woke up in another man's arms. It was cold and damp outside the bubble of comfort the blanket was providing our naked bodies. I could feel the clammy chill of the ground fog brushing against my face, but my back was warm where it was pressed up against Jimmy's front. The fire had burned out sometime in the wee hours of the night when we had exhausted ourselves enough to sleep, or passed out in a sex coma, either way. I knew I should feel some guilt, or some anger, maybe some resentment still over Will's ungrateful attempt to unmask me. But, the truth is I felt nothing. No pain anymore, so that's something, but there wasn't any passion either, which I don't think was such a good thing. I felt complete and total apathy. I had enjoyed last night. It had been some-thing you hear about in fantasy stories of knights in shining armor and princesses stuck in castles…well, not the kids' versions, the ones we ladies talk about. The kind Queen Marissa would drool over. But I didn't know if I really cared for Jimmy. No, that's a bullshit lie. I did care for him, but did I love him? I wasn't so sure that I still loved Will. Hell, I didn't even love myself anymore, and you can delude your-selves all you want but everyone, everywhere, in every when, has always loved themselves first and foremost. When we stop loving ourselves? Oh boy, I think you're in real danger then. I didn't hate myself either, which would have been a preferable alternative, I suppose. I mean at least hate is some measure of emotion, right?

I felt nothing, nada, zip, zero, zilch as I lie there with my back spooned against Jimmy. A pretty young man who had his problems, and might or might not be falling in love with someone, me, for the first time in his tragic life. I couldn't even feel empathy, sympathy, or guilt over that. You want to know what thought popped into my head? Shit happens. How pathetic is that? Feeling nothing, all I wanted to do was hide. No, not hide, disappear completely, that's what I wanted, to disappear. I just wanted to say forget it, let the world get by on its own. I was tired. Does that count as a feeling? Bone weary, deep down into my core, dead to the world tired.

I could feel Jimmy shifting behind me as he woke up. His left arm was draped over me and his hand was tucked under my arm, cupping my breast. It felt nice, soothing, maybe a bit adventurous, to have someone else touching me in such a personal manner. Okay, so maybe I was being a tad overly dramatic when I said I didn't feel anything. I wasn't dead on the inside or out. I could still feel. It's just when the rug gets yanked out from under you sometimes when you land as hard on your ass as I had you start lying, maybe over exaggerating a bit, to make yourself feel better. I don't know.

163

I realized how much pain I could still feel when my eyes focused on the mostly burned red maple leaf resting on the edge of the cold campfire. It must have landed there or been brushed into the fire while Jimmy and I were going at it like horny monkeys last night. It was stupid. It shouldn't have started me crying again, but I was a wreck. It was just a leaf, but it felt like I'd let my whole past burn up in that campfire, just brushed it aside, for one moment of weakness. That I did feel, hard, piercing and twisting, right behind that handsome young man's hand, deep in my chest. No melodrama there, it hurt, seeing that red maple leaf burned crispy, edges black and gray. That hurt more than Will's entrapment, Jimmy's infatuation that I'd encouraged, my own flaws and failures weren't the problem, it was the idea that Papa had seen those flaws somehow, and vicariously through that leaf, that tie to my past, had thrown himself into the fire instead of watching me give in to my weakness. That's what hurt.

I lay there, pretending to still be asleep, so Jimmy wouldn't hear me cry. I didn't do my gagging walrus weeping this time. Funny how I could do the dainty ladylike leaky drop tears when the pain hurt the most. Give the boy credit though, when my leaking tears rolled down onto his other arm, he didn't thrust that morning-wood I could feel pressing between my ass cheeks home. No, ever the gentleman, he slid out from under me and sitting up he pulled me into a hug, saying, "It's alright, Gale. I'm here."

The Knight's Wife

Oh good, more pain, see I knew it had to be there somewhere. The poor kid had no idea that his being there was a big heaping part of why I was crying. Odd how a month ago, maybe two, and this never would have happened - none of it. I'd have laughed off Jimmy's advances. I'd have seen Will's trap coming a mile away and would have avoided it. I would have seen that stupid sneaky troll hiding in the damn bushes and slit its throat before it ambushed Will. I guess it comes down to one last feather tipping the scales. That's too poetic for my life. It's more like one more turd toppling the scales of crap.

So, like always, I had to play the hardass. It was either that or fall apart again. Neither is pretty or fun, but I'd had my moment of weakness. My moment to let someone else be strong for me. Now I had to get my shit together, gather up the crap from the toppled scales of my life and go back at it. What was I going to do about Will? I didn't have a clue, but I'd cross that bridge when I got there. Papa's voice came back to me, "You can't always worry about hurting other people's feelings. Their feelings are theirs to protect, and if you hurt them, as long as it wasn't on purpose, then it's their problem to solve, not yours, little Nightingale." Maybe it was me stopping feeling sorry for myself, maybe it was all in my head, but it was nice to hear his voice. Whether it was me forgiving myself, or if Papa really would have cared if I'd had a breakdown and slept with some sad boy looking for love, I didn't know.

This all probably sounds like the ravings and ramblings of some hussy trying to justify her skanky ways. I just didn't know what to do, not really. Have you ever been so flustered, so lost, that you don't seem to know what to do? I don't suppose that excuses *who* you do, but it's still hard. Maybe you've been there and maybe you haven't, I don't know.

I pushed away from Jimmy's young, strong chest, where I'd been resting my head while I wrestled with my thoughts. Pulling the half-burned leaf away from the ashes with one hand I reached up and patted his cheek affectionately with the other. It was hard to look into those sultry blue eyes and say, "Thank you, Jimmy. I appreciate that. What happened…" It turns out it wasn't just hard to say it, but Jimmy wouldn't let me. He interrupted me, looking more like a damn puppy dog than ever as he said, "Of course, Gale. I'll always be there for you. I love you. That's what you do for people you love, right? Just like why you helped Sir William all these years, because of love."

Crap. Papa, any advice? But the damn leaf was silent. No words of wisdom from the past…except I could have sworn I heard his familiar chuckle softly echo as I looked into Jimmy's earnest face.

Twenty-two

With the silent, lack of advice from that place in my head where I hear my papa's voice, I had to stare at Jimmy's open admission of love without support, imagined or otherwise. What do you say when someone tells you that they love you, but you only care for them, you don't want them to die or anything, you enjoy being around them, but do you love them? Um, I'd have to get back to you on that. Jimmy, it turned out, was okay with that too, because he said, "No, you don't have to say anything. Actually, Gale, I'd kind of prefer it if you didn't. I understand this is harder for you than it is for me. I know you still love Will, and that was what had you so upset last night. This is… complicated …for everybody. I just wanted you to know it, to hear me say it, and well…just for me to have the chance to say it to someone, and really mean it."

Well, I didn't know what to say to that either, so I sort of silently stared at him for a while. I mean, saying something stupid like, "Thank you" or "I know" seemed really paltry after the kid had put so much thought and heart into his rationale, so, I guess, go with vague? I pulled his face toward me again and kissed him, but the gentle kiss of what I hoped was affection, not the ram my tongue down his throat let's go at it again like inebriated rabbits kind of kiss. To end the embrace I stood up and started gathering my scattered armor and clothes. I've always found it awkward to get dressed in front of somebody you've just had sex with. It's weird to say that when you think of where things, parts, hands, tongues, and lips have been, but I always want to cover those parts back up quickly, as if saying, "Look you had your fun, now that isn't going to happen again in the immediate future, maybe never again, so just let me get things tucked away and covered up so we can move on."

Easier said than done of course; you try squeezing your boobs into a leather armor bustier with anything approaching delicacy and speed – nothing quick or easy about that. As I stood there, stuffing, poking, and prodding all the pieces parts back into the right places, Jimmy lounged back with the camp blanket draped appropriately over his lap for a hint of modesty. Only a hint, mind you, morning Jimmy was still more than excited to rise with the sun and provide a tent in the blanket for a family of chipmunks to camp under – extended family too: a huge clan of chipmunks could have thrown one hell of a reunion under there. He grinned at me with that stupid male grin. You know the one, right? Basically that grin translates to *Ha ha, I see boobies.* You've all seen that grin, am I right? And if you haven't yet girls, don't worry, you will, sooner or later, no matter how big or small your breasts are you'll have some guy stare at them with that dopey grin as if it were a religious holiday he's basking in the glow of Boob Day! Gentlemen, boys, lords, knights, guys,

and kings gather round please. Let us start this holi-
est of holy holidays with a Boob Day carol, followed
by Boob Day games, and the ever popular Boob Day
feast!

"What?" I snapped at Jimmy as he grinned. He
was sharp enough to at least not say, "Ha ha, I see
boobies," aloud. No, he still grinned that grin but
said, "I'm just so impressed by what a badass you
are, Gale." He sat back up, pulling the blanket
around his shoulders. Sorry chipmunks, you'd have
to find a new tent. I looked at him questioningly for
an elaboration, and he gestured with a brush of his
fingers, saying, "All that armor, all those weapons. I
can handle a sword, but not like you. I mean, I
wouldn't even know where half of it went and I took
it off of you. Or, even what it's all called. Like that,"
he pointed toward the kris I was strapping to my
shin, "what's that squiggly curved knife-thing
called?"

"It's a kris, Jimmy," I said, rolling my eyes and
cinching the buckle.

"See," he said, shaking his head, "I had no clue!"

He was a cute, charming, innocent kid. He deserved better than what he'd been given in life and
he definitely deserved better than to be wedged into
my chaotic mess of a life, too. I started to say,
"Look, Jimmy…"

"No, Gale," he interrupted me, "remember, I don't want or need to hear it. Now is not the time. I think you need to figure out what you're going to do anyway. Don't worry about me."

He was right.

"I have a plan, Jimmy," I lied.

"Oh really?" he called my bluff. "What is it? Can I help?" But, he meant the last part and wasn't just being a smartass. I could tell by the set of those earnest blue eyes. Sighing, I said, "My plan is to make it up as I go along, Jimmy…and, thank you, but right now I have to do this alone." I leaned down and kissed his forehead where those eyes were now showing concern. Not to hurt his feelings, I added, "I promise to let you know if and when you can help, alright?"

He smiled and nodded, happy or at least satisfied with my promise. Smile changing to chagrin, he asked, "Can I keep the blanket for now? I think I'll stoke the fire back to life and rest here for a bit." Looking down toward his lap, he scrunched his face up and said, "I'm a little sore and tired from last night…" he then smirked the I see boobies grin again and added, "my lady."

Sigh. Rolling my eyes, I said, "Sure, Jimmy." And patting him on the shoulder, I asked, "Can you find your way back? I need to move, now, if I'm going to try and salvage some of this mess into something resembling my life."

He nodded, saying, "Absolutely," as he leaned back, placing his right hand behind his head and started to doze back off. Then, pulling the blanket up under his chin, he added as an afterthought, "Be careful, little Nightingale."

Okay, that was kind of weird and creepy. I'd have to tell him not to use that particular pet-name. I didn't like people calling me by nicknames and pet-names to begin with - you can call me a hypocrite if you like because I have no problem giving other people nicknames, go figure - but you don't want the handsome young man you just screwed raw calling you by the same pet-name your father did. Ew. Gross.

I took off at a run following the doubled up prints both Jimmy and I had left along the marshy forest floor yesterday. I didn't bother to say any more to Jimmy at that time, knowing full well, at some point, there would have to be a lot more to say. It couldn't be as easy as, *I love you, Gale. You don't have to love me. No problem!* It doesn't work that way. Life doesn't work that way. Guys like Jimmy, guys that can have any woman they want pretty much on demand, don't chase after a woman like he did with me and just be satisfied with one night of crazy, passionate sex by a campfire. No, complications were coming. I could feel it in the damn humid

171

air as I panted running back through the forest and swamp I had blindly fled into yesterday. It hadn't rained, thank the stars, and I was able to follow both my tracks and Jimmy's the entire way back to the dwarves' camp. It seemed like I had barely traveled an hour, when yesterday it was an endless journey of tears and stumbling. They always say the trip back goes faster anyway.

It was still very early in the morning, too early for a band of thieving lazy-ass dwarves to be out of bed, when I edged up to their camp. Two hulking, burlap-covered lumps, snored and wheezed, close to the restored fire I had sent into a cloud of boiled fish and steam during my escape. The guards I assumed. There was no real need for the dwarves to set guards out here. The villagers were fishermen, not fighters, and the dangerous creatures of the swamps would give a dwarf camp a wide berth. Why mess with a bunch of pugnacious alcoholics who loved axes when there were easier pickings elsewhere? The guards were a formality only, as was obvious by the snores, sleeping wheezes, and occasional comically loud farts. If the one cutting loose so much rolled in his sleep any closer to the fire, he might actually combust.

The other dwarves, not playing guard, must have been asleep in the accompanying tents. From where I was perched, high in a nearby maple tree, I could see several empty beer and mead barrels scattered around the camp. A few were stacked like children's building blocks and I saw a third blanketed form curled up atop those, rocking the empty caskets back and forth with his snores. They must have spent the sliver Will had paid them on one heck of a party last night after I left. With unnecessary stealth - the farting guard dwarf was louder than my footsteps - I crept down and started to search the tents. I was looking for Droopy. I figured if any of these stocky thugs had information, it would be him. The first and second tents were a bust, containing a fat blond dwarf and the second one had a fat red bearded dwarf hugging a sheep. Both looked happy so I let it be, who was I to judge? I was about to pull back the flap on the third, when I saw Droopy stumble out of the fourth tent, pecker in hand and dipping a bit as he aimed for the nearest bush. He groaned loudly, leaning against a tree trunk, when he was clear enough to let fly.

Droopy had the side of his head resting on his arm, which was in turn supporting his weight against the tree. He was muttering some dwarfish curse about too much beer, when I slipped my left arm under his, locking in a half-nelson hold on his neck and resting my stiletto under his exposed dwarf-hood. He gulped loudly and I leaned down, whispering in his ear, "Hold very still and say nothing, Droopy. Or I'll be changing my nickname for you to Stubby, understand?"

He nodded.

"Good," I hissed, voice muffled by my mask which I had put back in place after leaving Jimmy. Hey, no need to risk identification now, even if the real me was virtually unknown to most of the kingdom outside Thistledown city and the castle proper. Alcohol addled mind or not, Droopy was a sharp dwarf. He cursed softly again and without even attempting to look out of the corner of his bloodshot eyes at me he said, "Damn it sheila! Didn't you do enough to me camp yesterday? Did you have to come back and take me dignity too?"

Laughing slightly, I said, "If I let go, will you cooperate and answer my questions? Or will you make me make you regret it?"

"Aye, sheila," he agreed, nodding again, vigorously this time. "I'll be good, just let me finish up here and let me put me prick away. Me boys and me drank a right lot last night and I still have more to pass."

I stepped back and let Droopy finish his business. Let me tell you this, a dwarf can hold a lot, I mean *a lot* of pee! That's not information I suppose that has much practical use, but you never know. I would have believed that Droopy had drank all those barrels himself with the length of time it took him to empty his bladder. Sighing heavily and grunting with the effort, Droopy turned around, shaking his dwarf-hood a couple of times before putting it away. And, let me say this while I'm on that subject,

174

though it may not have been my cup of tea, Snow White definitely had her reasons for shacking up with seven of these guys if Droopy were any gauge of size and girth. Witness protection from her wicked stepmother my ass! She had other reasons. Droopy grinned when he saw me staring, that other wonderful male grin, it's a close proximate to the *Ha, ha I see boobies grin*, but this one is slightly more grownup and translates to *Yeah baby, you like?* Rolling my eyes, I said, "Cough it up, Droopy. What happened after I left?"

Rubbing the back of his neck the dwarf stumbled over to a nearby log and plopped down with a grunt. After gesturing for me to do the same, he said, "Well sheila, after that acrobatic escape o'yours, me and me boys helped that there Sir William get dried off some, those clothes of his were right soaked, and he had himself quite a few nasty burns on his chest and legs, too."

Crap. I had been worried about that. Steam burns are nasty if you can't get cold water (or in the winter, ice) on them quickly because the flesh keeps cooking after it's been burned. The dwarves took a risk in removing his clothes. They probably didn't know any better, but if the burns had been severe enough they may have pulled away some of his skin with the damp cloth. Not pretty, not fun.

Nodding his head as if he could see my mental remonstrations, Droopy continued, "Aye, I figured you didn't want to hurt the bloke none. You could have kicked his arse right then and there if that had been your plan, but you didn't. So, don't worry about it overmuch. He was hurt some, but not anything permanent. He'll heal up in a few days. I sent him on his way about two hours ago, maybe three, maybe four, it was still dark I know that much. I've been drinking if you hadn't noticed." He thumped on his chest with a massive hairy fist for emphasis, aiding the release of a giant belch of a size and duration to make any mother dwarf proud.

Spying what appeared to be a still half-full flagon of mead, Droopy leaned over, snatched it up and took a swig. Wiping his drooping mustache with the back of his hand he belched (more daintily and don't tell him I said this *elf-like* that time) and continued, "After we tended to his wounds, me and me boys dressed Sir William in some o'our castoff clothes. He was right funny looking, arms and legs sticking way out like a crane wearing a towel! Ha! Well, we felt sorry for him, since his whole plan backfired and all, so we opened up our reserves and had us one hell'o our own Sir William Day party!" He exclaimed, slapping his knee, and took another, lengthy pull from his flagon.

"What was his plan?" I asked when Droopy was done drinking and belching.

Looking sternly at me, he dropped his now empty flagon to his side, and pointed at me with a grubby finger. "About a week ago Sir William comes riding hard and fast into me camp. He's got bits of leaves and twigs in his hair, and he's just a right mess. His horse was panting like it'd been run ragged. We was all set for a fight. We figured at some point the king would send his champion out to run us off, so it wasn't all that big of a surprise. But, Sir William held his hands out and said, 'Easy good dwarves! If thee would palaver with me, I would make thee all a deal.' Firstly I says, 'What the fuck is a palaver?' and secondly I says, 'What do you want?' Well it turns out that the Great Sir William has some wild rabid sheila on his trail, been following him around he says. We figured it to be some damn fool groupie or ignored housewife that got obsessed with the good knight and was following him around." At this Droopy gestured to me adding, "You, I take it?"

I nodded and said, "But I'm not much of the groupie type."

"Aye, that's easy to see sheila," he agreed and continued. "Well, Sir William said he'd make a deal with the fishermen. I don't know what or how, for us to stay if we'd help him with his woman problems and stage us a little play for her benefit, and when the time was right, he'd pounce and find out who she was. Who you were I guess." He shrugged his shoulders and looked around for another unfinished drink.

177

Will must have ridden Duke very hard indeed if he made it all the way here and back in that single night he had supposedly stayed in Thistledown for what I now knew had to be a fake tavern opening. Crap. I should have noticed how tired either he or Duke was last week, and in retrospect I could remember them both being a bit sluggish when they returned, but I chalked that up to too much celebration and complementary booze.

"What's your deal with him then?" Droopy asked, pulling me out of my thoughts. "Sure'n you ain't the groupie sort, I agree there, but there's got to be some connection. Mayhap you're the obsessed housewife, eh?" Glancing at my armaments and weapons he added, "Doubtful that, so there must be some other connection, I'm thinking."

Looking up sharply, I hissed, "It's none of your business!"

Placing his palms out in placation toward me, Droopy said, "Easy sheila, you're right, it's none o'me business. I was just curious. It seems a mite strange is all. The Great Sir William, slayer o'a thousand monsters and righter o'a thousand wrongs, trying to unmask one wily swordswoman. I'd have thought if he'd had a problem with you, he'd have just pinned you down somewhere and the two of you could have gone at it till you was both dead or married with a cluster o'kids."

The Knight's Wife

He was, whether accidently or not, coming awfully close to the truth for my tastes. He continued, scratching at his mustache in thought, "In fact, that whole tripping into that stone thing he did when he tried to trap you looked really damned convincing to me. Either Sir William is one hell o'an actor or..." he trailed off.

I could have bribed him. I could have threatened him. But either of those options would have confirmed what he was supposing. I wasn't in the mood. Pointing over his shoulder, I said, "Looks like there's another full keg of beer over there."

He spun quickly to look and asked, "Where?"

Before he could turn back around I kicked Droopy, hard, I'm talking roundhouse spin kick, in the head. You can't go easy on a dwarf. If you're going to strike one, do it hard and fast, or it'll just piss the dwarf off. I'd been both hard and fast enough to knock Droopy out cold. I pulled him back into his tent, a more difficult task than expected for something that looks so short, covered him with his blanket, and for good measure found another half-full keg, and after dribbling some into his mustache and bedding, I tucked the keg under his arm like a pillow. If I was lucky, he'd wake up, hours from now and if he remembered any of this he'd think it was only a drunken dream.

Yeah, I know, so much for cutting back on kicking people in the head, huh?

Twenty-three

It wasn't hard to catch up to Will and Duke, both were very hung-over and moving at an appropriately snail-like pace. And yeah, you heard me right, both. Have you ever been to a Dwarf party? I've only been to a few, but let me tell you their one simple rule: everybody drinks. That means every living thing within the radius of what the dwarves throwing the celebration deem the *Party Zone* has to drink. Translation – they give booze to everything: dwarves, people, dwarves, horses, dwarves, livestock, dwarves, elves, dwarves...well you get the point. I even saw a drunk squirrel once when I went to a dwarf party with Papa. I was a little girl, and to appease the *Party Zone* rule, Papa let me have one mug of mead. The dwarves who threw the party thought it was hilarious when I got the hiccups.

So, *Party Zoned* out, I caught up to Duke a little north of the fishing village, not far past where Jimmy and I had spent the night in the traders' camp. I kept pace behind them for a while, attempting to give myself time to come up with a plan. I was starting to have the maybe beginnings, of a maybe half-assed plan. I wasn't sure. My impulse was to hightail it around the two of them, push on through the night and make it home early the next morning so I'd have everything set up and ready for when Will returned. Just like always, we could bury our heads in the sand

and pretend that nothing was the matter, that good old axiom of long married couples everywhere: *Ignore it and it will go away*. Though, unlike all the years before, I doubted Will would be in a particularly great mood and ignoring something is harder when it keeps cropping up in self-doubt. But, he'd get over it in time, right?

Yeah, I know, I doubted that too, that's why my plan was gaining a bit of momentum - less half-ass and a bit more whole-ass. I didn't have the far scoped planning skills of a chess master. Papa taught me to play, but I never had the patience to get really good at it. I was the kind of girl who'd try and distract Papa and swap pieces while he wasn't looking instead. He'd ignore it and still win, so when it came to plans and strategy, I found it best to just dive right in. Screw the cause and effect down the road; act now! You've seen how well that's worked for me so far, right? I mean, why learn from my mistakes when I could just make all new ones that made the old ones look paltry by comparison. Healing and emotional growth by Dr. Gale: keep fucking up and sooner or later you won't feel so bad about the original mistake!

Yeah, I know, I'm full of crap sometimes. No need to beat me up over it verbally though, I do that enough to myself. I got you covered.

But I figured crap or not, I'd utilize that very anti-strategy as I slowly crept behind and waited until

181

Will unsaddled Duke for the night. He'd picked another beautiful campsite, nestled in some old oaks by a small waterfall trickling down an exposed hillside and still a day and a half's ride from Thistledown; almost two from our cottage at the pace they were traveling. Once Duke was secured to a tree and set to munch on his supper, I decided to jump right in and see what happened. Will was crouched over, attempting to start a fire, and…well, okay so maybe I was still a little mad, but I didn't take it out on him too hard, honest. I kicked him in the ass. More of a push with the end of my boot really - nothing to brag about - and not a concussive blow to the head so don't roll your eyes, please.

Will stumbled over the stack of tinder and leaves he had been trying to light. Hands sprawled out to catch himself from falling completely and landing face first in the brush pile. He turned around, glaring and spluttering, "How dare you?"

But, I think my sword pointed inches from his chin answered nicely enough. Remaining silent, I stared down my blade's length at Will as he accused, "You!"

Using my husky - probably sounding like a cheap village whore that smokes too much voice - I said, "Yes, me!" Circling around his prone form, I added, "Go ahead and start your fire, Sir William. I figure you have questions, and if you're lucky, I may have answers."

He looked surprised. He started to speak then stopped. Finally shaking his head in disbelief, he managed to utter, "I don't understand, I…"

"What?" I asked, caustic and accusing, "you thought a surprise trap in a dwarf camp would be a better, more relaxed atmosphere for our little tête-à-tête? Did it ever cross your little mind to simply ask me? Wait around during some mission for me to show up and then ask, 'So, you follow me around often'?"

"Ah…well," he stumbled. Eloquence under pressure is just another of the many failings of the Great Sir William. Sorry swooning maidens, no poetic stanzas to sweep your skirt over your head here, only, "Ah…well," and if you're real lucky it'll be accompanied by the *Ha ha, I see boobies* grin. "Start the fire pretty boy," I ordered, sheathing my sword.

Will worked at starting the fire and I paced a bit, making sure to stay out of arm's reach. Remember I did tell you Will is actually a decent in-fighter and after yesterday I didn't want to give him a chance to seize the upper hand, no matter how compliant I was pretending to be. He watched me over the fire once it was blazing, giving the chill of the early autumn dusk an edge of warmth. Neither one of us said anything for quite some time. Will, I'm sure, was planning what he wanted to ask. This was the opportunity of two decades of wondering mind you, so I'm sure he had more questions than he could keep track of, and me? I was planning what I was going to tell him. It's not that easy, you know. Lying…well, okay, maybe sometimes it is, but still if it's going to work and be believable and not some nonsense excuse like, *oops, it must be magic*, then you have to put forth a bit of effort. I had cooked up about three dozen really good lies. Ones that were far out in left field the, oops magic type lies, ones that he would have to be a completely self-deluding moron to believe. He'd already proven he wasn't that. So, the one about me being an elven vigilante that had been quested with his protection because of a life debt to his great grandfather was out and the one about enchanted mushroom poisoning was a pass, too. So, when night had fallen completely, I figured I'd let him ask his questions, keeping me from pulling out the outrageous ones and I'd fill him in with the most believable lies as they came. It was the best I could do, right? I mean the truth was not going to work, not if I wanted to stay…well, did I? I mean, Jimmy was a sweet kid, but I did love Will, didn't I? How could I come this far down my life's path and still have to ask myself that question? Was the fact that I had to ask that question at all an answer in and of itself?

Crap. Stupid conscience!

Hey wait! He was the one that was supposed to be asking the questions, not me. Attempting to shut my own mind up, I sat down on a log and said, "Okay, Sir William. What do you want to know?

184

Bear in mind that just because you ask, does not mean you'll get an answer, alright?"

He nodded his head, but still didn't say anything. Folding his hands in his lap, he sat there and stared at me across the fire. Our eyes locked. The flames danced and splashed, leaching all color and character from his eyes, eyes I knew very well, and giving me a moment's hesitation and unease was the thought that I hoped the fire did the same for mine. I did not want him to recognize even the slightest detail, like the color or shape of my eyes. Sighing heavily, he finally asked, "Who are you?"

"Ha," I laughed huskily, or tried to; it's not something I practice. "Come now handsome, do you really think it would be that easy?"

He smiled a small, almost pathetic attempt at the gesture, a wounded animal smile, and said, "I had to try. Okay then, how about this, have you been saving me all these years?"

Time for easy lie number one. "No," I said, resolutely and shook my head. Let's see what he makes of that.

Will mulled it over for a few minutes in silence, only the fire popping and crackling with the occasional katydid chirp and cricket screech breaking the quiet. Deciding not to pursue with another question, Will stated, "But you had to have. Somebody has to.

I…well, I guess you know already…I'm not what everybody thinks I am."

I smiled even though he couldn't see it with my mask on. I had a sudden realization that I knew how to play this. "Sure you are."

"What?" Will stammered. "You've at least seen how that troll nearly choked the life out of me and that trip where I conked my head on that rock in the dwarves' camp?" He jerked his thumb over his shoulder in the direction he'd hoped was south I assumed as a reference. He was actually pointing east if you're interested. Bringing his hands back to his lap after his incorrect pointing, he continued, "That was no acting, that was all me, the Great Phony Sir William!" He said the last and buried his face in his hands. At first I thought he was hiding his exasperation, just frustrated and not sure what to do, but when his huge shoulders started to shake I realized he was weeping.

Oh Will.

I've tried to see it from his perspective in the past. It's not really an easy thing to do. Most people envy and emulate their heroes, thinking *I wish I could be like them*. Can you imagine having this huge legend built up around you and you basically have no idea how it has happened? You keep going out on quests for your king and your country to slay monsters and right wrongs, but you have no idea how you are doing it. You can't see very well and

186

every mission you nearly end up dying? But somehow you live to see another day, and everybody calls you a hero. I really don't think the fame would be worth it, and seeing Will weep at his own failings, his own – albeit unwitting hypocrisy – I started to regret what I had been doing all these years. Not saving him, no, but I should have come clean the very first time. I should have stayed with him until he woke up and told him what happened. He could have told King Theodore the truth, the monster was gone, but he was too injured to do so again and he needed to take on a duty more appropriate for his handicap, head of the palace guard or something. Stars above I was a fool! Sure I was very young back then, so was Will, but that is never a satisfying excuse, is it? No, young and dumb, the world's favorite scapegoats don't really make us feel better in our secret heart of hearts when we see someone we love in pain as a result.

With that thought I realized I needed to work this out. Not only to clear the slate, not only as a play to save my marriage…and despite last night's very long and very thorough affair; I still loved Will, but as a chance to rectify the recklessness of youth. It's not often you have the opportunity to utilize that perfectly clear hindsight. And seeing Will weak and crushed like this only made it worse, or better, or crap! I don't know! Whatever my screwed up psyche needed it to be for me to want to fix it. I stood up and walked around the fire. When I was standing behind Will I leaned over and rested my hand on his shaking shoulder, and gently said, "But you *are* the Great Sir William."

It took him several minutes to compose himself, but when he did, Will slid a hand down his face wiping away his tears, and said, "Please, don't patronize me. You've done quite enough already."

"No, Will," I said quickly remembering to lower my voice as I was too close to sounding like his wife there. "Sure, you are a bumbling inept fool with a sword and a really crappy horseman. Not to mention a danger to everyone in Thistledown as an archer…" I trailed off when I realized listing his faults really wasn't going to help either of us at this point. Not much of a pick-me-up for him and if my plan was going to work I needed him to be a bit less self-defeatist. I continued in a more positive tone, "But, you still are the Great Sir William. Don't you understand? Your name, your image, your legend is just as important as whether or not you can swing a sword. The people need that name. It makes them feel safe. They need that hero who will standup for them because they can't. That's still you!"

He stared at me as I took my hand off his shoulder and sat back down. Watching my movements, he asked, "Then how long *have* you been helping me?"

He stressed the have, which really worked nicely for my plan, sometimes I even scare myself. I flipped my hands out dismissively as I said, "A few years now. Not all that many." And then I set the bait, "Not compared to the others. They've been do-ing it for much longer. I don't know how long for sure. How long have you been keeping Thistledown safe, hmm?"

"Um, twenty…" Will started, but pulled back to the real issue biting on my lie like a fish on a hook, and asked, "Others?"

Smiling again, though he still obviously couldn't see it, I said, "Yes, others, lots of them too. Look, Will, I don't know how or where it started. We aren't some kind of secret order or cult, but some-where along the way somebody noticed that you needed some help, and they lent a hand. It could have been a farmer, a rancher, a blacksmith, a rang-er. I don't know." See, use some of the truth – a ker-nel of fact that he could cling to, but let him make his own conclusions. "They helped you but didn't want you to be embarrassed. Maybe they did it a few more times, who knows? Then someone else took over. We don't have monthly club meetings of the fraternal order of Help Sir William. That's why sometimes I see others out in the woods in disguise too. We don't talk about what we're doing but we all know what it is just the same. Thistledown is a safer place because of who you are - what the legends say you are and none of us wants to ruin that. We want to help, Will, so let us."

There. It would either work or I'd have to pull a whole new concept out of my ass. Either way it

189

would be best to leave it at that for him. Let him turn it over as he tried to sleep. Don't let him complicate it anymore right now with questions that I'd have to dodge. He could stew over what I had told him in the next few weeks at home. Then when he was done drawing his own conclusions, I could build the rest of the plan from there. I could still salvage this. I could still make it work. It was dark enough he couldn't safely follow me. His eyes were bad in the light, so without it he's all but blind. I stood up and walking past the fire, I squeezed Will again on the shoulder in passing and drove the point home, saying, "Please, let us help."

I walked away, back to the road and another long night's journey. I didn't look back; even when he shouted, "Wait maiden! Please, at least tell me your name! Please!"

No, I had done and said all I could risk for one night. And if I was lucky enough, and my plan came together enough, well, maybe that would be the last time Will spoke with the masked woman…yeah right, when the hell have I ever been lucky?

Twenty-four

Running by starlight has actually been a favorite activity of mine ever since I was a little girl. I know, I've told you how dangerous it can be and it is, especial if you're in unfamiliar woods, but on a well-marked road, with little risk of trip hazards? It's a joy. I ran all through the night. The sky was completely clear and it held that crisp autumn chill that lets you know winter is right around the corner, stalking you like a mountain lion, waiting to pounce and send your old joints to aching with the damp and the chill…but it isn't upon you yet. I could smell the fallen leaves I was crunching under-foot and though I knew I had tons of work and hassles ahead of me, somehow with the autumn air filling my lungs, the blood whooshing through my veins and pounding in my ears, I knew things would work out. At the very least I could pretend I was a little girl again as I ran under the same constellations. Sometimes only pretending is enough to get us through, isn't it?

Dawn was lightening the eastern tree line when I stumbled, sweat-soaked and exhausted onto my front porch. I had made terrific time. It would take Will and Duke until tomorrow evening or tonight at the earliest to travel the same distance, but the sheer joy of running through the night had lent me speed. Flopping around on the porch until I caught by breath, I wanted to rush inside and stoke the fire so I could scrub up with some warm water. I smelled. I smelled really bad. Good lord how I smelled! Four days of hard travel and exertions and well…it wasn't like I had a handy washcloth and soap with me out on the trail so toss the wild sex with Jimmy in that mix and I was one ripe onion. I was even heaving myself back up into a semi-upright position to go draw that much needed bath when the scratchy feel of the burned red maple leaf caught my attention instead. Looking down I could see a blackened edge creeping out from under my bracer. It looked pathetic, sad, and depressing. I've brought home some sorry, beat to shit leaves over the years since Papa died, but this was by far the worst.

Putting my much-needed cleansing on hold, I went back and to the side where the maple tree looked out over my humble homestead. I left that part of the yard alone except for when I wanted to visit Papa. I didn't bother to plant flowers, rake away the leaves, or hack back the taller grasses and weeds. I left that part of my home, that part of my life, wild and untamed just like my father. A cold mist was rolling in off the river, hanging low over my gardens and small meadow. I'd been an emotional wreck the last few weeks, ever since that stupid troll turned my world upside down. This was the first leaf I'd brought home since that incident and it sort of washed over me in one grand sweeping tidal wave of guilt, anger, self-loathing, depression, disgust, a little more anger, and finally I collapsed in a heap next to the tree. A tree that's roots dug down deep into the soil, through the earth, and through the bones of my father. I could never touch my papa's stubble-covered chin again, but I could run my hand along the rough gray bark and imagine that some of who and what my papa was had lent this tree strength. It was all I had...I suppose it was more than most people have. The tree at least went on living. A monument to the fallen that needs to breathe and drink is more relatable than a cold stone grave marker any day.

I lie there, weeping, head buried in my arms, with my right hand still brushing up against the bark seeking solace from a tree. I felt pathetic; pathetic and tired, very, very tired. I don't know when I fell asleep. But when I woke up I knew I was still dreaming. You ever do that? Wake up in a dream, only to know you're still dreaming? It's weird and disconcerting. I knew I was dreaming, not only because it was early spring, but because the barn slash stable was still a shed. Papa never kept livestock when I was growing up and the shed was used to store extra furs for trading or maybe other surplus items he had lying about. When I turned around the red maple tree was gone. In its place was Papa, looking younger and healthier than he had those last few years. No old worn man this time, when he smiled at me he looked like the rugged man of the woods I always remembered him as - the Hawk. Dreams suck. They're just a little mental tease, something we want or fear will happen in reality, but never does or can't, like seeing somebody we love again who has died. Suck or not, I wasn't going to pass up that impossible opportunity, even in a dream. I ran over to hug my papa. He caught me deftly and spun me around saying, "Hold on there, little Nightingale. I may look younger, but you're still a grown woman. You nearly knocked me over."

Laughing as he put me down, I said, "Come on Papa! You're a dream. You could arm-wrestle a giant and win."

"Am I?" he asked, scratching at the rough stubble on his neck and chin that I missed so much. "Maybe I am. Maybe I'm not. The world is bigger than you and me, little Nightingale. There are all sorts of doors, windows, and who knows what else. We see what we want to see and sometimes we see what we think we're supposed to see. Maybe we call it a dream. Maybe we call it a vision. That's a matter of personal choice, I guess."

Crying a bit at getting to hear his voice again, and not just an echo in my head, I said, "Well, whatever you are, you at least got the character right. Even dead you have something to teach me, huh?"

He smiled, and pulling me in for another less gymnastic hug, he said, "That's why I'm here, Gale. You're having a hard time right now. It happens to everybody. If life were easy it wouldn't be worth living, but you have to listen to me, sweetheart. It's okay to lose yourself…for a while. Shit, most people don't even know who they are and they still manage to lose themselves all the damn time, but the trick, the reason I'm talking to you – dream or not – is that you need to find yourself again. It doesn't have to be right now, but you need to at some point. If you don't, you'll be no better than the rest of them, and that wouldn't do me, that bumbling moose you married, that sad boy, your momma, or anybody else that loves you any good. You're better than the rest, Gale, but you're human, too. Remember that. Weakness is part of being human, but so is strength. You have too much of the later to lose yourself for long, little Nightingale. Take care of the others...but remember to take care of yourself, too."

I wanted to say something, say, "I will," or "I love you, Papa!" or anything else, but he leaned in, kissed me on the forehead, and that's when I woke up. It was midday and I still had my arm wrapped around the maple trunk. There was a litter of leaves covering me in a beautiful red autumnal blanket. I was still sad. I still wanted my papa back, but I felt better. I felt like I could move forward again. Sure, it could have simply been some sleep and rest, lending my completely exhausted body the chance to recoup. Or, maybe it had really been him. Dream or vision? It didn't matter which, not really. What mattered was that I could move forward. I needed to move forward. I not only should, but now could, keep going. I had the strength to do what needed to be done. And right now what really needed to be done was I needed a hot bath. Judging by the aroma coming off of me as I stood up I had either, fallen on a mole and crushed it in my sleep, or I needed that bath worse than I had thought.

Twenty-five

Cleaned and no longer reeking of four days of trail, sweat, and sex…and possibly a dead mole, too, I felt alive enough to gather my thoughts and prepare the house to look as if I had been busy about my housewifely duties this better part of a week. So, when Will returned all would be as it should on that particular front at least. The fire was stoked, warming the autumn chill that had ridden in with the fog this morning and refused to be banished by the sun. I had cleaned and laundered all my trail clothes and armor. They were dry and neatly stashed away once more. There was a chicken, plucked, gutted, and soaking in a pot of salt water just waiting for me to fry up when Will returned. I had no way of knowing if he would be home tonight, tomorrow, or if he decided to really drag his feet or Duke's hooves I guess, it could even be the day after.

I tried to keep my hands busy that day. I'm not really one to sit around and do nothing. Some people call it *relaxing*. I tried that once when I was younger, but it turned out to be too much work trying to make myself relax. It doesn't count as relaxing if you sit in a corner and keep mentally yelling at yourself to relax. I always thought that idle hands and minds stuff was a bunch of horse crap, but the busier I kept myself, the less I thought about the shit-storm my life had become lately. Scrub that mud off the back step, really hard and vigorously; instead of thinking about Jimmy. Scour the stained kitchen table and re-wax it; instead of thinking about Will. Jar as many of the vegetables as I could gather before early frosts could nip and wilt them; instead of thinking about Papa. Who needs to relax? It's overrated I say.

It had been fully dark for more than an hour when I gave up on Will coming home that night and I cut off a wing and a leg from my soaking chicken to fry up for myself. I had roasted some small red potatoes in garlic, butter, and rosemary to keep busy once the sun set. There was fresh cornbread, too. I'd eaten many meals alone before so it shouldn't have bothered me, but the funny thing was it did. I knew better than to expect Will to be home so soon. Failed trap or not, he had still been charged by King Theodore to settle the dwarf problem, so even if he'd traveled at a good clip, he probably was staying the night at Thistledown Castle. Stars above! Marissa was probably having him open more pickle jars at that very moment.

With nothing left to distract me, that got me to thinking about Jimmy. What the hell was I going to do about that? I actually needed his help if I was going to pull my plan off. What kind of twisted, messed up universe makes it so an adulteress has to ask her adulteree? Adult-accomplice? Adult-a-whatever, the guy she slept with! Fine, lover. What kind of cruel world makes a woman have to ask her lover for help to save her marriage? Maybe those of you who've never had an affair will call it payback, or justice, or something. And maybe you'd be right…it still sucks though.

Lost in my thoughts, I almost burned my chicken. Swearing loudly and splattering oil everywhere, I did miss Will come in the backdoor. I didn't even realize he was there until he said, "Fried chicken? Wonderful I'm starving."

I jumped, splattering more oil and burning my fingers in the process. Will said, "I'm sorry, Gale. I didn't mean to startle you. Are you alright?" He dashed around the table to check on me and struck his head on the same pan he had on Sir William Day eve. Only this time he was moving so fast the pan knocked him off his feet. I stood there sucking on my burned fingers and watched him shake his head and try to sit up…and, I kid you not, he had struck the pan so hard in the rack that the pan swayed a few times, hanging directly over his head. It was like a bad comedic stage play, watching the pan rock slowly right over his head, and sure enough, it slipped its hook and fell, conking Will on the head a second time. The universe plays cruel, twisted jokes on all of us I guess.

Will sat there on the floor, rubbing his head in two places and only said, "Ow."

Sighing to keep myself from laughing, I helped Will to his feet, guiding him over to his same, often used chair. It still protested his weight, just as the table did when he leaned on it. The strange comforts of familiarity – do we love them for their reliability or hold them in contempt from our overexposure? To Will I said, "Sit down dear. Here, let me see, is it bleeding?" again familiar overused words in this house. I moved his head around and pulled back his hair to find only two large and quickly rising welts, but no open wounds. Patting his shoulder, I added, "Let me get you some dinner."

I placed the almost burnt chicken and a large serving of potatoes and cornbread in front of him and went back to the stove to cook some more for myself. I always had trouble sounding nonchalant when I asked Will how things went on his missions. It was even worse this time, when so much had happened, but I asked as innocently as I could, "How'd things go at Lake Weldon?"

I think I sounded pretty convincingly ignorant, all things considered. Will caught nothing amiss either and said, "Not as well as I would have liked."

See, this is the kind of crap that sucks about my situation. I have to really pretend to be two different women. One, the doting wife, whose only concern is chores and caring for her husband, so as that woman I had to ask, "Oh dear, why not?" Even though, as the other woman – the cold killing masked woman – I already knew. The only interesting part would be to see how much he was willing to share with me, the doting wife, versus how much he opened up to the masked woman. I can count on one hand the number of times I had seen Will cry as his wife, and he cried upon the third meeting with the masked woman. Emotions are strange things, don't I know it, but still that kind of hurt the more I thought about it. He'd open up to a stranger, albeit at a very low point for him, and not me.

He tucked in ravenously to the bowl of potatoes, and around a mouthful said, "The dwarves actually turned out to be decent fellows when I got to know them. Once our initial disagreement was out of the way we got along smashingly. Speaking of, I have a few burns I need you to look at after supper."

Not really a lie there, I suppose.

Will continued, "I convinced them to either lend a hand around the village, sort of pay for the fish they've been taking through labor, or clear the swamps out of any pesky kobolds, giant snakes, or whatever other bog loving monsters may be there. That way the fishermen and their families could have less to worry about and then King Theodore would rarely, if ever, have to send me down to the lake country. I hope they choose that option. The ride south is such a long one on my aching old back." He reached around and rubbed at his lower back for good measure.

"What did the king say?" I asked, sitting down with my own plate across the table from Will. I poured him a glass of cider from the carafe I brought with me, guiding his hands to it so he wouldn't knock it over. Routine, familiar. Shaking his head, Will said, "Thank you," for the cider, and, "that's part of my hoping for the later. I was too tired to ride into Thistledown tonight. I wanted to sleep in my own bed after that long journey. I'll go see King Theodore tomorrow."

"I'm sure he understands," I said, patting Will's hand. I realized that if I was going to move ahead with my plan, I needed to contact Jimmy, so I needed to see Marissa. I needed to talk her into sending for Will so she in turn could send Jimmy out to me. What a mess, it's my plan and even I'm having trouble following it. To Will I said, "I'll go with you. I could use some new yarn," not a lie, I had to knit a new travel blanket incase Jimmy kept mine, "and I've been meaning to have an excuse to go visit Queen Marissa. The poor old thing needs people to talk to, being queen is quite boring I imagine." Not a lie there either, after all the stories I'd had to make up for her entertainment, I knew just how bored she was firsthand.

Will nodded. There was nothing out of place about any of what we'd said to each other. Mostly truths shaded in lies, you know, like any couple that's been together for years. Comfortable and familiar. Finishing off his cornbread, Will reached across the table toward the platter for another piece, and knocked over his cider in the process. Yeah, familiar.

Twenty-six

The next morning we were in Thistledown proper. Will left me at the stables to go report to the king. I told him I'd be in the market and if Queen Marissa were around to tell her I'd be there. He agreed and wandered off, bumping into a trash barrel and falling over a vendor's cart laden with every type of apple imaginable, sending them cascading down in a torrent of reds, greens, and yellows. The farmer was apologizing all the while as Will helped him pick them up, saying it was his fault for leaving his cart there and not the Great Sir William's.

Shaking my head, I wandered over toward the small section of the central square where King Theodore allows vendors and farmers to sell their bumper crops or crafts and whatnot. All without a tax or fee, see what I mean about the *Good* King Theodore? Does that happen in your land? Anyway, there was a woman who scoured and dyed her own wool. It was the best yarn you'll find in any kingdom and she typically set up her booth as close to the thistle fountain as she could. I headed over that way. It was a gorgeous autumn morning, the breeze was blowing a fine mist off the fountain and the water splashed just inches from her baskets of wool. Making conversation, I asked, "Isn't that a risky place to leave your yarn?"

She smiled; I can never remember her name. I'm ashamed to admit it, but she doesn't have any teeth – I mean *any* – so I always think of her as Turtle. Because, she's old and wrinkly, and when she smiles sans teeth...well, she looks like a turtle. Turtle said, "No deary, it's the perfect place. It shows I have confidence in my product, it does. My wool won't shrink!" She said the last with such vehemence that a small bit of spit shot out of her mouth.

"Well, then I'll take five skeins of royal blue," I said, trying to banish all mental reptile comparisons. She was a sweet old woman and I already had enough black marks on my inner scale of good versus bad person as it was. I didn't need to add cruelty to the elderly on there as well. She had barely finished digging out the skeins of the color I had wanted when Queen Marissa came running up behind me. She placed her hands on my shoulders maternally, and leaning over to see what I had purchased, she said, "Oh, Turtle has the best yarn doesn't she?"

I spun around quick, giving her that look. You know the one? Your eyebrows rise up and you stare real hard, trying to say, "I can't believe you just said that!" but sending the statement with your mind instead, so it kind of looks like you may or may not be constipated instead. Marissa scrunched her shoulders up, asking, "What?"

I nodded my head toward Turtle - crap - I mean the old woman. "What?" Marissa asked again, "she looks like a turtle, so I always call her that. Don't I?" She directed that last part at the old...well Turtle I guess, and she nodded, smiling her toothless smile. "See," Marissa said, and slowly starting to walk away she added, "Besides I'm the queen I'll call anybody by whatever name I like."

She looked down her nose at me and overdramatically said, "Chicken Legs, yes from this day forth you are now Chicken Legs. I am the queen and I have spoken." Turning away from Turtle's baskets of yarn and walking toward the fruit vendors, she added, "Come Chicken Legs, attend to your queen."

Rolling my eyes, I followed after her as she started to pick up random apples, pears, and peaches, pretending she could actually tell which were good and which were not. Lingering at the same cart that Will had tripped over earlier, Marissa examined a few apples and said, "Very good, I'll take a dozen of these Galas, please."

The farmer hopped to and pulled a clean basket from the bottom of his stack and started filling her order. I leaned over her shoulder and said, "Those are Granny Smith's not Gala, your majesty."

She glanced shrewdly at me from the corner of her eye. Touching a hand to her chest she gave me a single word reply, "Queen." Oh great she was in a sassy mood today, which of course meant she was expecting an elaborate tale of my sex shenanigans with Jimmy. Oddly enough I actually had real experiences to draw from this time and I found myself not only not wanting to tell them, but more than a little embarrassed by the prospect of doing so. When the famer finished picking the best of his stock for the queen, she gestured to me saying, "Chicken Legs will carry them, thank you."

She casually strolled away while I balanced her damn apples along with my yarn and followed again as she headed toward the stables. I grumbled at her back, "Chicken Legs? Seriously?"

She grinned slyly at me and said, under her breath since we were still out among the people, "Well, I could have come up with quite a few more creative ones," she bobbed her eyebrows solicitously, "but I figured they weren't as public appropriate as Chicken Legs."

Sighing, I said, "That's actually one of the reasons I came today, Marissa. I need to see Jimmy again. Can you send him out to me sometime this week with some sort of excuse to summon Will to the castle for something?"

We were down an alley by then, between two multistory houses, without anyone to overhear us so Marissa stopped and said, "By the gods woman! You just had him for most of a week. Is he really that good that you have to have him back so soon, or is it the end of life change come calling that has you so randy?"

The Knight's Wife

Hmm, hormones or Jimmy, which was the better excuse that would keep this conversation short and get me what I wanted at the same time? I went with hormones. It involved less use of Lewd Larry's repertoire and was more likely for the queen (who as I've said was several years my senior) to identify with. But just to be on the safe side I kept it vague … since that worked *so* well in the past, right? I said, "I don't know, maybe he's that good, but more than likely it could be hormones. Who knows? I need to see him, Marissa, just for an afternoon."

Taking pity and the bait, Marissa patted my shoulder, saying, "Of course my dear. I've been there you know: the hot flashes, and certain places become a dry desert valley one minute then a raging flood the next, and the arousal can be over the littlest things. Why even once, while I was at the height of the change, I almost jumped Marcus the baker while he was kneading some dough. He has those huge hands you know and his fingers were rubbing and pushing and tugging…" Her eyes were rolling up a bit as she described it. The things I'd told her Jimmy and I had done were much, much worse, but still, the list of verbs was obviously still a memory she relished as she continued. "…pounding and prodding that soft white dough until it had taken the shape he desired."

When she finished she fluttered her hand in front of her face as a fan. Huh? Who knew making bread could be so sexy? Catching her breath, Marissa said,

"Of course I'll send him out for you. Perhaps I'll wait until next week, but I will send him out to you whenever you need it. I understand. I'll come up with some errand I need Will for-"

"No pickle jars!" I interrupted her. She laughed, saying, "Alright, I had worried I'd gone overboard with that, but I was unprepared. I promise I'll come up with a list this time before I send for him."

"Send for whom?" Will's voice asked from the alleyway entrance, causing us both to jump and me to spill Marissa's apples everywhere. I bent to pick them up, but realized as Marissa stumbled over a few, "Ums" and "Ers" that I was the better liar and I shoved the half-full basket into her hands and covered us with the truth … mostly.

"For you, Will" I said and handed him my five bundles of yarn. He balanced them carefully in his arms and I continued, "I was teasing Marissa about all those pickle jars she had you open last time, and I said, 'If you're going to steal my man away for random household work, then at least make a list before he gets there, so you aren't bombarding him with silly things'."

See, all truth. The lies are always in the omissions. Isn't that how life goes?

Smiling that handsome smile that had won the hearts and loins of maidens all over the kingdom, Will said, "Oh I don't mind. If her majesty wanted me to open every pickle jar in Thistledown, I'd glad-ly do so and more."

Marissa smiled, Will smiled, I smiled, we all smiled; one happy circle of grinning liars. Still smil-ing, Will precariously pulled a folded blanket out from under his arm, and said, "I wanted to ask your majesty, what that very nice young entertainers name was? You know the one who performed at the…well…at my celebration? The juggler I think. He stuck around after the other performers left."

My heart dropped out of my chest, down way past my stomach, and shot right out my ass. I swear I heard it plop on the cobblestones when I noticed that the blanket Will was holding was my trail blanket. The one I had last seen a naked Jimmy wrapped up in. Will continued, "He stopped me in the hallway and said his sister had made this for me, but she was too embarrassed to give it me herself. It's a very nice blanket." He patted it and handed it to me, smiling and saying, "It's so nice I would have sworn my Gale made it." And he kissed me on the top of the head.

You hear that squish just then? Well I did, that was Will accidently stepping on my heart where it was floundering around at my feet. "She's the best seamstress in all of Thistledown. I can't wait to see what she has planned for this. Her sewing only falls into second place behind her cooking. " He hefted the yarn I'd pawned off on him and started to walk down the alley, calling over his shoulder, "Don't mind me. You two keep on talking. I'll load this up on Duke and be at the stables when you're ready to go, Gale. And a good day to you, your majesty."

We watched him go, stumbling to carry the yarn and completely oblivious of the omissions between the truths I'd given him. He didn't even pause to let Marissa tell him Jimmy's name. When he was out of sight, Marissa turned to me and very seriously, very quietly, asked, "Do you still want me to send him out to you?"

Sigh. Thank you universe for that nice little piece of guilt, sincerely Lady Gale. But nodding my head, I said, "Yes…I…I don't want to, Marissa. But…but I need to. Does that make any sense?"

She smiled and finished gathering up her apples. When she was done she patted me on the shoulder as she walked away and said, "Yes and no, dear. It's all up to you. It's your choice. You know what you're doing. You're a big girl. You have to take care of yourself sometimes too, Gale."

The words of my dream, or vision, or ghost, or whatever version of Papa echoed in Marissa's. Yes, I had to take care of myself, but, the thing was I'd already done that. I knew who I was and now it was just a matter of cleaning up the mess I'd made when I fell apart. I hoped when it was all over things could go back to the way they were. Funny how we get bored by the same old same old, day to day, but when something disrupts that monotony we realize we'd give anything to go back to being bored.

Twenty-seven

The ride home was uneventful. In fact the following few weeks proved to be uneventful. Marissa came down with an illness. Every land calls their maladies by different names. They all mean the same thing no matter how you say it. I've heard it called the autumn gripes, a cold, the flu, a pox, demon possession, you know, different names, same laid up in bed with coughing, sneezing, and pretty much wishing to die. So, incapacitated as she was, Marissa did not make good on her promise and it was weeks, almost at the end of the harvest season, until she sent Jimmy out to me with a summons from the king. It proved to be no army of pickle jars, but a legitimate request for Will to go see Theodore about a band of highwaymen that had been raiding the western roads. They had been lying in ambush and stealing from traders that had come from Thistledown's nearest neighbor to the west, Amberea.

Will left on Duke a mere quarter of an hour after Jimmy departed having delivered his message. The highwaymen were news not to be taken lightly. Thistledown and all the nearby kingdoms rely on the goodwill of their neighbors. Thieves running amuck, claiming no king or crown and taking as they wished, were not good for any land. And that went doubly so for Theodore because some saw his beneficence, the qualities that made him the *Good* King Theodore, as a weakness to be exploited.

I waited a half an hour after Will's departure before taking two cups of hot cider out to the sturdy wooden bench I had positioned to overlook my herb garden. Within moments Jimmy slid into the open seat next to me and picked up the second mug I'd left there with lifted eyebrows asking if it was for him. I nodded and said, "I need to talk to you, Jimmy."

He started nervously rambling, "If it's about the blanket, I'm sorry. I didn't know if that would be alright or not. Sir William seems like a nice guy. I figured since, you know, what you and I had done…" he trailed off for a second; letting memories of that night creep back for him, just as they were for me. He took a deep breath, then closed his eyes for a second attempting to firm his voice and resolve, and collect his thoughts I imagine. Oddly enough, when he did speak again he sounded more adult-like. "After we'd had an affair, I wanted to actually meet the man whose wife I had slept with and not just be a delivery boy. Talk to him, man to man, even if it was a stupid lie about a blanket."

He sipped at his cider, burning his lips a little and pulling away quickly. That one small gesture banished the grownup James that young Jimmy had worked so hard to bring forth. Stars above! What was he? Nineteen? Twenty? Patting his knee, I said,

213

"It's alright, Jimmy. It's not about the blanket. Will actually thinks you're a very nice young man. Of course he doesn't know about what we did. That would probably make him change his mind if he did... And that's what I need to talk to you about, Jimmy. Well, some of it anyway, the *did* part. The past tense."

He looked at me over his mug, trying to sip again without injury - another wide-eyed young Jimmy gesture. It wouldn't have been out of place for him to ask for some cookies and milk, too.

"Look," I said, turning on the bench to face him. "I don't know what you thought would happen. I don't know why I did what I did. I mean I do...it's just complicated, Jimmy. I love Will. I always have and I do have feelings for you also. I think you're a very caring person who has more to him than the surface good looks that the world sees. I...I just don't see myself, who I am, as an affair type woman...I mean, sure it was amazing, but all the sneaking around on top of all the other sneaking around I have to do already is just too much. Look, right here." I pointed to a patch of gray that I had noticed appear in my hair over the last few weeks. "You see that? It wasn't there last month, Jimmy. I can't do this."

He continued to stare at me over his mug. The steam drifted up and around his face in the late autumn sun, blurring his features slightly. He went from cute boyish charming stare to, is he having a seizure stare, to do I have a booger hanging out of my nose stare. Finally getting uncomfortable with the silence, I said, "Come on, Jimmy. Talk to me, give me something here."

Snapping out of his trance and placing his mug down at his feet, he took both of my hands in his and said, "My lady, Gale…I…I'm sorry if what I said about loving you, gave you the wrong impression. I…I do love you, but I never thought we would be anything more than a fling. When I told you I'd never loved anyone like you loved Sir William I meant that I envied you and I realized if things had been different between us, another time, another place, that maybe you would have done the same for me. But I never saw us as anything more than an affair. An affair to come and go at your whim. If you want that to have been one night of passion and love, then that is all it was. If you tell me to carry you into your bedroom and make you scream my name out right now, then I'll do that too."

I smiled. I was confused, but I smiled.

He continued, "Maybe I don't love you like other people love each other, Gale. I don't know. Does every person love the same way? Is that possible? For me I'm happy to have had what time I did with you, and I'm happy to spend time with you like this. Love for me - since you're the only person I've loved - is just wanting to be around the person you

215

love. I don't care in what way. I bet love is different for everybody: men and women, families, friends. I don't know. All I've had is you, so I'll take you whatever way I can have you."

And there it was. I didn't have to be a hussy or a multiple time adulteress. I could be what I wanted, like my papa had told me. It's sad sometimes when you get what you want, but you still want more. For some people it's that grass is greener idea, for others it's that inability to satisfy. For me it was sad because Jimmy was right, in another time or place I do think we could have been something more than ships passing in the night. I could have loved Jimmy, but life set me to sailing earlier. Sometimes you're sad for good reasons, weird. I squeezed Jimmy's hands and said, "Thank you, Jimmy. I do love you, but we cannot be more than this."

He nodded and squeezed my hand back. I could have sworn I saw the flash of something behind his eyes. I don't mean anger or sadness, but more of a *damn, I'd hoped she'd ask for one more go* if that look can be summed up in a flash, I guess. Any implied flashes, imagined or real, gone, we turned and sat in silence for a while, watching the sun dance on my now mostly brown, dried out herb garden and drank our cooling cider. It was nice, just to sit with someone who wasn't Will, wasn't Marissa and her pesky libido, just someone to quietly pass the time with. It was a long, quiet, and warm autumn afternoon, the type that stand out in your memory when you're huddled by the stove two months later freezing and cursing the snow. It was in that tranquil autumn setting that I asked Jimmy if he'd help me save my marriage. I knew he would. I hadn't ever doubted that part of my plan, but after what he'd said I realized I could have asked him anything and he would have done it. I could have asked him to jump off a bridge and he would have done it. I could have asked him to run through fire and he would have done it. I could have asked him to throw his life away for me, in any number of ways, and he would have done it. The sad part is looking back, that's exactly what I did.

Twenty-eight

Will returned home late that afternoon. He was in quite the mood. Apparently Lord Morgan of Amberea had threatened to declare war on Thistledown, claiming that King Theodore was behind the highwaymen robbing his people. The thieves would only strike after the Ambereans had sold their goods and were returning home. It did look suspicious from Lord Morgan's perspective – goods entered Thistledown and not only did his people return with no trade, but no gold for their troubles either. See what I mean about these small kingdoms depending on goodwill. If one person starts to act or speak inappropriately it can spread like wildfire and then before you know it, you're at war with another land, a fight that you're drug into even though you had nothing to do with it. With that kind of gravity behind the situation, Will was set to go charging off that night, but I convinced him it was too late and he should wait until morning when he was fully rested. It wasn't easy. I had help from his cider, which I'd spiked to calm him down. Groggy and bleary-eyed after supper he agreed to turn in early so he could get that much of an earlier start in the morning.

With Will in such a state I was glad Jimmy had agreed to my plan and he was spending the night out in the barn with Duke as he had done before. Once Will was asleep - I waited until he was snoring heavily - I carefully crept out with the leftovers from supper to tell Jimmy our plans for the morning. While he ate I helped outfit him for the next day's mission. It was convenient that Will and Jimmy were about the same size. I stored more than just my armor out in the shed; Will's worn and piecemeal castoffs were stored there as well: a gauntlet here, a vambrace there, enough greaves for a six-legged man, and pauldrons to spare. I instructed Jimmy that he was to take what he wanted, but he needed to disguise himself and still be fully protected, too. Not having the time to custom tailor a mask to his features like I wore, we settled for a black band of cloth with holes cut out for him to see through, wrapped around and tied into his hair. When I added the same coal around his eyes that I used, he was disguised enough for Will's poor vision. To be honest he actually looked very dashing and roughish. We had found mostly black leather armor, with a russet breastplate. Combine that with his black eye band and long flowing black hair and he looked like a schoolgirl's fantasy of the bad boy – the dark warrior that she wishes would ravish her, pinned to a wall, maybe struggling a bit, hands restrained firmly overhead while…uh, well, he looked really good, alright?

When I snuck back into bed with Will he was still snoring away. I hardly slept a wink, wide eyes staring at every crack and corner, worrying about taking a kid almost half my age into battle. There was a nice depressing thought to aid my insomnia.

The half the age part not the battle part, and it would be a battle, too. If the reports Will received were accurate the band of thieves was eight strong. Even if Will were half of what the legends claim him to be, he could not have taken on eight skilled fighters on his own. Sure, it's great for bedtime stories. Kids love to hear about swashbuckling pirates and such singlehandedly fighting an army, but overwhelming numbers will take down even the greatest fighter. But also, what if the multiple opponents are practiced in fighting together against their foe, instead of lining up one at a time to fight the hero like in the stories? Please, it's impossible. If the hero is fighting like a madman there will still be plenty of moments where a back or flank is unprotected… and that's all it takes – a moment – and no more hero. I've fought and defeated three men at once, and I was lucky at that. One man (or woman of course) against an army is impossible…maybe a wizard or something could stand his ground, but I've never met one who would. They'd rather have their nose buried in a book and when the army was at their door, they may notice enough to say, "Now what the devil is that?" right before an arrow lands in their neck.

So I was worried. Eight men, one woman saddled with one inept husband who was as much of a liability and danger to himself in the field as anything plus one young man with some skill at tracking and, as far as I knew, enough swordsmanship to know which end was the pointy one, but in love with me and willing to do whatever I asked him. Balance that equation out and it equals crap. Any way you look at it, crap, crap, crap. Yeah, I guess worry would have been an understatement.

When the late autumn sun started to lighten the shutters in my bedroom, I rose out of bed – yes, Will was still snoring – and went to the kitchen to stoke the fire and start on breakfast. I knew I should eat a large breakfast. I didn't want to. I was sick to my stomach with worry and stress, but with two hard days of over country hiking, I'd have to eat something or I'd run out of steam quickly. If Jimmy and I were to travel together in the autumn foliage reduced forest, parallel to the road, we'd have to stay deeper in, breaking trail as often as not, so as not to be seen. I set bacon and eggs to frying for Will, plus some extra for Jimmy once Will left, and while Will was still passed out I gathered what hardtack we'd need to feed two people in the woods for up to four days. If the mission took longer than four days we could be hurting by the end. There was little to gather in the woods this late in the year, so I couldn't count on supplementing our diet with wild greens and nuts or berries. The animals would have picked most of the good wild edibles bare by then to stock up for the winter. The damn squirrels are the worst. The little bastards hoard their foodstuffs like greedy old misers clinging to their gold until they die. Hopefully we could hunt down a deer or some fowl along the way for a larger meal, or a damn squirrel come to that, but I couldn't count on it either.

My larder was looking quite bare once I was through packing for everyone. Wrapping our provisions into two separate blankets, I tucked them away behind an old armoire just in time to hear Will stumbling out of bed. I served him his breakfast of champions when he eased into his groaning chair: six slices of bacon, four eggs, three sausage patties, and half a dozen hotcakes. Then I had my heaping bowl of oatmeal with raisins and roasted almonds. It would weigh me down for a while, but it would last, and it wouldn't keep popping for an encore performance in the back of my mouth as I ran like it would have if I had eaten what Will did. He was riding a horse, not running; the lucky bastard could burp bacon all day and not gag.

We ate our separate breakfasts in silence. I don't know why. Maybe it was the implied long good bye, or the possibility of a last shared meal, who knows? When I think about it, we never have spoken when we eat breakfast the day we leave on a quest. I guess most times we were in our separate worlds; me worrying over how things would go and Will doing the same, but until recently he could only stab in the dark as to how he was doing it. Now he knew that he had help, so who knew what he was thinking? Maybe he was more confident knowing there was somebody watching out for him. Not the secret cabal of do-good vigilantes I had led him to believe, but only his worried wife and the man she had cheated on him with, nice huh? I admit that's more than a little messed up, but we take what we're given sometimes … or we give up.

I wasn't ready to give up. I don't think Will was either, and, when I looked out the kitchen window, I could see Jimmy peeking out from behind the stable, waiting and ready so when Will saddled Duke up he wouldn't notice him. So I guess Jimmy wasn't ready to give up either. Wonderful, what a merry band of optimistic perseveres we were!

The frost hadn't even started to thaw off the grass when Will kissed me goodbye and rode off on Duke. I stood on our front porch, leaning on the weathered handrail, and watched them ride away. I stood there, worrying and leaning, until quarter of an hour later Jimmy came around the front of the cottage, hesitantly searching for me. Still looking like the fantasy bad boy but sounding more like an innocent school boy as he asked, "Gale, are you alright?"

I nodded and said, "Yes, Jimmy." Sighing internally, I let my head droop. With soon to be bound up hair hanging in my face, I breathed slowly and hoped he wouldn't back out when I asked, "Are you sure you want to do this?"

"Of course," he said with only the enthusiasm of those who haven't had their first hemorrhoid can muster. "You need my help. You can't do this alone. Not this time, so I'm in. Anyway, I'm kind of looking forward to adding my skills and deeds to the Great Sir William mythology…even if only you and

I will know about it." He smiled that grin, not the *Ha ha, I see boobies* grin, but the *I'm confident and cool, check me out* grin.

Whether he was or not didn't matter. What did was that he was willing to help me when I needed it. Out of love or lust, doesn't matter, not really, when your back's to the wall if someone helps you, beggars can't be choosers on their helper's rationale or intentions. Smiling back at him, I asked, "Did you find weapons you felt comfortable wielding?"

Jimmy continued to grin his *check me out* grin and artfully pulled two short swords from their scabbards on his back. In a flourish he spun, the blades becoming deadly extensions of his arms. Most of you have probably never hefted a sword in your lives. That's a good thing. If you've never had to, then your lands must be quite safe indeed, but if you have then you can testify to the difficultly of wielding two weapons of equal size accurately, and not end up looking like a mental patient swinging wildly at imaginary bees the size of pixies. Jimmy not only didn't look like a mental patient, he looked like he knew what he was doing. Jimmy had picked up some very deadly skills at swordsmanship somewhere along the hard road of his life. A weight was lifted from my chest. If Jimmy was as competent as his practice routine suggested, especially with weapons he had only had a few hours to familiarize himself with, then I may just pull this off as planned. No one dead, no one hurt…well except for the highwaymen we were supposed to go hurt. They would of course be hurt and probably die, but you know what I meant.

Jimmy ended his routine by sliding the blades easily back into their scabbards and bowed his grand stage bow that had me laughing once upon a time in a dark orchard. Seemingly a lifetime ago from where we were. Nodding my approval, and even giving him a light round of applause, I said, "Wait here. I'll get dressed and bring out our packs."

In less than half an hour we were off and quickly on Will's heels.

Twenty-nine

"Come on, Jimmy, chop-chop, move!" I prodded my new sidekick. It had been two hard days of travel, over backwoods that ran parallel to the western road. Just because most of the leaves had fallen did not mean that the creepers, vines, and thorns had died back yet. We'd need the crushing weight of ice and snow, piling up over the winter to push those obstacles out of our way. So, it had been two days of snags, catches, muttered curses, and loudly sworn profanity. Jimmy was stumbling along behind me, panting and winded from the long march. Between gasps he added, "And you do this every time Sir William is sent on a mission? No wonder you're in such good shape for a woman your age." He said the last with the needling hint of the smartass I was finding him to be (which of course I loved, birds of a smart-assed feather flock together) in our extended time together. Whether it was still flirtatious or not, I didn't care, it was nice to have someone to talk to and keep me company. I hadn't realized how lonely things had been for me until then. I had always considered myself the self-reliant type – the aloof Lady Gale, remember? Funny how sometimes we don't realize we're hurting, badly so too, until somebody points it out to us. Jimmy teasing me and me teasing him back pointed more of my wounds out to me than I would have believed possible. His company was a balm on those wounds and it made what typically would have been two days of brutal exhaustion almost into a vacation.

We crested the rise we were climbing, brittle shale interspersed with scraggly brown grasses barely holding the deteriorating hillside in place. When we looked down from the higher vantage point we saw a dense pine forest and, as my tracking skills had rightfully promised, our quarry. The highwaymen had set up camp in a thicket, a natural concavity in the thick pines where a lightning strike had toppled a few of the coniferous giants years ago and their smaller progeny had grown in their place to the height of a tall man, providing the perfect screen for privacy. Their fires would be sheltered from anyone traveling by the road, but they'd still be close enough to wander up and down it, attacking tradesmen from different places as to not give away the exact location of their camp…except to those of us who knew what to look for. Will was still an hour or so's ride behind us. He was traveling on the footsteps of a heavily laden caravan in hopes that the traders would prove too tempting of bait for the thieves and he could ride to the rescue. How do I know that, you ask? We followed close enough the previous day to overhear Will saying so to Duke. Why he talks to the horse so much is always a surprise to me…but…well, I guess it shouldn't be, should it? If I could realize how lonely I was, I can't imagine what it was like for Will. He had to be twice as lonely, so talking to a horse for company wasn't really a big deal. Now if he started talking back as the horse…that might be a bit more serious and weird. If he needed someone to talk to that's fine, I just wish he wouldn't speak so loudly to Duke. It's a wonder he isn't ambushed more often with the volume he speaks at - the forest can carry your voice far distances if you aren't careful. Will isn't exactly Mr. Caution if you hadn't noticed.

On top of the rise we had time - time to catch our breath, hiding behind the large boulders that were scattered along the hillcrest, and time to plan our attack for when the highwaymen struck. I explained to Jimmy that we had to let Will try and resolve it first on his own. Actually I had done that several times along the way, but I figured one more lecture couldn't hurt, to which, every time, Jimmy pointed out the catastrophe with the troll and suggested a new method that I'd shoot down. Finally, upon seeing what we were up against, he decided to suggest preemptive strike. Pointing down at the thieves, he said, "But, Gale, look at them. It's late, the sun is fading and they're all settled in for the night. If their watchman even notices the caravan it will be a miracle. Why don't we wait until full dark and slaughter them in their sleep?" Though I applauded Jimmy's ability to think like a cold killer, such things are easier said than done. I reached over, cupped his strong chin in my hand, and looking into his eager blue eyes, I asked, "Jimmy, have you ever killed someone in their sleep?"

"I've killed," he said a bit petulantly. "You know that."

"That's not the same thing, Jimmy," I corrected. "Trust me. To face someone who has hurt you, to strike back in defense, to strike back when someone has struck you is human nature. It's survival. But, to kill another creature, let alone a person, while they sleep? That is something you don't have in you." He had shut his eyes as if in shame that I was right, that he couldn't kill someone indiscriminately. Sliding my hand up from his chin to his temple, I rubbed at the corner of his closed lid with my thumb until he looked at me again. I said, "That's a good thing, Jimmy. It proves you still have a heart…it…it's why I love you too. It's nothing to be ashamed of." I know he wanted me to kiss him then. I could feel him leaning into my touch and part of me, a big part, a really big part that screamed, "Do him! Do him again! Right here! Right now! On top of a boulder, it'll be fun!" wishes that I had. But I didn't. I had traveled down that path before and didn't need the distraction at the moment so I turned away, letting his face fall from my grasp, and said, "We wait. Let them attack the caravan and let Will have his chance. If it bites me in the ass again, if Will gets injured or dies, it would tear me apart…but sometimes, some things just have to be done a certain way. It doesn't matter if there is a more rational solution. If this is going to work, then this is how we do it."

"Alright," Jimmy agreed nodding and listening as I outlined what I wanted him to do, where I needed him to be when the attack came, if it came, and where I would be, perched up on our high vantage point, where some of the other skills Papa had taught me could be put to use. With my plan imparted, Jimmy wandered down the opposite side of the rise all silent and stealthy. Watching him go I felt better about having him follow me so many times and not noticing him. He was good. He disappeared into the pine forest, his black armor making him another shadow among many. Then we waited again. I had a moment to hope, or worry (depending on the quantity of water in the glass), that the light wouldn't hold long enough for this to happen. I was a skilled archer, but shooting arrows off into the pitch black was asking for trouble. Just because I thought it was an enemy didn't mean that it wasn't Will, or Jimmy, or possibly one of the traders if they were jackass enough to stick around once the melee started. Friendly fire, I've heard it called. I think accident sounds better, or cluster fuck maybe, there's nothing friendly about shooting an arrow into your companions' ribs.

I could hear the voices of the caravan drivers pushing their oxen drifting up to me on the evening breeze. This close to Amberea they must have been attempting to return straight home, riding through the night, and with the word of the highwaymen sweeping across the land, who could blame them? It would be a close thing, but it looked as if their paths would cross before full night. From my vantage point, tucked in and hopefully blending among the moss-covered boulders along the ridge, I was a couple hundred yards away. Close enough to send an arrow through a heart with a favorable wind, but not close enough to really make out personal details. I counted seven heads around the thieves' campfire, in various positions of repose. As long as there was only one lookout the count of eight we had heard was true. Still, even with Jimmy's apparent skill, eight to two…minus a handicap of half a fighter for Will getting in the way, and we'd be at about eight to one and a half, not good odds.

Maybe it was just a sense, or a way that they moved, but these men looked tough. They did not give me the impression of fighters gone to seed that Droopy and his band of dwarves gave off. No these men seemed lean and hard. Dangerous, calculating men who were cold killers, living off the work of others but not so much that they were living a life of luxury either, not the type I wanted to send my bumbling honest husband and a mincing stage performing pretty boy up against. If I hadn't really meant what I'd said to Jimmy. If it had been just me and not him as well, I may have done as he suggested and wandered among them as they slept, an angel of death collecting unwary souls one slit throat at a time.

But, that was not to be the case as the lookout came racing back into camp. I couldn't hear what he said, but he was pointing, gesturing, and nodding his head to a tall lanky fellow, who I mentally marked as their leader. With a few barked orders from tall and lanky the eight thieves moved out with the flow of an organized fighting unit. Crap. They shot off, fully loaded and fully comfortable with their surroundings, even with dusk darkening the woods. Crap again. I would catch a glimpse here or there as they wound through the trees, headed away from their camp and back toward the approaching caravan. I counted myself lucky that their leader didn't just wait for the cover of darkness. It's what I would have done in his place, but thankfully, for whatever reason, he decided to make their move while there was still enough light for me to conveniently kill them from afar. It's so nice when the bad guys cooperate like that. Hopefully while I was practicing my archery, Jimmy would make his presence known to Will; confirming the story that I, as the masked woman, had told him. All nice and easy... hey, you never know.

I saw Jimmy sneaking up behind the well-organized thugs and worried again about having drug that poor kid into my troubles. I honestly think affairs, if you're absolutely set on having one, are better when it's just sex and no shared emotion. Just a one-night-stand to mutually get off and a thank you so much for a fun time now we'll go about our separate ways. I suppose really, what had me so worried was that I was now watching over two men that

I cared about instead of just one…see, I told you it was going to bite me in the ass.

Down along the roadside, the lanky leader stepped out from the underbrush and blocked the caravan's progress. Funny, if the oxen's driver had pushed them forward right then, running the cocky bastard over, they might have actually gotten away with it. But, people tend to respond compassionately at first. Even in troubled times the human instinct is to lend a hand instead of kicking dirt in someone's face. Maybe this man needed their help, right? They probably knew better, but felt compelled to help anyway. They definitely knew better once they had stopped and four of the band poured out of the woods with drawn swords, surrounding the lead wagon, leaving three still hidden in the trees, probably as archery cover just like I was. I could hear a few heated shouts, but when one of the thugs struck the head wagon's driver, knocking him off his seat and into the dirt, the others cooperated and started handing over their hard-earned pieces of silver and gold. That was when the Great Sir William rode upon the scene, shouting, "Halt! That is enough you ruffians! Leave these good people alone and leave my king's lands! You are not welcome in Thistledown!"

He actually managed to dismount with some measure of grace, no stumbles or trips, only a high leg over the saddle, and he stuck the landing. Good job, honey! The highwaymen were the hardened soldiers of the road that I had feared, though. There was no exchange of banter, no "Who's going to make us?" type nonsense. Lanky made a motion with his right hand and one of the hidden thieves burst out of the brush right next to Will. Instead of drawing a blade the thief tackled Will, bowling him over and the two grappled. I told you before that Will is a vicious infighter, that stupid sneaky troll up north only got the better of him because of his size and the element of surprise. This thief had surprise, but not size on his side. They grappled and wrestled for a few minutes, both grunting and cursing, with everyone looking on, the thieves and traders alike. Will had both size and skill on the thief. It was always a satisfying surprise to see the Great Sir William actually act and look like his legend. It's not often I see Will so aggressive and angry, though. He was savagely going at the thief, wrenching and gouging and punching. I don't know if it was all the stress of this last summer and autumn, coming face to face with his own flaws, or the threat of war on his beloved Thistledown, but whatever the motivation, my sweet, nearly blind husband put a hand to either side of that thief's head and snapped his neck like piece of dry kindling. I swear I could hear the crack all the way up on the hillside.

In the orange light of the fading sun a hushed silence fell over the crowd. I caught Jimmy looking questioningly up in my direction from where he had positioned himself behind another of the hidden thieves. I doubted he could see it, but I shrugged my shoulders anyway. With blood dripping from his nose, Will spat some more out of his mouth and rose to his feet. Standing at his full, intimidating six and a half feet of height, Will grabbed hold of the dead thief's ankle and drug him toward the others, growling, "I warned you once. This is your last chance…leave!" He shouted and tossed the limp body at their leader's feet. Very impressive and very dramatic. If we pulled this off they'd be singing about that in Amberea tomorrow night, and probably in Thistledown by next week.

Everything slowed down, like it always does for me in moments of high-tension. I saw the lanky leader slowly spit on his companion's corpse and shake his head. The caravan driver hopped back up into place and with a slap of the reins sent the oxen to plodding off as fast as oxen can plod. The surviving six highwaymen rushed out of the woods and onto the road to back up their leader with weapons drawn as the wagons made their escape. I imagine the leader assumed they could kill Will and run down the caravan in the night when they were done. The leader drew his sword and started toward Will, who had yet to pull his weapon free. I would have sent at least somebody after the loot if I was a criminal, but hey, that's just me. I also didn't have that testosterone fueled machismo driving me on to grunt monkey-like at my challenger as the lanky leader did. He was angry and ready to show Will who the bigger monkey was as he took two steps toward my husband, hand poised to draw his blade as he went.

So, I sent an arrow through his throat before he took a third step – two down, six to go.

The other thieves hadn't realized their leader was dead and continued to charge Will. Sword finally free, he'd lost the earlier grace and had been amateurishly jerking at it. He circled, trying to keep his back from being exposed. That was impossible, six on one? Another arrow, this one through a heart, improved the odds, and Jimmy, charging out of the tree line, looking once again like the bad boy black knight took the heads from two more before the last three realized they had had their ambushing days reversed and now they were the ones caught by surprise. Will managed to run another through in the resulting confusion. Wow, way to go dear! I downed one more through the chest and Jimmy easily finished off the last.

When the younger man pulled his blades free from the gurgling corpse of the last thief, he then performed his dramatic stage bow to Will. Nice, Jimmy, real subtle, good thing Will isn't as observant as I am, or he'd have recognized you by that move alone. Jimmy turned in a flourish and headed back toward the almost complete dark of the woods when Will shouted, "Wait! Who are you? I was expecting someone else."

No Jimmy, just keep going back into the woods. You're not supposed to add to the story, just confirm the one I've already told, and…Crap! Damn it, Jimmy! Into the woods! Into the woods! Bad pretty boy! He headed back toward Will and bowed again. I couldn't hear what he said, but Will nodded, and looked around at the night. He waved what I figured was meant to be a thank you gesture to me in the wrong direction and out of some weird compulsion I shot an arrow down. It stuck fast, buried halfway up the shaft, only a foot or two from Will's boots. He turned around and waved up to where I was, shouting, "Thank you maiden!"

He couldn't see me, but I waved anyway. I sat and waited for Jimmy to make his way back up and around to me. Then we'd climb up and over to the other side of the rise where we could keep an eye on Will for the return journey and still be out of sight. So…that time it worked. All according to plan. Yay, go Gale! I didn't know if it would continue to work, but that was enough for me to breathe easily again, for what seemed like the first time in months. I leaned my head against the boulder my back was to and looked up at the stars. I could hear Jimmy occasionally snapping a twig or stepping on a dried leaf as he climbed the hillside to get to me. In the relative quiet I pulled the drying red leaf out from its hiding place and rubbing it I looked back at the stars and whispered, "Thanks Papa."

Thirty

The return journey was probably the nicest stroll I've had through the Thistledown countryside since I was a little girl. The sun was riding high, warming the fields and forest evenly while we strolled along behind Will as he rode back toward the castle with the good news. Thankfully King Theodore didn't ask for any heads like poor old Gar Jinkins did with the troll. Will's word was as good as gold in Thistledown; if he said the highwaymen were no longer a problem then it was a fact. No decapitation required.

It was nice to take my time and not rush about frantically. Jimmy and I could keep at a slow, almost sedate pace and still remain a quarter of a mile ahead of Will. I stopped and picked a bunch of wild mums that I noticed blossoming at the base of an abandoned and crumbling stone wall. I picked flowers! When was the last time I had that luxury while on a mission, or was at that much ease to do it and not worry about how I should be doing something else? It was wonderful; there is no other way to describe it. I didn't want it to end. I didn't want to go back to the high-strung, stick a lump of coal up my ass and I'll give you a diamond in a day worry, which I knew was waiting right around the corner. I wanted to still help those people who couldn't help themselves. Help the people of Thistledown, my people, but I didn't want to have to do it so secretly. I didn't want Will's fame and notoriety. I didn't want to ride in to save the day in a blaze of glory. I just wanted to do things as I always had, but out in the open. Walk with the warm autumn sunshine lightening my step and pick flowers if I felt like it…but don't we all? Fighters or not, don't we all want to be ourselves and not hide it – especially from those that we love?

Jimmy and I had a picnic supper under an old oak tree that had managed to hang onto its golden leaves late in the season. The dried leaves rattled in the breeze as we finished off the supplies we had brought with us. It was like a date, sitting there under the sun without a care in the world, relaxed. We talked and joked about random things, nothing too personal, we'd done that already, we didn't need to open old wounds. I had shut that relationship door on Jimmy, with some regret, but it was pleasant to have that feeling of courtship without the anxiety. I don't know if a man and a woman can ever really be *just friends*. There is always that undercurrent, subconscious or not, that if you are close enough to be attracted to each other then you will be … and it's all downhill from there. You enjoy each other's company, the conversations, the commonalities; you laugh, you smile, you relate, you find out you love so much about the other person, and then you back off and say no to that last ultimate expression of love. I hadn't done that with Jimmy, we pushed on all the way past that. Maybe that was why there was no awkwardness or anxiety? We had jumped to the last step most "friends" draw that line at and we were now filling in the beginning few we had hurdled over…or, just maybe it was because for the first time since Papa died I wasn't alone.

Will was with me of course, but you see, Will is only ever with Gale – his wife, the daughter of the man who once upon a time saved his life in the woods. He is never with all of me, both Gale and the masked woman. The cold killer who would do whatever she needed to protect those she loved. Would Will love me, all of me, like Papa did, or as fate had deemed it Jimmy did? It's weird that you could be with someone for so long and still be worried about what they would think of you if they knew the *real* you.

I won't say that those thoughts took the wind out of my sails on the last leg of that gorgeous trip home, but I won't lie, they did nip a bit of the spring from my step, just a little. We watched Will ride through the gates of Thistledown Castle to the resounding cheers from the commoners as word spread that war would not be upon them. Mission accomplished, plan followed through to fruition, we would live to see another day and my secret was still safe. Sighing I started to head back toward our cottage when Jimmy lightly touched my arm, saying, "I'll leave you here too, Gale, if that's alright?"

It's stupid, I knew I wasn't going to keep him with me like some pet, like the love-struck puppy dog I had been comparing him to, camped out in my barn with my horse so I could have a friend to talk to and play with when I needed to fight evil. He was a person who had his own life to live and not be my lapdog and companion. But, all the same, I didn't want to say goodbye. I did want to keep him in my barn…but I couldn't…could I? No alright, fine I couldn't…but I wanted to.

Instead of kicking him in the head and dragging him back to my barn, I fought the impulse, it was there, but instead I said, "Sure, Jimmy," and shrugged my shoulders to let him know it was no big deal. "That's probably a good idea. I need to get home and make the place look *lived-in* while we were gone."

I think he wanted to offer to help with that, too. Something about the set of his eyes or the way he leaned a little toward me as if he was ready to follow me if I'd asked. But, I think sometime during that wonderful trip home, Jimmy realized the same shift in our relationship that I had. He may not have truly believed me last week when I told him we were not going to be together. I think somewhere in the back of his mind, the little boy that wasn't loved, thought that I would still run away with him off into the sunset. It's a hard thing to watch when a child becomes an adult. It's not something you see often; in fact I don't think it's something you see at all. Most of the time it's a gradual shift over years, so subtle no one sees it. That's why you always hear people say things like, "Wow you've grown up" or "When did you get to be an adult" but the thing was … I got to see it with Jimmy. When I didn't invite him back or ask for his help, he didn't throw himself to the ground and have a tantrum, he didn't beg me to be his one true love. No, he just nodded his head and smiled at me. He turned away first and started to walk around to the rear of Thistledown Castle. He had gone a dozen yards or so when I shouted, "Jimmy?"

He turned, but he didn't look as if he hoped I'd changed my mind. He looked at me like any friend would when their name is called. Hurting more than a little inside, but proud too, I said, "Thank you."

He smiled, nodded, and waved that time, before returning to wherever it was he was sleeping when he was not in my barn.

Thirty-one

Winter swept in with a vengeance, early storms and squalls leaving that warm pleasant autumn stroll to seem more like a dream than a memory every time I looked out the window to see the snow drifting and piling up against the barn. With the winter came more problems, not just for me, but for Thistledown as well.

Will returned home after the incident with the highwaymen weeks ago, but he wasn't the victorious hero I had expected. He was bashful and even a bit coy about the whole thing when I prodded him for details. He would only say, "It was nothing, Gale. I did my duty and that's all." That was really surprising since this was the first time he had actually done some of the badass work, so to speak. I was figuring on hour after hour of long-winded tales of how he beat those thieves to a bloody pulp, showing them not to mess with innocent bystanders traveling in lands guarded by the Great Sir William, but those stories were never told. It was always the same almost recruiting for the king's army spiel of *I did my duty* every time I we talked about it.

But, that wasn't the worst part. Instead of the typical at home comfortable companionship we typically shared in the lulls between missions, there was a distance between us. It was cold, and not just the snow and ice blowing through the cottage's cracks and crevices. It didn't feel like it was coming from me, even though I had realized what was missing from my life, a friend, and I was still missing him. It had been this way since that transformative goodbye where I had last seen Jimmy and I wanted to know how he was doing. No, it wasn't that. I kept those thoughts and feelings to myself. The cold between us was coming from Will. I admit there was a short stint of a few days where I wondered if Jimmy had told Will about our affair, but that faded quickly, not only did I trust Jimmy, it didn't feel like that type of cold. It didn't have that accusatory *I know what you've done* feel while Will kept his distance. It was more the opposite. He was jittery, paranoid, and nervous. He hardly ever responded to me physically, even if I initiated it. He would stare off out the window as if he were looking for something and jump three feet in the air if I tapped him on the shoulder and asked what he was doing. No, in our small snow-bound cottage it felt like Will had been the one to have the affair, not me.

That was only one of my problems. The other … well, the other can wait. Thistledown's problems, on the other hand, came with a rapid knock on our door one afternoon. The snow was blowing so hard that we couldn't open it or the wind would have kept us from reclosing it, even with Will's bull-like size pushing against it that's how bad the storms had been. In-between the wind's howling blasts, when it

244

was possible somebody may actually hear, Will shouted, "Go around back!"

I wasn't sure if our visitor had heard over the wind or not, but a minute later a knock at the kitchen door told me they had. The ball of ice and snow that tumbled through my kitchen door was a frozen sight for sore eyes. I actually didn't recognize Jimmy at first. It wasn't until he removed his fur hat and over-sized magenta balaclava (magenta, really? Well at least I knew what to knit for him as a birthday gift) that I realized it was him. I started to gasp out his name and rush to get him over to the fire, but I fought the impulse down when I remembered that as far as Will knew my acquaintance with the young man was only him delivering the occasional message to Will or from his stage performances as a juggler. Hugging and wrapping him in a blanket by the fire would probably be more than a bit suspicious. Will strode into the kitchen and quickly directed the young man toward the fire, doing what I longed to, and said, "James! Stars above lad, get by the fire before you catch your death! Gale, pour the poor boy a cup of tea, would you please?"

Jimmy let Will steer him toward a chair by the fire, saying, "Thank you Sir William. You're right about the cold. This storm has been going for weeks and the king's old soothsayer Bagley says it doesn't look to be letting up anytime soon."

I set a mug of tea next to Jimmy almost as soon as he'd sat down. I'd already added the honey and mint that I knew he liked, but I doubt Will was going to notice something so subtle. Jimmy nodded to me and wrapped his fingers around the ceramic mug, cradling it for warmth, and said, "Thank you my lady." I bundled his wet outerwear up, leaving his snowshoes by the back door and went into our bedroom. We kept a second stove in there for cold winter nights. I hung Jimmy's wet clothes over it to dry and brought a flannel blanket out with me to drape over his shoulders.

After a few sips of tea, Jimmy said, "The cold is part of why I'm here." He pulled a rolled decree out from inside his wool sweater. Handing it to Will, he said, "It's the poor northern ranchers again."

Bless his heart, he told us what the scroll said so Will wouldn't have to pull out his reading glasses. Setting the scroll on the table, Will devoted his attention to Jimmy instead as he continued. "The early winter is dumping feet and feet upon the ranchers at the base of the mountains, more than we are getting here. From what I'm told that isn't anything new. The ranchers are used to hard winters." He looked at both of us for confirmation and we both nodded in agreement. Continuing, Jimmy said, "The problem is with the cold and snow, a pair of Yeti have wandered in out of the deep mountain passes in which they typically roam and have started feeding on both livestock and ranchers indiscriminately."

The Knight's Wife

Crap. Remember me telling you there were worse things in the northern mountains than trolls? Yetis are one of those things. Forget all about the stories you may have heard involving cute, cuddly, white-furred misunderstood monsters that only want to help with holiday decorations. No, yetis are viscous, highly intelligent, cold (both literally and figuratively, the skin under their fur is blue and freezing to the touch) killers. If you managed to pull out all of a yeti's teeth, it wouldn't tame it. Please, you'd probably just piss it off worse and it would gum you to death like old Turtle the yarn merchant chewing on a bagel. Trust me; you do not want to mess with a yeti… let alone two. Crap.

Jimmy's story quieted the room of all but the howling wind and the crackling fire. We all knew what it meant. We all didn't want to face it. Oddly enough, the hero who was being called upon knew less than all of us. Will knew yetis were dangerous, but he didn't know that the two people in the room with him would be the ones most likely to face that danger and keep it from killing and eating him. Shaking his head at the prospect, Will said, "It's getting late. James, you'll be staying. You can sleep here by the stove. Gale and I have another one in our bedroom doing its best to fight back this infernal storm." At Jimmy's raised arm and attempted argument, Will added, "I won't take no for an answer, James. It must have taken you all day as it was to trek out here in those things," he pointed to Jimmy's dripping snowshoes where they sat perched in a corner. "No, Gale can cook you a hot meal and we can have a little company on this fierce winter night. Tomorrow you can head back into Thistledown with my mark upon that scroll so King Theodore knows I've seen it. I won't waste time telling him I am going to go. I'll head out for the northern ranches when you leave. I don't know if Duke can handle the high drifts…" he looked my way, an acknowledgment to my superior horsemanship, and I shook my head. "Alright then, I'll set out with my own shoes at first light. It will be hard going, but I won't let those poor people who have already suffered so much this year be in such danger a moment longer than they have to be."

So that night, as the winds continued their seemingly endless shrieking, I slept under the same roof with the only two men I had ever slept with, and worried about the coming storm … more than the currently raging one.

Thirty-two

Early the next morning Jimmy left to let King Theodore know Will was on the way. In passing as he left, he said, "I'll run to catch up. Don't worry; I'll be right behind you." And he headed off into the bright, white, snow-filled morning without looking back. He was true to his word and caught up to me by that night.

Will left at almost the same time and I followed, and all but right on his heels, too. In that blizzard it was pointless, or more precisely, it was dangerous to lose line of sight. My line of sight, not Will's thank goodness. It was a rare thing for any nasty creature, bad guy, villain, or monster to venture out to do naughty evil stuff in the cold and snow. Other than a few creatures like yetis or ice dragons, most monsters are just like you and me when it comes to ferocious winter weather. They wake up, maybe have a little breakfast of scrambled eggs and whatever leftover bits of human they may have sitting around, then sit down with a cup of tea, look out the entrance to their dastardly lair and see all that snow, ice, and wind and they say, "Screw the murder, mischief, and mayhem! I'm going back to bed."

The up side was that with the blanket of white, Will could barely take a wrong turn. Once he found the northern road all he had to do was push on down the middle of the lane until he made it to the north ranchlands. A leisurely day trip in good weather would be turned into three or four days of breaking trail in snow that varied in depth from ankle, to knee, to waist, depending on where the drifts were piling up. I stayed no less than twenty to thirty yards behind Will while he trudged. As I've said, blizzard condition missions are a rarity, but on those odd times when a snow loving baddie decides to come out and play, I wrap myself in a bleached white traveling cloak. It wouldn't work as very good camouflage against you or anybody else with good eyesight. I'd look like a kid playing ghost, "Boo, you don't see me. I'm ghost, boo."

But Will was never going to see me, wrapped in white, following behind him and taking advantage of his huge girth breaking trail ahead of me. For once I had an easier going trip than he did. Easier mind you, not completely easy. The wind was blowing so hard that half of the time it had filled Will's tracks mostly in by the time I got to them. Thinking ahead I had packed a spare white cloak in my rucksack for Jimmy. I didn't know what he'd think to bring, so I packed for both of us. I was already carrying more supplies than I normally would due to the cold, but I also had the added weight of supplying for two. So easier, not easy. But, the thing is, I didn't mind. It may sound selfish, and wrong of course given that people were dead, but I was glad for a chance to spend some time with my friend again. I had been trying to invent ways that I could visit with him or him with me without arising suspicion almost instantly after the last time. The problem was with my life the way it was, with the situation being what it was, I couldn't come up with any way to see him that didn't involve a real mission, like this one where other people had suffered or were dead. There were only so many pickle jars Will could open for Marissa. Funny how the first time she delayed Will because she thought Jimmy and I were going at it, then we actually did, and now I wanted her to help me find ways just so we could have a cup of tea or go for a walk. I don't know if you'd call that irony, coincidence, tragedy, or whatever... to be honest, I guess I'd call it life.

The sun had fallen, dimming what little light there was shining through the cloud cover to nil. When it was too cold to travel further, Will hunkered down by the side of the road, behind a large boulder and attempted to build a fire in the leeward side. We had only gone a third of the way, better than I expected truth be told, but still not great. The wind gusted, strong and violent, biting at my eyes, and forcing its way through my cloak to rob me of strength and heat. Shivering, I wished I could help Will. His survival skills are not poor, but they are also not anywhere near approaching the mastery Papa passed on to me. But how often does the subject of winter survival shelters come up around the dinner table? A large snow-laden pine tree was only a dozen or so yards away from Will's attempted bivouac. He wouldn't freeze to death, hopefully, but he wouldn't be as comfortable as I was either, after I dug down and found a four by six foot pocket of open space around the pine's trunk. "The best place to look for shelter in any blizzard is around the base of a large conifer, little Nightingale." Papa's voice echoed in my head as I excavated my camp. "Nature will do almost all of the work for you. All you need to do is dig your front door and be sure to light your fire *away* from the trunk, and it's instant home sweet home."

It didn't take long, not instant, but close enough. I had my fire going, small and stoked with coal I had brought with me, and was drifting in that semi-dosed sort of sleep you get sometimes when you're over-tired. Jimmy startled me even though I had been expecting him, when he peeked his head into my shelter entrance, and asked, "Gale, is that you?"

"Yes, Jimmy," I whispered after I'd jumped out of my doze. "Get in here so you don't freeze."

He tumbled in head over heels, pouring fresh snow into my cozy little cave, and muttering, "It's colder than a witch's tit out there! I actually passed you both. With this damn wind your tracks were all but gone. It wasn't until I turned around and saw Sir William tucked up against the backside of that boulder that I realized I'd gone too far."

"Is he alright?" I asked, seeing Jimmy snow-covered and almost yeti-like himself, I was no longer so sure Will wouldn't freeze to death.

The Knight's Wife

"Yes, I think so," Jimmy said nodding. Then shrugging his shoulders and adding sheepishly, "I checked on him. He was asleep, but shivering violently, so I added some of the coal I brought with me to his fire, guessing that you'd bring more than enough. He was only using some gathered deadwood." Holding his hands out to calm the growing irritation he could see in my eyes, he continued, "I know the rule, no contact, but I figured after last time he has to know we're out here somewhere, so why not check to make sure he was alright. If he woke up, he shouldn't be so surprised, right?"

Letting my agitation dissolve, I said, "Yes, Jimmy, you're right. Thank you."

He nodded without responding and squeezed in next to me, pressing our sides together and snuggling in under the blanket I had draped over my shoulders against the rough bark of the pine's trunk. We sat there in silence, both of us lightly dozing, bodies nearing exhaustion after so much hard travel. It was girlish and silly, but I wanted to visit. I wanted to talk to my friend, because though he had slept in my cottage last night, I didn't get to talk to him, not really. I could feel his level breathing against my side, through both of our armor, so I knew he had to have fallen deeply asleep. I sat there for a while, enjoying the rhythmic press and rub of his body against mine. Will had been so distant lately it was nice to feel connected to someone. I wasn't willing to open that relationship doorway on Jimmy again.

253

I'd been the one to close it, so it was up to me to keep it closed. It wouldn't be fair to him, to Will, or I guess to myself to keep opening it and closing it when I got too scared or upset and needed a shoulder to lean on. Papa, dream, memory, or whatever he was, was right. I could fall apart, but I had to make sure I found myself again…I had to think of someone other than myself when I did that. If I fell apart or lost myself again, even for one night, what would that do to Jimmy? Could he handle the constant pressures and strains from a relationship that was one minute friendship and the next physical pleasure? Or, was he just a guy and I was giving him too much credit and maturity? Would he be okay with the constant rigors of an on again off again sexual friendship? Or, was the whole thing just my desire to have someone warm to cling to on a cold, very cold, night?

I had one more secret I wanted, no not wanted, needed, I needed to share with Jimmy…but, but they say there is a time and a place for everything, right? Whoever *they* are? Sometimes I wish *they* would just shut up…life would be easier if *they* did. But, in my quiet little snow cave, with a nasty storm still howling around us, and my poor, bumbling husband, huddled next to a tiny fire shivering in his sleep, well, somehow that didn't seem like the right place or time to tell Jimmy I was pregnant with his child. What do you think?

Thirty-three

I was up before both Will and Jimmy the next morning. Not much of a surprise really, I don't remember sleeping much at all. Even when I'm exhausted I have trouble sleeping. I crept out of our snow shelter and went to check on Will. He was still huddled in a ball, snugged up against the leeward side of the boulder. The snow had drifted up around him in the night. He must have awoken at some point and rigged his extra blanket into a lean-to with a few large branches hastily hacked from a nearby pine. His small coal and wood fire had burned down to embers and I stoked it for him, so the heat may help thaw him before he pressed on. I'd have to check him for frostbite when we returned home; with that kind of exposure he could lose toes, maybe a foot if he wasn't careful.

Before I wiggled back into our shelter, I looked around, and for the first time it dawned on me that the storm had stopped. No new snow was adding to the current drifts. The wind wasn't even blowing, so the drifts weren't shifting. It was beautiful. I love the woods covered in a heavy snow, typically looking at it from my kitchen window where I sat curled up with a cup of tea next to the stove, but it was still pretty. It would still be hard travel through what had already accumulated, but at least we wouldn't be buffeted by winds and new snow. With a little luck we might make it to the northern ranches by night-fall. That wouldn't warm Jimmy and me up any, but Will could catch a break and thaw out after what had to have been a hard miserable night.

When I did worm my way back into the shelter, Jimmy was already awake and roasting some cold sausages over our meager coal fire. A small teakettle was nearly whistling from its perch on a flat rock next to the flames. He smiled when he saw me and around a mouthful of sausage, he asked, "How is Will?"

"Alive," I said, shaking off the snow that had found its way down the back of my neck despite my best efforts when I crawled in. "Cold, he may be in danger of some frostbite, but he's alive." I sat down next to Jimmy in the cramped space and he poured me a cup of tea. Wrapping my fingers around the tin mug, attempting to soak in some of the warmth, I said, "Thank you." He nodded and I added, "The storm's finally stopped."

"Good," he said around another bite of sausage. "Should be easier going then. I have never been a big winter person. I prefer warm sun and sandy beaches."

I chuckled a little, saying, "I used to feel that way, too. I still don't love the really nasty weather like this, but my papa used to always say, 'Nightingale, warm weather is good for a spell, but if things don't swing around from cold to hot and back to cold again, people tend to forget they are part of the world they live in. The seasons help us remember the cycle of life and death'."

I stopped talking for a second, thinking about winter and Papa always had me close to tears and I didn't want to choke on my words. It could have been the pregnancy hormones too, but I'd rather think it was the past causing the lump in my throat when I was finally able to finish. "Poetically, he died in the winter. I can't believe it must be almost fifteen years ago...and I still miss him like it was yesterday."

"I'm sorry," Jimmy said. He must have heard the tears in my voice.

Waving his apology away, I said, "It happens, like he said life and death, but the winter always reminds me of his passing. It makes me sadder than I should be, but I think if I moved somewhere where it was always warm, I might forget about him. Not some ridiculous complete amnesia or anything like that," I explained and Jimmy nodded that he understood what I meant. I continued, "I'd be worried that I'd remember him less and less as the years without a winter went by. I know the further we bury our past in time the more we forget about it...but I don't want to forget him. He was more than my father. He was my friend...and I've learned just how few of those we get in life."

I don't know if he realized I had meant him, or if he had his own ghosts that made him empathize, but I felt Jimmy's hand lace through mine. He didn't say anything. He simply slipped his fingers into mine until they were intertwined and he squeezed. He sat quietly and didn't ask any questions, even after a few minutes when I let go of his hand to pull a waxed red maple leaf out from under my bracer. I always make sure to preserve some with paraffin before they all fall, for such an occasion as this, and I ran my fingers over its glossy surface, lost in my own thoughts. We finished the rest of our breakfast in silence. Me trapped in my past, wishing for impossibilities, and daydreaming about never-will-bes…and lord knows what was going on inside Jimmy's head, maybe the same thoughts only the faces and names were different. I wish I'd told him then. I think maybe that was the time and place *they* are always talking about. Wouldn't it be nice if that perfect time and place came accompanied by some kind of ringing bell or something? Ding, ding, ding, Oh, goodie! I almost missed the perfect moment to say - *fill in your own blank* - Good thing there's that bell!

We took turns peeking out of the entrance to see if Will had started north again or not. It was a good hour later before Will drug his, what must have been very cold and weary, body up and started trudging north. We doused our fire and slipped into our white traveling cloaks – Jimmy looked better as the dark bad boy knight than the white shining armor type.

The Knight's Wife

The black eye band and his long black hair accompanied by the white cloak gave him a fallen angel look that was still very flattering.

We had another hard day's travel. Not as hard as before, or as difficult as it could have been, but still not something any sane person would go out and do unless people's lives were at stake.

I won't bore you with the details of another long day hiking through the snow. Think white, think cold, and think white some more and you have it. By the time the sun fell, dropping the temperature further, Will showed no signs of slowing down and we realized he planned on pushing along until he reached the ranches. That was actually a smart move on Will's part. I know I don't give him enough credit at times. Sure he may not have all of the survival skills that I do, but he was no fool either. The severity of the storm having dwindled and taken the clouds with it, left a crystal clear night sky, beautifully decorated with glittering stars that reflected off the snow drifts. The forest was a stunning sight like that – an absolutely stunning, deadly sight. The temperature was already freezing and without the clouds to trap some level of warmth on the ground for us fragile humans, camping out under those stars without proper shelter would most likely be a death sentence. So, evidencing a level of survival knowledge I didn't know he possessed, or it could have been shear obstinacy and determination too I suppose, Will trudged through the snow covering the northern road long after the sun fell and long into the winter night. Jimmy and I followed, farther behind without the wind blowing to mask our presence, but we kept our white cloaks' hoods up as a precaution. We were two ghosts moving in the night, haunting the steps of a hero who wasn't one, and the stars silently watched.

Jimmy and I hadn't talked much during the trip. It wasn't that we didn't want to, or maybe it was, when you're that cold you can easily mistake freezing for being taciturn. I knew I couldn't keep it secret from him forever that I was carrying his child, but that wasn't what held my tongue on the subject. It wasn't the cold either, if I'm going to be a realist. It wasn't the risk of Will overhearing us either, plunging through the snow drifts like a workhorse, he'd barely be able to hear more than the crunch of his snowshoes and the blood pounding in his ears. My silence was selfish I guess. We were quiet out of comfort. He was there with me and I was there with him. We didn't need to say anything. Occasionally his hand would slip into mine again or I'd lace mine through his elbow when I'd help him over a particularly deep drift and then I'd leave it there for a while as we walked. I know it may sound like I was leading him on. I know some people have real taboos about touching and physical contact – unless it's a parent and child, or family hugs, two grownups of approximate age, yes, I said approximate! I know I'd never see the other side of forty again, but it's close enough, thank you! But if you fall under those guidelines and you aren't married? Well touching is off limits, right? Given our past, maybe it should have been, but for me, I needed that contact, that touch. It was an emotional anchor when I was feeling adrift, and I didn't think it was right to be hands off and then at some point soon say, "Oh by the way, Jimmy. I don't want to touch you because you knocked me up!" That wasn't the case, of course, but I didn't want him to get that impression when I did tell him.

Foggy headed with those thoughts, I ran into Jimmy's back when he stopped. I started to ask what was wrong, but he pulled us down before I could make a sound. Hidden behind a large drift, he pointed further up the trail where the bright orange light of a bonfire was dancing on the snow. I hadn't realized how close we were to the northern ranches. The forest all looks the same when it's covered in feet of snow, but that's no excuse for my daydreaming. I was finding it harder and harder to be my old focused self. The gruff and husky voice of Gar Jinkins, shouted down the road, "Who goes there so late on such a gods forsaken night?"

I barely recognized Will's voice as stuttering and shaking with the cold as it was, but he yelled back as best he could. "It is I, Sir William! Gar, I hear you are having trouble again my friend. I came to help as quickly as I could, but that blasted storm was nearly the end of me last night."

"Sir William?" Gar asked hesitantly, because Will's speech did not come out anywhere as near to clear as the trained wifely ear translation that I gave you. It was garbled and slurred, but when Gar's sharp old rancher's eyes realized it was Will and not some creature out in the night about some malevolent errand, he shouted, "Stars and stones man! Get your frozen ass over here and warm up!"

The bonfire was enormous, ten to fifteen feet tall, blazing and crackling with what I'd guess to be an entire oak stump at its core, probably coated or soaked in tar and pitch before it was set alight to burn hotter and longer. There was a blanket wrapped around an old chest that Gar had been using for a seat and the old man yanked it off and threw it around Will's shoulders awkwardly. Sometime since last summer Gar had lost an arm. In the firelight he still looked as rough as ever, more so without the arm, but the pain of the last year had definitely taken its toll. His eyes were sunken further in and the lines on his face were etched deeper from a diet I'd guess that was more fluid and intoxicating than actual nourishing food. He pounded Will on the back with his single hand and passed him the steaming mug of whatever he had been drinking before we all arrived, saying, "It's good to see you, Sir William. I tell you we've been so bloody worried, we didn't know what to do. Two weeks ago when those snow buggering sons of whores yetis showed up, me and a few other ranchers went out and tried to run'em off. After that troll we decided we weren't going to let you fight all our battles for us, but," rubbing at the stump of his arm where it ended halfway between his shoulder and where his elbow should have been, Gar added, "Mayhap we should have."

Over the mug, Will chattered, "How many have been killed?"

"Oh, I should say a dozen," Gar said, scratching at his stubbly chin with his only hand. A fur hat with dangling earflaps covered most of his head. The tassels on the ends of the flaps bobbed slightly as he continued, "Lord knows why, but the Jinkins have been spared this time. Maybe whatever gods there are felt we'd suffered enough this last year. But the other clans haven't been so lucky." He gestured toward the bonfire, saying, "This here was my idea! Each ranch has four of these behemoths blazing away at the cardinal points. So far it's worked, but we've only been doing it for the last two nights. Once those snow devils get hungry enough I doubt a bit of fire will keep them away." He looked off toward the rest of his ranch where over the rise to east and west a soft glow could be seen dancing on the snow drifts. Nodding his head in approval and slapping Will hard on the back again, Gar added, "That's why I'm extra glad to see you! We're tough folk up here, salt of the earth and all that, but we need a man like you for the monsters. We can fight the land and the harsh weather she'll throw at us, but the creatures that come out of the dark? That's a different story all together. Now get your ass up to the house.

263

Don't worry about waking anyone. It's been two weeks of poor sleep. My missus will fix you up with a hot meal and a warm bed, don't you worry."

We watched Will trudge up to the glowing homestead on the hillside where, as Gar said, a hot meal and a warm bed were waiting for him. Jimmy looked over at me and whispered, "Should we find another large pine, or should we try and get closer to the house? Do we risk being spotted?"

"Another tree," I said and when Jimmy frowned a bit, I added, "hey, that's the downside to this whole secret hero game. It's not always sunny autumn camping."

He nodded and started off into the woods away from the light of Gar's bonfire. It would be a cold night, but between our meager fire and our body heat it wouldn't be too intolerable. Tomorrow should be fun though, trying to move about with all the ranchers on their guard and not make any noticeable tracks. Plus just because we were there to fight back the yetis, that didn't mean that the monsters wouldn't hunt and stalk us while we tried to do the same to them. Yeah, lots of fun, circling around through the woods, dodging, evading, sneaking, freezing, and trying to follow Will unnoticed; lots and lots of fun. My only hope was that Gar's mishap and missing limb would keep the other ranchers from grabbing their torches and pitchforks to help Will on his hunt. There'd be nothing worse than a damn mob trying to help and only getting in the way. Those wonderful thoughts followed me into another unsettling night's sleep.

Thirty-four

I slept in Jimmy's arms again. Not slept as in post-coitus, exhaustion sleep! Come on! With that much snow on the ground something would freeze, turn blue, and fall off. No, we slept intertwined to conserve body heat. I knew it was morning, not only by the light filtering in through the snow, but by the fact that our small fire had burned down to nothing. I still didn't want to move. It was warm were I was and cold, very cold, where I had to go. So, I snuggled tighter in Jimmy's arms and could tell by his regular breathing that he was awake as well. I don't know if he knew I was awake or not, but his voice was tentative like he almost didn't want me to hear him say, "Thank you, Gale."

I shifted so I could look up at him, when I asked, "For what?"

He seemed slightly embarrassed, perhaps he hadn't wanted me to hear after all, but he explained, "For including me. For not thinking of me as some pretty plaything to be tossed aside when you were done with me. I'm very happy… happier than I've been in my entire life actually. It may sound weird, but even being included in something so off the wall as this…" I could only assume he meant aiding and abetting in the continuation of the false legend of the Great Sir William. "…it's not something most people would be happy about, I suppose, but it makes me feel like a part of your family…and that's nice. Thank you."

Ding, ding, ding, Gale! That's the bell right there sweetheart. That is your perfect time, maybe not the perfect place, but the kid just poured his heart out to you about being included, now is the time to tell him about his child! Do it now, ding, ding, ding!

"Jimmy, I…" I started to stammer. I knew I could do it. I had to come right out and say it. No hemming or hawing, no Gale rambling on about something that only had the loosest of connections to what we were talking about, just come right out and say, "Jimmy I'm-"

"Gar! Gar! You crusty old coot, you still alive or are you an ugly old icicle?" The shouts interrupted me and we both peeked out from our shelter to see one of the younger ranch hands strolling down the hillside from the homestead shouting at the hunched over form of Gar, where he sat wrapped in a blanket and warming his single hand by the still raging bonfire. Yelling over his shoulder, Gar said, "O'course I am, Perkins, you slack-jawed idjit! It'd take more than one cold night to get the better of me, at any age!" Dropping the volume of his voice when Perkins drew closer, he asked, "How's Sir William? He looked to be in mighty bad shape last night when I sent him up to the house."

"He's all thawed out," Perkins said, sitting down on the old trunk next to Gar and passing the older man a fresh steaming mug. "A late supper, warm bed, and a big piping hot breakfast, done him a right lot of good."

Draining the mug in one pull then slapping some life back into his legs, Gar stood up and said, "That's good. That lad will take care of this nonsense, you mark my words. He done right by Daisy last summer. He'll do right for us again. Now keep this fire going. Half of me is starved and the other half is frozen. I need to fix at least one half if not both. I'll send Marcus down later to check on your wood supply, after I see Sir William off to the Gibson's place. That's were those blasted snow devils were seen last, right?"

"Yump," Perkins said as he jabbed at the fire with a large branch. "Hoss says Tony Gibson found fresh tracks out by his eastern boarder last night."

"Mmhmph," Gar grunted some unintelligible agreement and shuffled up toward the ranch.

Jimmy and I ate breakfast on the run. I knew where the Gibson's ranch was from trips I had taken with Papa. We both figured it would be better to arrive there before Will and follow him once he had the trail than to try and stay hidden while moving in and out of a place as busy as the Jinkins homestead was. It was a risk traveling about in the open dressed in our white travel cloaks. We looked like smaller, maybe pint-sized yetis. Jimmy looked more yeti-like then me though, he was closer in height. Yetis are about the same height as trolls, perhaps a bit smaller, but broader in the shoulders. The real difference between yetis and trolls is that yetis have mastered speech, which, of course, is what makes them more dangerous. We risked the cloaks because it was only a chance that we'd be spotted in them if we were unlucky, but in our dark leather armor we were sure to be spotted and from a greater distance against the snowy white backdrop. There were a lot of vigilant and nervous ranchers out and about. Two black shapes moving stealthily on the horizon were just as likely to be shot with an arrow before questions were asked, than not. We needed to blend in and hope for the best.

Gibson's ranch abutted the Jinkins' ranch on its western edge, and we crouched down, staying on Gar's land, but kept the Gibson's eastern bonfire in sight. We sat for an hour or more until Will crested a rise with Gar following in his wake. Crap.

My worry only lasted a few moments though, because after the obligatory shaking of hands, exchanging of introductions, and hail well met the Great Sir William, both the Gibson's boarder guard and Gar pointed to the yeti's tracks and stayed behind as Will plodded on, torch in one hand and his sword drawn in the other. Gar was right in what he had said to Will last night. The northern ranchers are hardy, stout people, they fight the land for every year they get, but that's just it, they fight the land. They don't and can't fight some of the monsters that walk that land. It may sound bad, but for Jimmy and me, Gar losing his arm in their attempt to drive off the yetis was a good thing. It reminded all of these stout and hardy people that raising cattle was their path in life, not slaying monsters…that wasn't Will's path either as you know more than well by now, but they didn't know that. So they let their hero go about his business without them tagging along and they went about theirs. Thistledown, and the rest of the world I guess, would be a better place if more people re-membered that. I'm not saying people can't be more than what they were born into, I only wish they'd recognize their limitations, at least it would mean less rescue missions on my part if they did. Jimmy and I slowly crept around to flank Will as he fol-lowed the tracks, going about *our* business.

It was another long cold afternoon of traveling, but this time it was over unfamiliar land which is always more difficult, as we left both the Jinkins' and Gibson's ranches behind. There are a few strag-gler clans even further north than the people I knew. By necessity their ranches were smaller because their land was at the very edge of the mountains; sometimes a brave soul even hacked into the exterior mountains to build on. Mostly they raised sheep and goats or other livestock that could handle the terrain. Their lands were steeper and craggier, and didn't abut each other like the cattle ranchers. Neighbors were far enough apart that they may not even know each other. These people were the stoutest of the stout and the hardiest of the hardy. Their backyard was often creatures like the yetis' front yard. The tracks Will was following were taking us up into the lands of those rugged few. I didn't like that, not one bit. These people rarely went beyond their small corner of the world. They were Thistledown residents only in name. If they were in trouble they relied on themselves…or…they died.

No I did not like it one bit that those deep, clawed footprints were leading us into the lands of people who didn't have the community protection of the northern ranchers like Gar. I didn't like it at all. Jimmy was proving to be a very deft learner at winter travel and how to and how not to step on drifts, what was the proper step and shuffle walk necessary for snowshoe hiking, and many other skills. Watching him maneuver over or around obstacles that would have knocked Will on his ass, I realized that my papa would have liked him. He didn't complain when he fell, he didn't bitch that he was hungry or that I was moving too fast. He kept pace and he kept quiet, yeah he was turning into Papa's type of person. He had changed a lot from the awkward young man who was pretending to be charming that I kept hitting last summer. I think Papa would have been proud that his grandchild came from Jimmy. Not happy that I'd had a child out of an extra-marital affair, but, you know, happy that it was with a good kid like Jimmy and not some random gigolo.

271

The smile on my face at the thought of the two of them sitting around a campfire, Papa and Jimmy, saying nothing but just hanging out listening to the sounds of the forest, vanished when I heard Will shout out, "Hello! Anybody home? Hello!"

I pulled myself out of my fantasies and looked up to see a small farm, smaller still than our cottage. The fence that was meant to keep goats in place was torn apart in several places without any livestock prancing, eating, or butting heads in sight. The front door to the cottage hung askew, flapping a bit in the gentle breeze. Snow had drifted up into the open doorway, clogging the entrance but for the pair of yeti tracks that plowed right on in. How did I know the fence was for goats? There was the top half off a goat's head, horns and some scalp, lying in the snow about three yards in front of me. That's how I knew. That and all the snow in the torn apart fenced area was pink and red with blood, garnished here and there with a dismembered goat piece.

Thirty-five

It was a scene to churn the stomach of even the coldest killer, either that or it was the pregnancy hormones, but blood and body parts indiscriminately strewn about with pieces of sinew and lord knows what else painting the drifts in various hues of scarlet and gross were probably the more likely candidates. You hear campfire stories about such grisly sights, but hopefully mass dismemberment and blood splattered snow are just things a storyteller uses to scare you, and not something you ever experience for yourself. Trust me, I give you my word as a cold killer, it's nasty.

I don't know if he was practically snow-blind on top of his already poor vision or if he simply hadn't noticed it, but Will kept shouting, "Hello, in the house! Anybody home?" Jimmy glanced over at me when I nudged the goat's head with my boot. It's not like I expected it to move or anything, but it was kind of an impulse action. You know what I mean, my body wanted to prove to my mind that what we were seeing was real and not some trippy moldy bread that we ate for breakfast making me hallucinate. The head rolled, what was left of it, and some dark blackish red dangling flap of something, scalp or brain or who knows what, made a wet plopping sound as it rolled, causing my trail-scarfed lunch to climb back up the back of my throat. Yeah, it was real alright.

I don't know if yetis are nocturnal or diurnal, or maybe Will's yelling woke this one up from a nap, but, the yeti stumbling up to the torn-apart backdoor looked grumpy as it rubbed its eyes with its free hand and clutched what looked like the arm from one of the homesteaders, I'd guess, with the other. Oh lord, it could have been Gar's arm for all I knew. The monster grumbled slash roared, "Who the hell are you?" The yeti looked almost as confused as it was agitated. Then again that could be the perpetual look a yeti has. Its features are more canine-like than human, with a pronounced muzzle and large nose. The only noticeable non dog-like aspect of its appearance was the complete lack of ears; coldblooded poor circulation I'd guess keeps them from having non-muscular appendages. So, the yeti tilted its head in confusion, looking like it expected Will to throw a stick for it to fetch.

The full impact of what had transpired hit Will about the same time as he realized that the seven foot tall yeti that was crouched in the doorway was talking to him. Will's face scrunched up, we could see both him and the yeti from where we were hiding in the snow-laden underbrush, his already exertion-flushed features deepened to a darker shade of red when he looked at the dismembered body parts scattered around the yard. He bellowed, "Monster! I would have let you leave to retreat to your home…"

The Knight's Wife

They never do, but yeah, he does always offer,
"…but for this I will destroy you!"

And that said, Will charged the yeti, sword in
one hand and burned out torch in the other. He
caught the yeti by surprise and almost drove his
blade through the creature's chest. It would have
been a miracle in that sad tragic corner of the world
if he had, but at the last second the yeti lifted the arm
it had been munching on and deflected the blow. Not
something you see every day there, hero with a
sword dueling a monster wielding a human
arm…well, not something I see anyway. If it's
commonplace to you, I suggest relocating to a safer
country. On the backswing the edge of Will's sword
grazed the monster's yellowish-white furred shoulder, opening a decent sized gash that painted the
yeti's fur to match the bloody snow. The yeti howled
and punched Will in the face with its free hand,
sending Will tumbling backward into the livestock
pen that was now a slaughter yard. Will landed on a
water trough. His large, armored back crushed the
rickety wooden trough on impact, sending shards of
ice and water spraying up all around him. He laid
there groaning as the yeti jumped off the front porch,
dropping its humorous weapon in the process - I
know, sorry, I had to - and stalked toward him, muttering, "Stupid furless pig whore! Cut my arm something good! We'll have roast pig whore for supper
tonight." Monsters, the ones that can talk anyway,
are always yammering on and on about eating people. It's really annoying and seems almost clichéd

like some sort of monster ethnic slur, but they do say it, so is it still a slur or stereotype if they do it? Would it be ethnically wrong to assume a giant would say, "Fee-fi-fo-fum?"

The yeti reached down and grabbed Will by the throat, hauling him to his feet. To his credit, Will tried to break the yeti's grasp with one hand while he punched the monster in its canine face with the other. The yeti growled and roared, especially when Will's gauntleted fist broke open a pressure cut below the yeti's right horn, just above its eye, causing fresh blood to run down its face. Grunting with the effort the yeti threw Will across the yard where he landed hard against the house, rattling and cracking the already damaged frame and dumping a ton of snow off the roof to pool around him where he came to a rest. When the pile of snow covering Will didn't move, that was my cue, grabbing Jimmy's hand in passing and squeezing, I said, "My turn, wait here and back me up."

He squeezed my hand back and nodded before I raced away, drawing both my short sword and stiletto as I went. Running up behind the yeti before it could finish Will off; I had a flashback to the troll where I had done something similar. Instead of risking this yeti being some badass winter-loving version of that troll, I slashed out with my sword in passing instead of jabbing and aiming for its heart, severing the brute's hamstrings. Adding more of its own blood to the already stained snow that it had helped to pollute, it screamed and fell to its knees. The yeti howled inarticulately and tried to reach around with its massive arms to stem the flow as my momentum carried me passed. I planted my feet, sending up a shower of fresh – well, fresh-ish with all that blood it was hard to call it fresh - snow, to splatter against the clapboard sided house. Before the yeti could gather its wits, I spun around and jammed my stiletto into its throat. The screams and roars subsided into a wet gurgle when my blade pierced its skull, bloody tip popping out on an angle from behind its nonexistent ear. Shaking with its death throes, the monster slid off my stiletto and fell face-first into the snow and bled out.

Breathing deeply and trying to calm my adrenaline spiked nerves, I crouched down and wiped my short sword and knife off on the yeti's matted pelt, keeping my eyes and ears perked for the other monster. I don't see how, but maybe our little racket out in the yard hadn't woken the other one if it was napping. Or, maybe it was off using the privy because human flesh does a number on the digestion? Who knows, but there was no sign of it as I watched the woods and back of the cottage. The pile of snow that was my husband started to moan and shook the roof-dropped load of snow off. He rose to his feet and groaned, holding the side of his head in one hand he said, "I would have had him. You should have given me more time."

I laughed, "Sure you did, William. Sure you did."

"No, seriously," Will added, gaining his bearings a bit more. "I stabbed it and opened a good-sized cut above its eye. I was wearing it down."

"Ha!" I laughed again and added, "absolutely, and the way you broke that water trough with your back? I can't believe the yeti didn't run away from such a display of manliness! Please, you were almost dinner and…" I trailed off when I heard shuffling and growling sounds from the nearby barn. It could have been a goat still alive wondering what all the noise was about, and probably a bit curious about where all the other goats went. I doubted it, but it could have been.

"I was doing fine," Will continued petulantly. You could tell that he'd been really proud of how he'd taken things up a notch in the hero department, killing two of the highwaymen in the autumn and not doing too shabby of a job fighting a yeti armed with an arm, and he wanted to prove to those of us helping him that he was capable. He almost sounded like a little boy stomping his feet when he said near-ly the same thing I had thought. "I don't always need you guys to come save me. I killed two of those highwaymen! I can handle myself."

The growling was moving in different directions and I couldn't follow it. Some of the snow drifts were throwing off a terrible echo and others were acting as mufflers. It was not a good situation to be distracted in, sounds carry oddly in snow. I needed to focus and Will yammering on, he was blathering the entire time I was attempting to locate the second yeti, was not helping matters. When he started in on, "I'm a damn good fist fighter, I'll have you know." I couldn't take it anymore. I needed to be able to concentrate, so I snapped at him. "Will, just shut the hell up for one minute!"

He went silent. Everything went silent: Will, the woods, the yeti, the blood rushing in my ears, everything. I realized in that moment of silence, that I had not given the slightest attempt to mask my voice. No husky, "How you doing there tall dark and handsome?" My face was still properly disguised, but my voice. The voice Will had heard snap at him hundreds of times in our life together, was not. No I spoke like me. I spoke just like his wife, and they say when a person has one weak or absent sense the others compensate. The deaf have better eyes, the mute have better eyes, oh screw it, everybody has better eyes except for those who can't see a damn thing! They get better hearing.

I had been creeping up toward the cottage to try and get a better look inside when I'd yelled at Will. I couldn't have been more than a couple of yards away. My back was to him. I held my breath for a second in that seemingly eternal silence. But, I closed my eyes and let my head drop to my chest when I heard him ask, "Gale?"

279

Thirty-six

Of all the stupid, crappy, moronic luck a person can have…I kept my back turned to Will's question. I didn't hear the other yeti growling and shuffling anymore. Maybe it really had been a loan surviving goat making good its escape into the woods. He should have known better by the set of my shoulder, the classic posture droop of the defeated, but Will may have thought I hadn't heard him. Then again, he was probably in such shock he wasn't noticing much, so he repeated his question. "Gale? Is that … is that really you?"

Crap. Crap, stupid, crappy luck!

After sheathing my stiletto in its wrist scabbard, I pulled on the neckline of my shirt where I tucked the mask in place. Working the seam up with my fingers so when I turned around, I pulled the mask off for Will and faced him down with the truth, never saying a word. I saw so many emotions race through his bad eyes at a pace that they were almost hard to follow: disbelief, sadness, worry, anger, fear, doubt, pity, and more feelings that don't really have names, but we feel them just the same. He shook his head and closed his eyes as he said, "All this time…I should have known. All this time, who else could be doing the things I couldn't, but you."

The Knight's Wife

The accusation slash remonstration (and kind of backhanded compliment) hung between us. I didn't know what to say. I really, for the first time – I know, shocking – had nothing to say. Will still looked down at his feet like an embarrassed little boy, who doesn't want to meet the gaze of the parental figure that has been looking out for him. He hadn't done anything wrong, but yet he was the one to act like it. People are weird creatures, we really are. We'll take the blame for things we didn't do, collect guilt we didn't earn, and accuse those who are innocent of the crimes we committed...weird, weird, weird.

A sprinkling of snow falling to my right caught my eye, and pulled it away from Will. I started to turn and look up at the sky to see if it was about to storm again, but Jimmy darting out of the woods, without his weapons drawn, arms pumping and running full steam, brought my gaze to the world below, not above. Every movement took on that high-stress slow-motion feel I get when things are beyond what my day to day mind expects to see. It's something that all knowing, always annoying *they* call hyper-awareness. It can save your life ... or, or well, it can make horrible moments that much more torturous. Jimmy slowly ran across the yard, yelling, "Sir William look out!" and slowly shoved Will aside as the second yeti slowly leapt down from the roof, slowly swinging a club so big that it could have been used as a camp stool. Will slowly stumbled into a nearby snow drift, but Jimmy was not so lucky. Everything sped up when the yeti landed the blow it had intended for Will across Jimmy's neck and shoulders. I heard a dull, wet snapping sound and my stomach churned and plunged as Jimmy's body fell to the snow limp.

There was a loud roar of anger, thunderous and ear-splitting. At first I thought it was the yeti bellowing some sort of revenge wail, but when Will kept roaring as he ploughed into the yeti, sending it back away from Jimmy with the amount of force its companion had so recently launched Will, I realized who was yelling. That was no small yeti. It wasn't the runt of whatever passed for litters among its kind. It had to have been seven and a half feet tall and twice the weight and girth of Will. But…but that didn't stop the Great Sir William. They came to rest on the wreckage of the water trough, a few shards of ice pierced the yeti's arms and ribs, so it leaked blood from several wounds. Will landed atop the massive beast's chest and pounded at its face with his gauntleted fists. I don't know how many blows he landed before the yeti was dead, but Will kept punching long after it stopped fighting back. It wouldn't have mattered if I had been counting because I was too busy screaming. I'm not the girly scream at a mouse or hairy spider type woman. I think by now you should know that. But I screamed. I knew, I mean I knew by that dull meaty sound the yeti's club had made when it landed that Jimmy was dead, but I screamed anyway, hoping against hope that he'd roll over, give me one of his many grins. Preferably of the cocky *aren't I hot shit* variety, and bound to his feet. Maybe even drop me that corny over-the-top stage performer's bow to boot.

He didn't. I still screamed as I scrambled over the few feet separating us. There were no open wounds for me to tend to or pretend to fix, but the angle of his neck and the almost instant discoloration of the exposed skin along his jaw and throat told me what my fingers were desperately trying to find and not. There was no pulse; Jimmy was dead. My friend was gone.

I don't know how much time passed. It felt like minutes but it could have been hours. At some point I had removed the silly, rakish black eye band I had made for Jimmy instead of a mask. I wrapped it around my hand, tightly for something to squeeze in anger and sadness, something to hold on to. It was my fault, no matter what platitudes I wanted to pamper myself with, I couldn't escape that he was dead because of me. Sure, I didn't land the fatal blow, but he was there to take that blow because of me. If I'd ignored him, if I'd kept him at arm's length, then he'd still be alive. He wouldn't have been my friend, he wouldn't have given me a child, but he would have been alive, and not cooling in my arms. It was my fault.

Some time in those minutes or hours, Will wandered over to where I was sitting with Jimmy's head in my lap. I'm sure he had many questions. Good lord! He deserved those questions and their rightful answers … but despite what I'm sure was an almost overpowering desire to ask them, Will stayed silent. He stood there behind me for a while, quiet, not accusing, just watching. Then he went away again and I don't know how much time passed, but I could hear him dragging the yetis' corpses around and gathering the body parts of the goats, while I stroked Jimmy's long black hair. He built a huge bonfire out of the torn apart fence posts and tossed the animals in. He burned the remnants of the cottage's occupants in a separate pyre, so not to sully or tarnish their remains by placing them in contact with their killer's. I don't know if that was their custom or not, but it seemed like the right thing to do. When he was done night had fallen, but both fires were burning brightly and reflecting off the snow almost to daylight proportions. I don't know how he managed it, but Will scooped both me and Jimmy up in the same load and carried us into the deserted cottage. He had lit a fire in the stove and done his best to clear away the massacre that the yetis had made of the poor homesteaders.

I don't know if a person's spirit stays on the earth when they depart. I have no doubt that there is a spirit, a soul, to each of us. But, does that soul linger, does it haunt? I don't know. I hope not or else that cabin, tucked away in the northern woods at the very base of the mountains, would be a very haunted place indeed. It probably would be forever, but I never went back after that night and I hope I never do. I'll see the yard and the carnage long enough in my nightmares to last an eternity.

Thirty-seven

We spent the night in the cabin. The ghosts of the dead haunted my sleep if not in reality. Better to lose sleep to the spirits than to freeze to death outside. At some point when I couldn't stand the pain and loneliness any longer, I left Jimmy's body and crawled over to where Will was curled up next to the stove. He wrapped his blanket around me and held me until morning without saying a word.

I slept at some point and woke up with red aching eyes and a tired worn-out mind. Will had attempted to cook us some breakfast, which was sweet, dangerous, really dangerous when I saw the blackened grease burns on his hands, but still sweet. He set a plate of half-burnt bacon and runny scrambled eggs on the floor in front of me, then sat down across from me and tucked into a plate of the same. I wasn't hungry, what with Jimmy's body still out in the corner and all, lying like cordwood next to the fireplace, but I didn't want to hurt Will's feelings either so I ate. When he was mostly finished with his food and I was still poking at mine, I said, "Thank you for not asking last night…what do you want to know?"

He took a while before he asked. He sat there looking at me, not angry or accusing anymore, just looking at me, like he hadn't really seen me in years.

286

Finally he said, not asked mind you, but said, "It was you the entire time. Not a group of vigilantes doing their best for Thistledown. Hawk saved me once and you kept on doing it. I should have seen that coming." He nodded his head agreeing with his last statement and chewed on a tough piece of bacon before continuing. He was looking over at the fire and I noticed a small tear glint in his eye as he stopped chewing. Dropping the last of his bacon so he could rub at his eyes and pinch at the bridge of his nose like he had a headache, he said, "I'm sorry, Gale. I owe you an apology."

What the hell now?

I didn't say that. I reached over and grabbed his hand. When he looked back and made eye contact, he saw my confusion and said, "I was so distant to you these last few weeks."

Um, yeah, so what?

Again, not aloud. He continued, "I had sort of fallen in love with you. I mean, not you *you*, but you." Oh good so now he was babbling, wonderful. "The masked woman!" He finally spluttered out. "I had fallen in love with the masked woman, which turned out to be you. But, I still feel sick about it. I didn't know it was you, but I was in love with her … but I realized yesterday that I was still in love with you. I'm sorry, is that alright?"

Crap. Big stupid ox. I reached over and kissed him fiercely, pulling his face toward mine. I kissed him with a passion that I hadn't since we'd grown too old and our relationship had turned to familiarity over fire. When I pulled away I whispered, "I love you too, and yes, Will, it's alright. It couldn't be more alright."

He smiled at me and for a second the years vanished. I was looking at the silly young knight who smiled at me over a bowl of chicken soup as I nursed him back to health. When he started speaking again his tone shifted to one of a questioner, no longer stating what he knew in his heart to be fact, no longer worried about mistakenly loving the same woman. He had put all the pieces he could together and from there he could only suppose. "You asked James to help you? How did you know he could fight so well? He took on those highwaymen without a hitch. Is that what he's been doing at the castle? Has he been acting as a bodyguard to Queen Marissa? I know I see him with her a lot…" He petered off, too many questions and no answers yet. He stared at me and waited, expectantly.

The truth was obviously out. After all that had happened I couldn't say, "Well, darling, he followed me around like a puppy for a while and one night in a moment of weakness I screwed his brains out. The fact that he could fight turned out to be a bonus. Oh, and I'm carrying his lovechild too, surprise!" The sick part was I didn't want to lie. I'd been lying to

Will for so long that I finally wanted everything on the table. I wanted him to know everything about the woman he loved, both Gale and the masked woman. If he loved us both, then he should know. But, he was all I had left … well, not all, but it was early in the pregnancy and I was, well not old, let's say not as young as I was, okay. I didn't want to jinx that, too. But, in my desire to clear the air between us I could drive in a wedge that wouldn't be there with a lie, or, worse yet, the truth could drive Will away. I came up with best lie that I could. It hurt to tell it. It hurt to say it…but after everything we'd been through I couldn't lose Will, not now. Not after Jimmy.

Reaching out and taking Will's other hand in mine, I started to lie, and every word was a damned dagger jammed further into my heart. "Will, do you remember how Papa used to go out trading for weeks at a time?" He nodded that he did, but looked a little confused as to why I was asking. As I continued pieces started to fall into place like they do for me when I lie. I link chains with words. Sometimes it surprises me and other times it makes me sick. This time it made me both. "This was a secret. One that Jimmy and I wanted to keep. You see, Hawk was so respected for how he raised me without my mother. How he had had his one love and she left him through no one's fault…but he was human, and he had desires." Sorry Papa, I know you'll understand. "He occasionally would sleep with a gypsy woman he fancied. It wasn't love. It was just need. I don't think people would think any less of his memory if they knew that, but he went to such lengths to keep it secret that when Jimmy and I found out we were siblings, we thought it would be best to keep it quiet like Papa did."

Will smacked himself on the forehead and said, "I'm so stupid! He tried to tell me and I didn't get it." At the inquisitive tilt of my head, he explained, "That blanket. The one I thought looked as good as one of yours? He said his *sister* had made it for me. You. How could I be so dense?"

I smiled slightly and nodded a little, but inside I was sick. See what I mean about those links and pieces? I'd actually forgotten all about the damn blanket until Will brought it back up. Substantiation for a lie I didn't want to tell, and it made me want to vomit. Will leaned over and pulled me into a hug, whispering, "I'm so sorry, Gale."

We both were...

In the aftermath of tears and apologies, we decided that Will and I would hike back to the northern road with him carrying Jimmy for me and I'd wait there for him. He'd take the horns from the yetis to Gar and let him know about what had happened out at the farthest reaches of Thistledown. I wanted to burn the cabin to the ground, eradicate and annihilate what remained of the only place in Thistledown that I now hated, but Will thought it'd be better if the ranchers could come and see for themselves. The other neighboring small farms like this may have been wiped out too and the ranchers would need to check them out. If not out of companionship and neighborly goodwill then at least as a precaution to find out if more yetis were venturing out of the mountains. I went with Will's suggestion. I wasn't in the mood to argue.

I waited with Jimmy's body in the same snow shelter we had shared only that night. The bonfire had been allowed to burn out when Will strode into view and declared the good news. I pulled Jimmy behind me on a makeshift sled the rest of the way and hid, in sight of a happy tableau that I couldn't take part in even if I had wanted to. I had wrapped Jimmy's body in clean linens from the deserted cottage before we transported it … him? … it, yes, it. Jimmy was gone and what we were taking with us was just a beaten shell. I kept the stupid eye wrap knotted in my hand, though. It gave me something to squeeze when my emotions threatened to overwhelm me. I squeezed it hard and tight many times while Will was being lauded as a hero once more. I could hear the cheers echoing down around the snow-covered hillside. Many ranchers had turned out at Gar's when the news spread and a potluck slash party had started at the Jinkins ranch in Will's honor.

Down in my cold quiet snow cave, Jimmy's head lay in my lap and I wanted to stroke his long black hair, but I couldn't so I squeezed the eye wrap harder. His hair was tucked up in what was to be his funeral shroud and pulling it out to see and touch again would only hurt more than it would help. I whispered, "I'm sorry, Jimmy. I meant to tell you. I should have told you…" But even then, to a dead body, I couldn't say it. So, I didn't. I wept until Will came and got me later that day.

We took turns pulling the sled back to our cottage. We pulled through the night. It was a cold dark and very hard journey, but the unspoken agreement being that we both wanted to be home. There would still be more questions from Will given time, I was sure, but right then we wanted to be in our home. To sleep in our bed, haunted though that sleep may be, it didn't matter. We wanted that comfort of familiarity in such an unfamiliar time. It was late the next morning when our cottage came into view. We pulled Jimmy's body alongside the back kitchen door and left him, out and in the cold, while we warmed and cleaned ourselves up. Then we passed out in that bed that had been calling us both from miles away.

I woke up once. It was late afternoon and the sun was falling. Will wasn't in bed next to me. At first I was scared. I was worried - terrified was more like it - that he had decided to leave me after all the lies I had told him. That he'd had enough of me, enough of the stories, lies, and half-truths - some he didn't even know about - and he up and left. Then I heard the grunting and chopping. Following the sounds to the back of the house, I looked out the kitchen window to see Will, two fires raging on either side of him to warm both him and the soil, out by the winter bare red maple tree. He was digging a grave for my *brother* so he could be with his *father*. I wanted to cry and be sick at the same time.

We buried Jimmy under the tree with Papa before nightfall. Will did all the work. I cried mostly. The next day he rode into Thistledown to let King Theodore know that the problem with the yetis was over. I don't know what Marissa thought. She and I have never spoken about it. Her illness seemed to take a lot of the wind out of her sails. She was never as spunky as she used to be after that winter. I only hope she thought Will caught scent of the affair and chased Jimmy off. I hope she didn't think that Will killed Jimmy out of jealousy. But, I guess it doesn't matter. She didn't ask, so that time I didn't have to lie. I guess there's always a first time, huh?

Thirty-eight

So that's the end of my story. I wish I had a better way to finish it for you. It'd be nice to say, "And they lived happily ever after." But how often does that really happen? Come on, be realistic, how many happily ever afters have you seen or heard about? I suppose they could happen somewhere to some really lucky people, I don't know, maybe. That bitch Cinderella seemed to really luck out, but something tells me when she gets those bloated pregnancy hippo-feet that I'm dealing with now, Prince Charming may have traded her in for a newer model. Maybe I'm just being spiteful because happily ever after is not for me, you've seen my luck, come on, really? I used up what little I had by keeping Will through everything that happened. Oh…and I hate to burst your bubble, but probably no happily ever afters for you either. Sure, we'll have our happy moments along the way but we'll have our crappy moments, too. That's life – Happily, crappily ever after.

How am I going to move on, you ask? I don't know. I'm still married to the man I love, but I'm pregnant with another man's baby. What will I do if King Theodore calls Will away on a mission when I'm pregnant? Or worse yet with an infant? I don't know. Maybe I'll get lucky, maybe that will be the happier portion of my ever after and all the evil monsters out there will decide to give Thistledown a wide berth with the Great Sir William still on the clock. Maybe my efforts over the last twenty some odd years will have driven caution into their thick monstrous skulls. Maybe we will be able to retire, both Will and me, and raise our daughter in peace. Only, I'll be the one with the secret. They can go about life happy and oblivious to the truth. Will can believe she is his daughter, and she can be raised believing the Great Sir William is her father. They can have the happily ever after part and I can be the one dealing with the pain. Maybe that will work, I don't know. I hope so. I've kept secrets before as you know, don't we all? I suppose I could keep this one, too.

Did I love Jimmy? Yes, yes I did very much. And...and is that really wrong? I don't know. Can you love more than one person at the same time? Of course, your love may hurt one of them, and you for that matter, but you *can* love more than one person. Maybe it's my need to justify my actions, but I think I needed something that was just *mine*. You can understand that, can't you? Ask anybody who does so much for other people, after a while of all the give, give, give a small voice inside your head starts screaming, "What about me? You keep giving to him, her, them, and everybody else under the damn sun, but me! What about me? Can't I have something, even the smallest, tiniest, most miniscule thing that is just *Mine*?" Or is that merely a justification for my actions? I don't know.

I guess that's all life is. A series of "I don't knows" followed by a round of "Maybes" and back and forth again and again. I don't know, maybe. You don't get the luxury of knowing much for certain. So you better hold on tight to those few certainties you are blessed with. I can tell you what some of my certainties are: I still love Will, I will love my daughter (I'm confident it's a girl), and if any of those previous "I don't knows" happen to come true and I have to go back into cold killer fighting mode, then another certainty is that I'll grab two red maple leaves off of my tree to take with me and hope that Jimmy … that James, forgives me. That he's looking down from the stars with my father watching me. That he sees his daughter and how she is loved. How she has a very different childhood than he had. That he is content and no longer scared. That's the certainty I can carry away from all this, two red maple leaves.

Author's Notes

Hello Again Reader, I hope you enjoyed *The Knight's Wife*. I can't promise you there will be more romances where that came from. As I'm sure you noticed I couldn't maintain the flippant, light-hearted style throughout the tale that I started with. But, when the hell is love ever completely flippant and simple? Again, I seem to have written something that doesn't have a genre. My overpowering need to add a measure of reality to all of my fantasy work to create relatable characters, I think, will always keep me from writing you a story that is completely blithesome...I'll let you be the judge as to whether that's a good or bad thing.

I refuse to go through that nonsense of telling you that all the characters are works of fiction. To be honest I hope Gale does resemble someone you know. She should, she is every woman. She's your wife, your sister, your mother, your partner, your daughter, your cousin, your aunt, your fourth grade math teacher, that checkout girl at the grocery store that you make small talk with for a decade and then one day she's gone: maybe she quit, or was fired, or was in a car accident after work and died but you never knew her name so you missed it in the paper. She's every woman who has ever loved.

Some of you may have noticed that the only physical description I gave you of Gale in the entire book was that she was of average height. That's it. She doesn't need a face because she has any one or all of the previously mentioned faces. Maybe she has the same eyes that look back at you from the mirror every morning? If I did my job well she does. I hope my story of realistic love didn't tarnish any silver-polished daydreams you have of the idea. Love is what it is. No description can ever do the emotion justice. Love is life, love is death, *maybe, I don't know.*

As always thanks for reading,

Nick Shamhart

About the Author

Nick Shamhart was born in Sandusky, Ohio on the winter solstice in the years before Americans started electing actors as President. He still lives in that mostly vowel state under protest from half of the voices in his head. The other half could care less where they reside, because they are too busy yammering on endlessly about everything from Sit-Com theme songs to theology and metaphysics. The voices help Nick write his books. If you like his books tell your friends all about them. The voices have many other stories yet to tell. They keep...*what?*....hold on please....*yes, I was just getting to...no...no...look, do you want to do this?...well you can't....no....no....yes, alright*. The voices say thanks for reading.

Nick Shamhart

Made in the USA
Charleston, SC
13 September 2013